# Praise for Nicholas Mosley

"Mosley is that rare bird: an English writer whose imagination is genuinely inspired by intellectual conundrums."
—Robert Nye, *Guardian*

"Mosley's dialogue is a deliciously dotty exercise in existential inquiry, reading at times like a poker-faced collaboration between Samuel Beckett and Gracie Allen."
—Michael Upchurch, *Seattle Times*

"Nicholas Mosley is a brilliant novelist who has received nothing like the recognition he deserves—either at home in England or in this country. . . . One can only hope that Mosley's reputation will someday be commensurate with the quality of his fiction."
—Robert Scholes, *Saturday Review*

"Dalkey Archive has in the English writer Nicholas Mosley a throw-back, a modernist mastodon whose project for fiction surpasses in grandiosity that of any American writer I know."
—Tom LeClair, *Washington Post*

"Mosley is ingenious and cunning. . . . Anybody who is serious about the state of English fiction should applaud Nicholas Mosley's audacity—his skill is unquestionable."
—Frank Rudman, *Spectator*

# Also by Nicholas Mosley

## FICTION

Spaces of the Dark
The Rainbearers
Corruption
Meeting Place
Accident
Assassins
Impossible Object
Natalie Natalia
Catastrophe Practice
Imago Bird
Serpent
Judith
Hopeful Monsters
Children of Darkness and Light
The Hesperides Tree

## NONFICTION

African Switchback
The Life of Raymond Raynes
Experience and Religion
The Assassination of Trotsky
Julian Grenfell
Rules of the Game
Beyond the Pale
Efforts at Truth

# Inventing
# God

by Nicholas Mosley

DALKEY ARCHIVE PRESS

Originally published in the United Kingdom by Secker & Warburg, 2003
Copyright © 2003 by Nicholas Mosley

First U.S. edition, 2003

Library of Congress Cataloging-in-Publication Data

Mosley, Nicholas, 1923-
    Inventing God / Nicholas Mosley.— 1st ed.
        p. cm.
    ISBN 1-56478-291-3 (acid-free paper)
        1. Middle East—Fiction. 2. Judaism—Relations—Islam—Fiction. 3.
    Islam—Relations—Judaism—Fiction. I. Title

PR6063.O82I5 2003
823'.914—dc21

                                                                2002041572


Partially funded by grants from the Lannan Foundation and the Illinois Arts Council, a state agency.

Dalkey Archive Press books are published by the Center for Book Culture, a nonprofit organization.

www.centerforbookculture.org

Printed on permanent/durable acid-free paper and bound in the United States of America.

If God did not exist it would be necessary to invent him.

Voltaire

**invent** / v.t. . . . 1. Find out, discover, esp. by search
or endeavour. Now *rare* or *obs.*

*The New Shorter Oxford English Dictionary*

# PART I

# I

Dr Richard Kahn, Lecturer in Anthropology and Social Studies at the American University of Beirut, was conducting an evening seminar to students who came from both Muslim and Christian families. The civil war in the Lebanon between factions of Muslims and Christians had been over for some years now, and the ex-belligerents were busily rebuilding the city that they had previously been destroying with such passion. They had each made use of their particular god as a justification for their ferocity – as if He were a jealous and needy warlord who demanded the blood of his enemies. Then after a time it seemed that they had become bored, or their gods had become satiated; though the protagonists still clung to their religious allegiances as if these were an insurance against further requirements of belligerence and self-justification.

It seemed to Richard that it was perhaps natural to require a god in time of war – as an excuse for killing and a way of giving meaning to dying. And was not antagonism, aggression, an essential component of human nature? Richard argued that people were likely to be Muslims or Christians more from a need to belong to a group that would provide emotional reassurance in a difficult world, rather than as a result of a personal search for truth and meaning. And then in peacetime there was a return to triviality. Richard wondered – Could there not be an idea of God that would make peace subtle and passionate?

These were matters that Richard put to his students in his seminars. Many of them showed little interest, allowing such intrusions into their preconceptions to die like sounds in a vacuum. Some appeared to allow an implication in and then let it fester briefly in hostility towards Richard. There were times when Richard felt he was foolhardy to be expressing such views in what was still a potentially explosive situation. However he hoped he might have some small role to play in diffusing the atmosphere of religious fanaticism which he felt absurd and dangerous. Also there was one very pretty black-eyed girl who sat at the back of the class and stared at him so intently that he felt she must be enthralled by the boldness of his opinions.

Richard was a compact, curly haired man in his mid-thirties. There was a confident wariness about him like that of a boxer.

On this particular evening he was saying 'As Voltaire said – If God did not exist it would be necessary to invent him.'

One of the male students said 'But surely that was intended to convey that God did not exist?'

'Something that seems necessary to invent must exist at least as a potentiality.'

'Why not simply a fabrication.'

The black-eyed girl at the back of the class said 'But whether it was a fabrication or a potentiality it would have to be tested.'

Richard said 'Indeed.'

The male student said 'You can test the existence of God?'

'That seems to me inevitable.'

Another student said 'But the Christian god was supposed to provide peace and justice and it didn't work.'

The girl said 'It would have to be tested in the way in which it was supposed to work.'

'And what is that?'

The girl looked at Richard. Richard said 'That might be part of what you would have to find out.'

Richard began to wonder if, after the seminar ended, the girl might be waiting for him in the campus grounds: indeed one could imagine anything as a potentiality. But there was still at this time an air of uncertainty in the city so that at night people did not linger but hurried home to their separate places of shelter. In some defiance against this Richard had taken to walking from the university buildings back to his flat through streets where gutted houses had not yet been rebuilt and street lamps were few and far between. This was a part of the town which had previously been a no man's land between warring Muslims and Christians, and the ruins had been left to serve as a sort of monument to human folly – or to the vagaries of gods. Also in this part of the town the bombing and shelling had uncovered certain archaeological remains that had been considered worth preserving, but the authorities had not got round to dealing with these yet, so empty buildings had become the haunt of squatters – people made homeless by war and around whom there proliferated stories of muggings and killings. Richard wondered – What do I imagine that the black-eyed girl and I might do – dally in some secret Roman courtyard or cellar? There had of course been no sign of the girl in the campus grounds.

Richard carried a stick with which he poked the ground in front of him, to give warning of holes or fallen masonry or to be ready to ward off imagined bands of robbers. He had ventured into these streets once or twice as a boy, when the war had just been getting under way and shells had come rending the air like torn paper. He remembered how in war, perhaps just because of the danger and fear, one felt that boldness had some autonomy. So was this, paradoxically, why God seemed prevalent in war? God was that which reassured humans of their freedom?

5

Around a corner, down a side street, a bright light suddenly came on. It was as if a security device had been activated by a sensor.

Richard stopped and peered cautiously down the side street. At some distance, at a crossroads, there was a pool of light. Within this there was a dark shape crouched on the ground: something caught by the light and keeping still in the hope that it would not be noticed? Richard imagined – It might be a mother bending over the body of her child: or a dog savaging a dead or dying victim. These were images that had become familiar through photographs of war. They jostled in Richard's mind; they tried to merge, but jumped from one to the other.

There was nothing to indicate what Richard should do. He could hurry across the opening to the side street with his head down; he could approach the pool of light cautiously and see what it was on the ground. Something was moving as part of or beneath the crouched figure: this could be a child; it could be a piece of material blown by the wind. Or – it suddenly struck him – might the whole occasion be a scene being shot for a film? There were such uses being made now of these settings of desolation. Then – but surely this was a trick of light – there seemed to be a shape rising up from the body like a giant shadow: it could be made by the headlights of a vehicle approaching. Richard backed into a doorway at the side of the road; he did not want to be seen; the vehicle might be a police car on the prowl for night-wanderers.

He remembered the Sufi story of a person searching at night on the brightly lit ground under a lamp-post. A passer-by stops and asks – For what are you searching? The person says – For the keys of my house. The passer-by says – Is this where you lost them? The person says – No, I lost them in the dark, but this is where the light is.

Richard had told this story to his students. They had listened gravely: it had seemed they were wondering whether or not to laugh. The girl at the back of the room had gazed

6

at him wide-eyed. He had thought he might say to her – It is in the dark that we might find what we desire.

Most of the buildings in this part of the old no man's land had seemed deserted, but there was no knowing whether stories of squatters and muggers were true. Towards the end of the war this was an area where sectarian gangs were said to have kept their hostages – as bargaining counters in the negotiations for a future peace. A friend of Richard's, visiting from England, had disappeared when walking in the town, and there had been speculation that he must have been taken hostage. He had come to lecture to Richard's students on the reasons why humans seemed to need and to like war. He had not been heard of again, and stories about his disappearance had spread.

Richard became aware of cold air coming from behind him; he seemed to be at the entrance to a passageway through to the centre of what had once been a substantial building. He moved a pace or two backwards with his hands out behind him: he was aware that if he turned he might see something of where he was going by the light that would reach him from the street, but he did not want to turn his back on whatever was happening outside. Eventually when he did turn, the light from the street abruptly went out. In the complete darkness he felt with alarm that he had no idea where he was: how far had he come down the passage? in what direction was the street which he had left? So now it was indeed as if he were the man who had lost his keys in the dark. He felt with his stick and tapped it against walls: but he felt he might be betraying his position if he made too much noise. But was he hiding? What else should he be doing? It seemed he should stay still until something further occurred to him.

But with no stimuli, no sight or sound or touch, how might anything be conveyed? He was in a vacuum. He joked to himself – What was all that stuff about the necessity of invention!

Then it seemed to him that something came out of the darkness and touched his sleeve.

It was unlikely that this was in fact happening; though why should it not be? He had known that there might be people in the building. Fear ran up his arm and exploded above the top of his head. He might be about to be taken hostage and chained to a radiator; he might be being called on to rescue a child such as the one he had imagined in the street. He remained quite still. Then the hand or whatever it was – surely just a current of air! – seemed to creep down his sleeve and briefly explore his own hand before it disappeared. He then had a fantasy that it might be the hand of the black-eyed girl from the seminar who had followed him. Of course this was madness! But what a happy invention.

Richard was making his way along the passage; he entered what seemed to be a side room. He was groping along a wall of this with an arm out when suddenly the ground seemed to disappear beneath him and he fell; he flung his hands out to break his fall and at first they encountered nothing and then it was as if they were being torn, bludgeoned. He tried to get a hold, he lost his stick, he scraped and tumbled; he came to rest heavily on rubble. He was on his side with one leg bent under him. There was no feeling in his leg; he did not know whether or not this meant that it was broken. He sneezed and spat; he was trying to get rid of dust from his mouth and eyes. He thought – Dear God, is this what I have invented? I am one of those hostages who has been trapped and is about to be tortured.

One of the stories that had circulated about his friend who had disappeared was that he had been taken prisoner by an extremist group who wanted to extract from him some specialist information that in fact he did not have.

Richard tried to make out by touch what kind of place he was in. He was among fallen plaster and masonry; he might have caused the collapse of the floor above, or others might have made the hole before him. There was an area of wall to one side of him that was cool but with a slight roughness; this might be the texture of mosaic. Through this the space

8

around him seemed for a moment to come alive; why should he not be in one of those not yet fully explored excavations – a classical courtyard, indeed, where there had once been fountains? He tried to reach further; to drag himself, to crawl; but pain came in violently: it was likely after all his leg was broken. But even if now he could not move, in the morning there would presumably be light coming in through the hole and he could make himself heard for someone to rescue him. He shifted himself with difficulty so that his back was propped against the wall and his leg was at an angle that was bearable if he kept still. He thought – The Romans were both hedonists and torturers.

At the other side of him to that on which there seemed to be mosaic there were some loose objects like sticks on the ground where his hand was resting. Perhaps earlier prisoners or squatters had been making a fire. Then the impression came to him that the sticks might be bones: someone had been chained and had died here: how could he tell? Should he pick up the sticks and feel their consistency? There was also some cloth with them, dry like paper but softer and more crumbling. He began to feel alarm again, going to the top of his head and not quite dispersing there. The cloth might be that which had once covered a body; the body might have turned to bones; but there were not enough bones for a body, there were just enough for instance for an arm. Then, as he leaned over, his cheek came across something cold and hard on the wall; it was metal. Twisting himself and causing himself renewed pain he reached for it and explored it with his other hand; it was a ring, or stanchion, attached to the wall. It was of a kind, yes, to which a prisoner might be fastened. It was directly above the cloth and the bundle of sticks or bones that might have been an arm. He had a vision of a hostage who had been kept in this cell and had been handcuffed to the ring in the wall; he had been abandoned and left to starve. If he had wanted to free himself he would have had to sever his arm – but would this have been possible? Could one cut off an arm and live? Two of the sticks on the floor were of the right size for a forearm, but would the smaller bones be enough or too much for a hand? He needed to try to make sense of this if he was to go on imagining it. Where was the rest of the body? What of the ghostly hand that had reached out to him in the darkness? He straightened himself and sat again with his back against the wall. It seemed that he should stay very still until morning. Of course the bones were just sticks! But might he not invent a story? His friend who had disappeared, Maurice Rotblatt, might he not have been entombed here? And have managed, against all the odds, miraculously to free himself? This was just the sort of story that Maurice himself would have appreciated. And he, Richard, could pass the remaining hours of the night by imagining how it might be made useful. What story might it remind one of? What God had tried to make peace possible rather than war?

# II

Carl Andros, Professor of Biology and Life Sciences at the University of North London, was on his way to deliver an evening lecture on to what extent humans could be said to be at the mercy of their genes: in what manner could one talk about chance, determinism, free will? Andros was walking the two miles or so between his flat and the university buildings because he hoped that thus he could prepare his mind for the lecture: or rather, as he sometimes liked to put it, that by being occupied physically he might leave his thoughts free to sort out themselves. About this latter idea he was apt to find himself open to some ridicule from his colleagues: the idea that there was an organising ability in mind – how could this be tested? Andros had argued that one could observe one's own experience and even to some extent carry out experiments with this: there might be no logic in the idea that a subject might treat itself as its own object, but how else in practice did people learn about themselves? Or was it being claimed that this was the one subject about which humans never learned? There was indeed, he suggested, some evidence for this. But if it was by experiment that one brought to consciousness an understanding of the environment, then could it not be by experimenting with consciousness that one learned about chance, determinism, free will?

The specific occasion for this lecture was the recent announcement by scientists that they had elucidated the complete sequence of the human genome – the hugely complex structure of genes and DNA that ordered the way in which humans were formed and maintained. So did this also control the way they behaved? Was determinism now irrefutable? Or was there in humans a capability of a different kind – perhaps just shown by the fact that they were able to discover and map and consider such a structure as the genome.

It had been suggested that humans would now be able to 'play God' – 'God' in the popular sense of being the controller of the universe. However it should be remembered, Andros liked to say, that in orthodox Christian understanding, for instance, God had given autonomy to His creation, and only interfered with it in the way of making information and occasional suggestions available to humans to whom for the most part He had handed over responsibility.

It was early spring, and Andros was walking through quiet residential streets where lights were beginning to come on. The façades of houses were like carapaces that had evolved to protect a softer substance within; the windows and doors were like the geometrical markings that are sometimes formed on shells. Or like, Andros ruminated, the blind eyes and silent mouths of actors' tragic masks hung on a wall. These two sets of images jostled one another and tried to merge: should it not be one of the propensities of mind to be able to hold apparently disparate ideas together?

There were few other walkers in the streets. Occasionally there was a lighted window with curtains undrawn and a glimpse of people standing, sitting, going about their daily tasks. Could they not imagine themselves also outside their windows looking in?

Andros was approaching a house which he recognised; he had been accustomed to come here some years ago. Now in the basement area some sort of struggle was going on: a mugging? a rape? someone trying to break in? Andros slowed in his walk. He could either go on past with his head down (was one not often told – Do not interfere with this sort of thing, you will only add yourself to the list of injured); or stop and at least look cautiously over the railings to see more of what was happening. And if this was in fact just two people making love, then surely he had reached an age when he might harmlessly take a prurient interest in such things. He might even test a theory of a fellow maverick colleague of his – that just by watching the backs of people's heads you could make them become aware of you and turn from what they were doing. Andros took hold of the railings above the basement area and looked down.

There was indeed a struggle going on. This could be, yes, either assault or some not too unusual foreplay to the business of making love: in some feminist circles indeed it was nowadays questioned whether between heterosexuals there was any difference. The two people in the basement were, yes, a man and a woman. But to an impartial observer there should surely be apparent the difference between rape and making love.

There were no more than slight gasping and grunting noises coming from the basement. The man however might be threatening the woman with a knife? It seemed that he, Andros, should be doing something either more or less than just watching – unless it was true that he might influence events by gazing at the back of the man's head. He tried this: he caught a glimpse of the woman's eyes peering up at him over the man's shoulder. She was young and pretty; perhaps no more than a teenager. The man then did pause in whatever he was doing and after a moment looked back over his shoulder. Andros thought – But he was responding to the girl who was responding to me; and was not I responding to the girl?

The man pushed the girl away from him and began to clamber up the basement steps. Andros thought – Well, now

13

I am about to learn the nature or outcome of this experiment: am I going to be attacked.

The man was young, with a wild, troubled face. When he got to the top of the steps he said 'For God's sake will you watch her?' Andros said 'Yes.' The man said 'She wants to do damage to herself.' Andros thought – What a strange way of putting it! He saw that the man was carrying a knife. But it was possible that he might have taken it off the girl? She called up from the basement, 'I only do when you try to stop me!' The man said 'How can that be if I have to try to stop you?' Andros thought – Well yes, that makes sense. The girl started coming up the area steps. Andros thought – But don't I know her? He said 'What happened?' The man said 'I think it would be best in the circumstances if I disappeared.' The girl said 'That's right, run away!' The man said 'I thought that's what you wanted me to do.' The girl said 'Yes that's what I said, I do.' Andros wondered – Well they seem to be stuck in a fairly commonplace pattern: perhaps I could help them? When the girl got to the top of the steps she said to Andros 'Don't you know me?' Andros said 'Yes I do.' Then – 'Who are you?' She said 'Aren't you giving the lecture?' Andros said 'Are you coming?' He thought – But I don't think she's just one of my students. The man said 'She thinks the world's unendurable and she has to take it out on herself.' The girl said 'Who else should I take it out on?' The man said 'Well on me, for instance.' She said 'I try, but you're too nice.'

Andros thought – Well you both seem to be doing not too badly.

They had begun to walk, the three of them, in the direction in which Andros had been heading. They moved slowly, with Andros in between, with their eyes cast down, as if they might be expecting to find something on the ground.

The girl said 'What are you going to talk about in your lecture?'

Andros said 'This sort of thing.'

'What?'

'You're walking along. You think you know what's happening. Then something turns up, and seems to be rearranging things.'

'What.'

'Were you really going to my lecture?'

The man said 'Yes, we were on our way.'

Andros said 'The odd thing is that things really do seem to sort themselves out.'

They were emerging from the quiet street onto a busy thoroughfare. They paused on the edge of the pavement like people who have come to the edge of a sea. Andros thought – Yes of course I know her! I knew her as a child. He said as if to the two of them 'Would you like to have supper afterwards?'

The girl stopped and put a hand to her head and said 'I think all this may be happening too quickly.'

Andros said 'Possibly.'

The young man said to the girl, 'Will you go home then?'

The girl put her arm through his and squeezed it and said 'Why, aren't you coming with me?' She laughed.

The man said to Andros 'You see?'

The girl said to Andros 'So what else do you think may be happening?'

Andros said 'Oh I don't know. Lots of things. Perhaps we'll find out.'

The man said to the girl 'No I want to go to the lecture.'

The girl let go of his arm. She said to Andros, 'You're a miracle worker. And I'm a nutcase. Why did I say I didn't want to have supper?'

'Perhaps we can meet some other time.'

'Yes I hope so.'

The young man said to the girl 'You said you wanted to come to the lecture!'

'Yes I did, didn't I.'

'Do you want your knife back?'

'No.' She turned and began running away from them along the pavement of the busy road.

Andros and the young man watched her go; then they made their way through the traffic across the road. The young man said 'I'm sorry about that.'

Andros said 'Don't be.' Then – 'You know how to get in touch with me if you'd like.'

'Aren't we going to have supper?'

'No not tonight.'

'You mean she fixed that?'

'We all contributed.'

Across the road there was the building that was known as the Old Biology Theatre. When Andros and the young man reached it they separated and Andros went to find the organiser of the lecture. In the theatre there were already rows of faces in front of him like volunteers for an experiment. He wondered – But what exactly is to be tested?

When the time came for him to speak he said –

'The occasion of my talking to you tonight is the successful mapping of the human genome – the complete set of human genes which, it has been claimed, is responsible for making us what we are and behave as we do. This mapping has been a remarkable achievement, and will give us powers that we have not had before to combat disease and organic abnormalities. It could also offer us chances to experiment with future structures of life. But how we are to use such powers will remain within our choice. Choice will be in a different area to that of the quite valid one of scientific discipline and determinism.

'This is why I have subtitled this lecture – Is it still necessary for God to be invented?

'It has become a truism even in this materialistic age that science cannot make judgments about value. Rational ethical systems have been formulated but cannot scientifically be shown as authentic. Traditionally, religion has been the means by which humans have tried to understand their condition and to commit themselves to ethical attitudes towards it. We have fashioned stories and beliefs to explain our situation, and these have seemed authentic in so far as they have been felt as relevant to our experience. But with regard to old stories this relevance has become less and less apparent. It is not clear if this is a failure of the stories and expressions of belief, or of our understanding of what such language is trying to do. Religious discourse is an attempt to refer to what is beyond the scope of rational language, but which is felt to be there and is required to be described.

'The old stories were understood properly as that which might give us confidence in our own judgment. God was not so much that which told us what to do (though it was easy to believe this), as that which gave us the experience of the validity of our freedom to choose. God was also that which was felt to provide enough information to make valid choice possible.'

Andros spoke slowly, with pauses between sentences. It was as if he were waiting for pennies in the minds of his audience to drop; or for some signal that this did not much matter.

'So just as important as the scientific achievement of the mapping of the genome, would be a grasp of the considerations by which proper choices concerning how to handle it might be made. Or perhaps a better way of putting this would be – a grasp of how states of mind might be encouraged by which proper choices might occur. We can, as a society, use our experience to make rules, and over wide areas such formulations can be effective. But there is always likely to be a predicament that has not been come across before; or one of such complexity that two or more traditions or prospects seem in conflict. And then judgments have to be made, and consequences endured, for which old formulations are of little help. Then we are aware of having to turn to discovery and invention: and what justification might we find for that?

'It was my intention to argue in this lecture that all

religions, all ethical systems, are inventions, but none the less can be authentic. Voltaire famously said that if God did not exist it would be necessary to invent Him; and this has been often taken to suggest that in reality He is an illusion. But if an invention is seen to be necessary – necessary for an understanding or an ordering of the way things work – in what sense can it be said not to exist? Truly religious people are those who do not claim to know *a priori* what to believe, but who through questioning, observation and experience form impressions, and then appear to find that what they have conjectured works.'

Andros looked at the rows of faces that were lined up like laboratory specimens in front of him. He could see the young man in a row at the back but not, as was to be expected, the girl.

He said –

'It was the contention of my old friend and colleague Maurice Rotblatt – he who disappeared some years ago and about whom, as you may have seen, stories have sprung into the news again – that we had to stop talking and start watching and listening; that concerning the chances of making proper choices, pointers and patterns would occur if we were attentive and did not try to force them into shape. He believed, that is, that we can tell what is right and wrong in a way that artists can tell when they confront their work in the process of its formation. And although I myself remain essentially a scientist –'

He broke off. He thought – How on earth am I to go on with this?

– Am I not saying that this is essentially unsayable?

'– I do not see a contradiction here.'

There was an elderly man hurrying down the aisle. He was making gestures of admonition or warning. He murmured 'I'm so sorry.' Andros thought – He is the cavalry to my rescue? He is bringing a message from my old friend Maurice Rotblatt?

The man clambered up onto the platform and said 'I regret to announce that we will have to evacuate this building. A bomb threat has been received. The police suggest the telephone call might be genuine. Will you please make your way in an orderly manner into the street.'

Andros thought – That girl has made the telephone call?

Then – Maurice would have liked this story!

People began sluggishly to leave their seats and drift towards the exits.

The elderly man flung his arms out and announced 'No panic!'

The young man in the audience was standing up and looking at Andros excitedly.

Andros thought – Yes, we will have more to say.

# III

A twenty-five-year-old Muslim called Hafiz was engaged in post-graduate work at the American University of Beirut. His subject was genetics – the study of the way in which the characteristics of a species are maintained and passed on and occasionally modified. His family belonged to a fundamentalist sect who believed in Mohammed as the one true prophet, and in the virtue of a holy war against the enemies of Islam. Hafiz was more interested in the unorthodox Sufi idea of a holy war against tendencies to hatred and violence in oneself.

In his scientific work Hafiz had become one of a team enquiring into whether genetic differences between ethnic groups might be discernible in terms of the structure of DNA. This work was not part of the university curriculum, but it was being backed by an outside authority in the hope, it seemed, that one day it might lead to the construction of a weapon for biological warfare. If it could be found, that is, that there were distinctive genetic differences between one set of people and another, then in theory a lethal virus might be engineered which would affect some ethnic groups while leaving others untouched. And thus there might be carried out, efficiently and even without leaving traces of intention, the sort of ethnic or religious cleansing that extremists locally and in neighbouring countries said they so ardently desired, but present methods to achieve which were cumbersome and led to bad publicity.

Hafiz thought this a fruitless line of enquiry, because there were no clear scientific categories by which could be defined this or that ethnic group. However at least one religious leader had argued that since Allah had decreed there were essential differences between Muslims and infidels, it was reasonable to suppose, since Allah was the Lord of everything, that these differences would be reflected in the structure of DNA. Hafiz had risked suggesting that the evidence seemed to be that Allah had decreed such differences to be indefinable; but he had soon learned it was wise to keep such speculation to himself. The politics of the time and place were such that funding was found and given unofficially to this work; and Hafiz used the opportunity to pursue, haphazardly and mostly in secret, an enquiry of his own – which was to see whether there might be any genetic components that could be identified as leading to needless rivalry and aggression. He could pursue this solitary line because the work of his team was supposed to be secret anyway, and in fact each member did not know much of what the others were doing. But Hafiz realised increasingly that his own imagined categories were impossible to define: some aggression seemed necessary for self-preservation and discovery, however much other forms might seem grotesque and simply destructive.

Hafiz had a friend called Joshua whose family were members of the Maronite Christian Church, which in Lebanon was the traditional enemy of Islam. Hafiz and Joshua had been close to each other as children, but then the civil war had got under way and it had been difficult for them to meet: their families lived on opposite sides of what became a no man's land in Beirut. The war had been between Maronite Christians on the one hand and various Muslim sects on the other, but the latter often found themselves at enmity between themselves, and the fighting had been further confused when Palestine guerrillas took refuge in the outskirts of the city and the Israelis had pursued them and encouraged the Christians to slaughter the refugees.

However even in the war Hafiz and Joshua had occasionally managed to meet by making use of a system of cellars and linking passages that stretched beneath the strip of ground that was no man's land. These passages were frequented mostly by those who wished not to be hindered from making money in time of war: this was known about by the combatants, but the latter did not try to prevent it because it seemed even to them that it was useful to have some underground trafficking in war. Thus both Hafiz and Joshua had grown up with the idea that on a deeper level than that of a commitment to causes, there was some common sense in human nature that with boldness could be distanced from the demands of war.

Later, when the war was over and it was aggression that seemed for a time to go underground, Hafiz and Joshua used to go down to the beach, which even during the fighting had been kept as a kind of playground. They would lie on the sand and watch the waves coming in ceaselessly. Hafiz said 'It does seem that some sort of aggression is necessary in the rhythm of things.'

Joshua said 'But it should be contained, as in music.'

'The waves have their own limitations?'

'Though every now and then there would be some cataclysm.'

Joshua's subjects as a post-graduate student at the American University of Beirut were anthropology and archaeology – the study of how human characteristics and artefacts had evolved more through social and historical forces than through the influence of genes. He as well as Hafiz had distanced himself from his family: he had made a study of the heretical Christian Gnostic sects that had flourished in the Middle East. He and Hafiz sat and watched the strangely controlled and beautiful dance that went on between the land and the sea.

Hafiz said 'There's all the talk of mapping the human genome. One may then have more power to contain and combat disease.'

'But not change human nature.'

'Well, not be in control of such a change, no.'

'Do people think they are in control of the work you are supposed to be doing?'

When they had been younger Hafiz and Joshua had been in love with one another. They had hardly talked of this: it had seemed to be a condition that could flourish only if it were not put into words. Recently however Hafiz had moved towards an interest in girls, although Joshua had remained faithful, thus causing some unease to both of them.

Hafiz said 'There's this absurd talk, you know, about being able to find a genetic component that would establish the difference between Arabs and Jews. Or even, God help us, between Muslims and Christians.'

'But it can't be done.'

'No. But who's going to say that.'

'So you'll continue to get funding?'

'Yes.'

'But does anyone in fact believe such a weapon can be made?'

'Who knows any more what anyone thinks or believes? You believe what you want.'

'Even if it kills you.'

'What's stopped a biological weapon being used up till now is the fear that the stuff will be blown back on oneself. If it's imagined that it will harm only one's enemies, then someone will be tempted to use it.'

'And it would still be blown back on oneself.'

'Yes.'

'But it's said that the Israelis are working on such a bomb.'

'Well they may have to say that, but they wouldn't be daft enough to trust it.'

'I don't know. The hatred between Arabs and Jews is by now daft enough for anything.'

They sat with their hands on their knees and watched the women sunbathing; the young boys enjoying throwing sand at each other and wrestling.

Joshua said 'I sometimes think that some cataclysm will have to happen if human nature is to change. It's becoming too daft to remain viable as it is.'

Hafiz said 'And cockroaches will survive.'

'So mightn't there be a case for pretending to believe that such a weapon might work, while knowing all the time that it wouldn't?'

'You mean to scare the enemy, and indeed oneself, shitless?'

'Exactly.'

'But surely that's not the sort of subtlety that human nature requires.'

There had been a day when Joshua and Hafiz had been children when they had gone on one of their expeditions in the cellars of abandoned buildings in no man's land, and down a hole they had come across a chamber which seemed to have been newly exposed by a hand grenade or a bomb. They had explored it with their torches; on the walls there were faint representations of birds and foliage; it seemed they might have stumbled on some Aladdin's cave. Then from some further reach in the darkness there had come a scream, and the smell of burning. They had become very frightened and had switched off their torches; then they had seemed to be lost in the dark. There was the impression of shadowy figures moving past them; they had remained for some time as if paralysed. When they had eventually found their way out of the maze they had determined not to play their under-ground games again. But to Joshua there had remained the memory of strange and esoteric imagery on the walls; this being juxtaposed with the impression of someone being tortured.

Now, years later on the beach, Joshua said 'Do you think we ought to have done something in that cellar?'

'Done what?'

'About that scream.'

'What could we have done? We remember it.'

'You think that's enough?'

'Haven't we learned something?'

Quite soon after this conversation on the beach someone in Hafiz's laboratory claimed to have made a breakthrough in the search for an identifiable genetic component which distinguished followers of Islam from others. It was unlikely that anyone believed this, but it seemed prudent not to dismiss outright the claim, for whoever did might be branded as unreliable, and squeezed out of his job, or worse. And indeed with the emphasis on secrecy it was easy for people neither to challenge the claim nor endorse it. And funding for the project could continue at least until an attempt was made for the claim to be tested.

Hafiz and Joshua met in a café in the town where social life now went on with the heedlessness of post-war years. Joshua said 'But this is appalling.'

Hafiz said 'It's a game of bluff being played out between lunatic scientists and deceitful politicians. Nothing will happen.'

'But if they get as far as testing it then something will happen. If no one backs down, then something may have been produced that will wipe out everyone.'

'I thought you didn't think that would be a bad thing.'

'One still has to try to stop it.'

'Of course, the dream of our people is that such a weapon or the threat of it might be used against the Israelis.'

'What is it about us and the Israelis? You mean we might want to obliterate them even if we don't really think they might obliterate us first?'

'We should go and talk to Richard Kahn.'

'What will he know about it?'

'He knew that man who was taken hostage years ago and disappeared. He was supposed to have had some secret information about all this.'

As students both Joshua and Hafiz had gone to lectures by Richard Kahn. They had been excited by the way in which his interests seemed to spread beyond any particular discipline; also by the often amused and amusing style in which he spoke of things which others took so ponderously. The three of them became friends, and used to meet in the evenings.

Joshua said 'I thought that when Richard fell down that hole it was his common sense that seemed to disappear.'

'No, I'm serious.'

'Do you think it was the same hole?'

'As what? As our hole?' Then – 'Oh Lord, I don't know!' They found they were both blushing.

That evening they went to visit Richard Kahn in his flat where he lived with his girlfriend Leila, who had dark hair and bright black eyes and until recently had been a student of Richard's. There was a story (stories proliferated at the time) that she had found Richard when he had been mugged or had been drunk one night and had fallen down a hole when on his way home from work; he had broken his leg, and Leila had somehow come across him or perhaps had followed him to keep an eye on him. Anyway she had got him home and had then moved in with him to nurse him. Richard used to say that the breaking of his leg and the lengthy complications that ensued were amongst the best things that had ever happened to him. In order to earn money while Richard was convalescing Leila got a job as a dancer in a nightclub. Richard stayed at home and was said to be writing a book about humour and wit in religion.

Hafiz and Joshua found Richard seated on a prayer mat in his sitting room in front of his computer. He was naked except for a loincloth; his leg in its heavy plaster cast stretched out on the floor in front of him. Another story about Richard was that in addition to his semi-mystical practices he was also nowadays involved in intelligence work for the Americans or Israelis.

Hafiz said to Richard 'You know about this man in my department who says he's found a genetic distinction between Arabs and Jews –'

Richard said 'I thought if you breathed a word of this you were likely to be shot.'

'Well now I've passed on the information to you you're likely to be shot too.'

'So let's hope everyone knows it's all nonsense.'

'They say some substance is going to be tested.'

'So everyone may be wiped out? And it will have been finally and triumphantly demonstrated that there's no significant distinction between Arabs and Jews?'

Hafiz knelt on the floor by Richard's computer and studied the text that was on the screen. He said 'Who was that man who was kidnapped and held hostage years ago? Didn't you know him?'

'Maurice?'

'Didn't he have some inside knowledge about this sort of thing?'

'No, people just thought he did.'

'Why?'

'He was that sort of person.'

'That was why he was kidnapped?'

'Perhaps he wasn't.'

'I thought you found some bones.'

'Oh, they could have been anyone's.'

Joshua said 'I always thought that story was a joke.'

'Well not only a joke.'

'You said he was like Jesus.'

Hafiz said 'What, the empty tomb? The discarded bits and pieces? Is that the sort of thing they're putting out on the Net?'

27

Joshua said 'Anyone can put out anything on the Net.'

Hafiz said 'But no one knows what effect it has.'

Richard put his computer on hold and the screen went blank. He leaned back and closed his eyes.

Joshua said 'So what could we put out on the Net about this weapon.'

Hafiz said 'Let's put out that the Israelis have got it.'

'What would be the point of that?'

'The Israelis wouldn't use it except in retaliation.'

'But no one believes the Israelis.'

'But they wouldn't have it.'

Richard said 'I suppose you two think you're being frightfully amusing.'

Joshua said 'Mightn't that be the point?' Then – 'Well what is it about the Jews?'

Richard said 'What is what about the Jews?'

'Why does everyone pick on them?'

Hafiz said 'Don't they think they've been picked on themselves?'

Richard said 'Yes but what for. That's the question.'

# IV

A sixteen-year-old Israeli girl called Lisa lived in Jerusalem and was being taught the history of the terrible sufferings of her race. She and her fellow school-pupils were instructed about the atrocities that had been inflicted on their parents' and grandparents' generations: these events, it was said, were of an evil that was unique and incomprehensible; they must never be forgotten so that nothing like them should happen again. Lisa felt the force of what was being said; but did not see how the insistence that something was incomprehensible could prevent it from happening again.

Lisa sometimes tried to imagine how she would have behaved at the time of the Holocaust. The question that had troubled many of her generation was – How was it that whole communities at that time seemed to have been led to the slaughter without putting up a fight? It had been explained – People then had no effective organisation nor weapons: it was because of the helplessness of their situation that there had been such urgency about the creation of the State of Israel – and why there is such passion about its strength and security now.

Also, it was pointed out, it had been the belief of many of their parents' and grandparents' generations that so long as they kept to their religious faith and observances then what happened to them was the will of God, however inexplicable and shattering this might be. This fatalism had largely changed with the establishment of Israel: it was now accepted that the state should be protected by political and military force. Lisa wondered – God changes his will?

She found it impossible to talk of these things with her immediate family. Her mother said that on account of what had happened at the time of the Holocaust she had ceased to believe in God – how could God allow such things to happen? Her father said that anyone who read history could see that such things had often happened, and so was she saying that no one should have ever believed in God? Lisa had some cousins in a settlement in the country who said that whatever had been God's will in the past, it was certainly His will now that Israel should not yield an inch of the ground that had been promised to them. Lisa thought – But if I were God I would get fed up with people telling me what is or is not my will.

She tried to imagine herself as a designated victim at the time of the Holocaust. She saw herself lined up on a station platform with her mother and aunts and a crowd of neighbours: her father, she imagined, would have been taken away earlier. She and those with her were to be put on a train and taken to – but indeed how could they have known where – to a place of work? a factory? Would not this have made sense in wartime? Who could have imagined that their enemies would be so irrational!

Lisa was having a daydream of this one day at school. The teacher was writing mathematical equations on the blackboard. Lisa was thinking – But if everything is determined like mathematics, can anyone be held responsible?

Lisa imagined herself getting out of the train at the end of the journey onto flat black earth where there was no platform – just the railway lines ending in front of a gateway. The gateway had a squat tower above it like the one which had been shown in so many photographs. Beyond this photographers had not gone: there was darkness. Lisa was thinking – Do we have to go into the dark, to find what is otherwise incomprehensible?

On the flat muddy ground there were soldiers with rifles slung behind their shoulders like wings. They might be devils. Did not Christians believe in devils? There were so many paintings like this – of figures with pitchforks shovelling people into the fire. So what was it that people said they did not understand – that humans themselves might be responsible for hell?

On the blackboard the teacher was writing the equation that represented the transformation of matter into energy. Lisa thought – Do we not all now want a hand in the ability to make hell?

In her imagination in front of the gateway there was a young soldier with his rifle sticking up from his shoulder like a broken wing. He was instructing people where to leave the suitcases which contained their belongings. Lisa thought she might go up to him and say – I am a mutant, a changeling; I have no family, no belongings; I do not want to belong to the human race as it is. The young soldier had the mark of a terrible wound on his face. She might say – Can you not think of something more fitting for both of us than hell?

The class was packing up. The teacher was wiping out the figures on the blackboard. Lisa was thinking – But two plus two do not always equal four? Somewhere I have read that they need not.

In the evenings Lisa went to classes in nursing – the alleviation of sickness; the healing of wounds. She had become especially absorbed in the study of obstetrics – the bringing of new life into the world.

Lisa had a great-uncle who was Professor of Comparative Religion at the University of Jerusalem. She sometimes went to visit him on her way home from school or to her evening classes. He was an old man who lived on his own at the top of a high-rise block by the university compound: he had fallen out with the authorities because he thought that in their policies and their teaching they were too much haunted by stories of victimisation; these seemed to be taking the place of the old religious stories as a means of ensuring Jewish identity and cohesion. Lisa could talk with her uncle about such things which she could not talk about with either her school-fellows or the closer members of her family. She went to see her uncle this day after school. He was sitting in his wheelchair by a window that looked out over the Old City. She said 'Why is it that we Jews don't feel responsible for ourselves?'

He said 'But now we do.'

She said 'Once it was God. Now it's our enemies.'

Her uncle had a way of moving his lips inside his mouth as if he were chewing his words before swallowing them or spitting them out.

He said 'God is properly that which enables us to be responsible for ourselves.'

'How?'

'God is that which guarantees our freedom.'

'That's not what we are taught.'

'Maybe not.'

'We still think it right to blame our enemies.'

Lisa sometimes had the impression when she was with her uncle that she had come up against that blank wall, or gateway, beyond which there was darkness.

He said 'They've been teaching you about the Holocaust?'

'They've been teaching us mathematics.'

'And that makes you feel helpless?'

'No.' Then – 'But why shouldn't we be responsible for our enemies.'

Her uncle sometimes seemed to chew so hard on what was difficult to swallow that it was as if it were gagging him and preventing him from speaking.

Lisa said 'I mean I sometimes wonder, if I'd been alive at the time of the Holocaust, if there would have been anything that I could have done. I mean, could I have said that I had nothing to do with my family?'

'No.'

'Why not?'

'Because it wouldn't have been true.'

'But can't we change? Why do we go on insisting that we have been victims?'

'Because we think by that things will change.'

'But it seems just to result in our still being surrounded by enemies.'

'We feel ourselves to have a special task. And they feel us feeling this.'

'But what do we feel is this special task?'

Lisa was imagining herself standing outside that gateway. She held a hand out to the young soldier as if there might be a way through; or she might touch the wound on his face.

She said 'Weren't we ever told we might be responsible for our enemies?'

Sometimes her uncle became so still that it was as if he were listening for something just out of earshot.

After a time he said 'There have been times when prophets have seemed to suggest that we might be responsible. There's the book of Jonah. Bits of Isaiah. But that's more what Christians think. And they have proved to be remarkably ill-equipped to do what they say.'

'You mean, it is we who should be running the world but we're not?'

'Oh my dear, how does one run the world? God's freedom cannot be fixed. One's responsibility is to watch and listen.'

'And guide.'

'You can't say that.'

'All right. But without even knowing that you're doing it.'

He said 'It's true you have to learn.' And then more gently – 'It's also true that God is more to do with what you don't know, than with what you do.'

Lisa sometimes felt that she should go and sit on her uncle's lap and put her arms around him. Then the brittle sky above them might crack and fall to earth like broken glass. And they could stop worrying.

She said 'I think we're still waiting for something to learn.'

When she left her uncle Lisa liked to walk or run along the road that led beneath the wall of the great platform on which King Solomon's temple had once stood, where there was now the Islamic Dome of the Rock. This was thus an area sacred to both Jews and Muslims. Round a corner there was an archaeological site where excavations were spasmodically continuing at the base of where the wall was at its highest. The site was fenced off and was closed in the evenings, but Lisa had found a broken piece of fence through which she could climb, and she liked to make her way to where she could be in solitude away from the noise and crowds of the town. There she could sit or lie while darkness came down. This site was supposed to be the place where prophets had once spoken; where King David had danced; before the Temple had been built like a great tombstone on top of it.

She tried to remember what her uncle had been saying. There had been a time when prophets had suggested that Jews should be responsible for people other than themselves? What was the book of Jonah? Hadn't he been swallowed by a whale?

– This was like something waiting to be born?

This evening when darkness was coming down and the moon was like an eye watching through a peephole, Lisa made her way through the fence and was in an area of sunken paths between the stones of what had once been dwellings. The noise of traffic faded; the huge structure of the Temple platform reared above her. She had no classes this evening, and was reluctant to go home. She had a favourite spot where she could lie with her head against a stone beside wild flowers. She was sometimes apprehensive of what ghosts there might be around her. On the platform was the rock on which it was said that Abraham had been about to sacrifice Isaac; within it was said to be the secret chamber where the Ark of the Covenant had been stored; on a stone there was written the unspeakable name of God. What did these old stories mean? Muslims believed that from this platform Mohammed had ascended to heaven; Christians had believed that on the Day of Judgment a rope would be stretched from here across the valley to the Mount of Olives and souls setting out along it would either reach paradise or fall to hell. So many ghosts! They jostled and fought like rowdy children. But Lisa did not for long stay apprehensive. She lay on the cool earth with her hands behind her head and stared back at the moon. She said to herself— Well, old God, can't we move on from your box of magic tricks?

This was a time, she well knew, when her countrymen were in some confusion about current apprehensions. For years there had been war or the threat of war, and enemies had been clearly marked on the map and in the mind. Then efforts had been made for peace, and it had sometimes been difficult to know who was an enemy and who was not. On each side of old dividing lines there were now those who wanted peace and those who preferred the simplicities of war; the latter from each side sometimes seemed to join in impractical alliance; each set of peacemakers sometimes appeared sickened by their new friends. So did not war indeed make more sense than peace? Certainly, it seemed that violence was now on the increase again because it was felt there was nothing better to do.

Close to where Lisa was lying was an excavation where a recent shaft had been dug: she had noticed this the last time she had come to this spot. The excavation was up against the base of the massive wall of the Temple Mount. Lisa had wondered — What if terrorists have taken advantage of the work of archaeologists and are extending a tunnel under the Mount? The archaeological work was being done by Israelis; but there were enough people of all kinds who might wish to

35

damage the Mount and thus destroy the chance of peace. Directly above her at the top of the high wall was the al-Aqsa Mosque that was in daily devotional use by Muslims – and about which there had indeed been rumours from time to time that an attempt might be made to blow it up. Such threats could come from Israeli extremists outraged that a mosque should exist on Israel's most holy spot; or from Arab political extremists who might be ready to desecrate even one of their own shrines if it would be seen by the rest of the world as a sacrilege by Israelis – so that then there might be justification for neighbouring Arab countries to launch a missile attack on Israel – possibly, even, with biological weapons. There had once been Israelis ready to do violence to those of their people who had attempted to make what they saw as a shameful peace.

Lisa remembered one of the strange jokes that her father liked to tell – You are on your own at night in the desert and you come across a party of armed Arabs: what could be worse? And the answer was, of course – To come across a party of Jews. And her father would do his strange clicking laugh behind his teeth while the rest of the family protested. Lisa thought – You mean our jokes might be a recognition of the dark?

She thought she should see if any more work had been done on the recent excavation at the base of the wall. The whole earthwork of the Mount was in fact said to be riddled with only partly rediscovered tunnels which had been dug at the time of King Zedekiah either as escape routes or supply routes when the city had been besieged. If some new tunnel had been uncovered might this not indeed provide a means by which terrorists could get at the mosque? Or might it lead to the lost resting place of the Ark of the Covenant, or to the stone on which there was written the unspeakable name of God. Lisa crawled, trying to keep out of sight – but from whom? from that all-seeing eye? from whoever even now might be lurking in or at the entrance to the tunnel? Then when she came to the hole in the ground that she had previously noticed she found there was now placed in it a vertical ladder. She felt an impulse to run; yet if she did, how would she ever learn how one might be responsible! It was as if she might be at the entrance to that gateway. And that, to be sure, had been no fairy story. She thought she might go down the ladder and then up again quickly; just to say to herself that she had done it. She tried to laugh: how self-important she was becoming! She needed one of her father's terrible jokes. She stood on the ladder.

Light from the moon was cut off halfway down; she could still look up at it when she had reached the bottom. She lowered herself: she imagined she did not have much farther to go when she thought she heard footsteps above her. Or might they be the wing-beats of a great black bird come to get her. In her alarm she missed her footing and slipped; she hung dangling from her arms. She thought – I am a fool; this is the result of thinking I might be responsible for everything. She regained a foothold and stumbled down the last few rungs of the ladder. She crouched at the bottom and felt around with her hands. The shaft she was in was quite narrow; but behind her, yes, was a tunnel. She thought she should crawl a short way along in order to be out of sight of anyone above her. What was it she had imagined she could say to that soldier by the gate – I am a mutation, a foundling: I have nothing to do with the past: if I could choose, I would like to be born again. Can one not choose this? But this was what could be done only by God. She moved backwards down the tunnel on her hands and knees; like this she felt safe. Or was she like Jonah going down into the womb of a whale? It seemed important to recognise that what she was doing made no sense; but then the old stories had made no sense; or had they? They had told of impossible coincidences, and trust. Perhaps she could become part of a new story, a new myth. She thought – Perhaps I am like that caterpillar that is paralysed by the sting of a wasp and is dragged down into the wasp's lair so that the wasp's offspring can have a living body to feed off all winter.

There seemed to be an opening, or alcove, in the tunnel to one side of her; she felt her way into this with her feet and hands. She thought – I will stay here for a time until the danger is past, or until I am given some other indication from the outside world. There was a sound like that of a stone falling to the bottom of the shaft: then what seemed to be a flash of light and a violent pressure on her eyes and ears. She thought – And now there will be darkness: and I suppose I shall never know just what has happened at this moment.

# V

Laura Simmons was in the drawing room of her country house in Oxfordshire. She was arranging flowers in a vase on a grand piano. She thought – I am an actress in a play so old-fashioned that stage hands must surely soon come to take me away. Between the blue of the delphiniums and the gold of the lilies there were spaces which seemed there to give form to colour. Laura tried to remember – Do our minds make colours or are they part of the flowers which grow?

There was the sound of a car arriving on the gravel of the drive outside. This too was like something in a script. She thought – Am I supposed to know my part, or to make it up as I go along?

– One day I will move on from being a feminist with a past.

Her niece Maisie put her head round the door. She said 'Did you expect me or shall I go away?'

'No I didn't expect you.'

'Well, if you're sure.'

Maisie came on into the room. She wore a white blouse and a short skirt over black tights. She said 'We tried to break in but neither the bit of plastic nor a knife would work.'

'Who's we?'

'This man I met.'

'He's driven you here?'

'Well, he wanted to meet you, but he's gone away.'

'Why?'

'Perhaps because I'm now here.'

Maisie went to a sofa and lay down and kicked her shoes off. There was the sound of a car driving away outside.

Laura said 'Are you all right?'

'No I'm absolutely not.'

'It doesn't matter if you couldn't get in. The stuff I wanted isn't important.'

'We bumped into your friend Professor Andros. He caught us in the basement snogging. I mean we had to make out we were snogging because otherwise it would have seemed we were trying to break in. He was on his way to give a lecture. We said we were on our way to the lecture too. As a matter of fact I would have liked to have gone, but I was being horrible. He wants to come and talk to you about your friend Maurice.'

'Who, Andros?'

'No, not Andros, though I'm sure he would too. This man I was with. He's called Dario.'

'How did you meet him?'

'He wants to write something about Maurice.'

'He came to see you?'

'Oh I think one just bumps into people. Things happen. That is, if it's important. Or is that schizophrenic?'

'I don't know, is it?'

'I don't think he knew it was your flat.'

'Your young man? How should he? You let him think you were trying to break in so you could be snogging?'

'No, Andros. My young man knew.'

'How? But of course Andros knew it was my flat! He used to come there.'

'I told him you were the love of Maurice's life. I mean my young man. He was in fact on his way to the lecture. I don't know if he knew who Andros was or not.'

40

'You're not making sense.'

'I know that. So am I the only person who knows that about themselves?'

Laura left the piano where she had been arranging flowers and came and looked down at Maisie on the sofa.

She said 'What was the lecture about?'

'Chance, determinism, free will. Or so he said. I didn't go. Dario did. Does anyone in fact think they make sense?'

'Did Andros know you?'

'I don't think so.'

'Of course Andros knew you!'

'Were you two-timing Maurice with him?'

'No. In a way. But Maurice had gone.'

'I think Andros would have quite liked to be two-timing someone or something with me.'

'That's ridiculous.'

'That's what I'm saying. But it might be true.'

Laura went back to the piano and stared at the flowers in the vase. She said 'You make things up.'

'I think people do.'

'That's what Maurice would have said. Also that most people don't know it. But you do, is that what you're saying?'

'I don't know anything. I don't know why people behave as they do. I don't know why I behave as I do.'

'And that doesn't worry you?'

'Yes it does. I think because of this I'm a specially privileged person.'

Laura put a hand out as if to arrange flowers. Then she gave up.

Maisie said 'My latest hero is a man who blew his brains out when he was thirty because he became obsessed by the idea that we can never know things as they really are, but only by what our brains tell us. So he got fed up and blew them out.'

'Kleist.'

'Yes. I bet you got Kleist from Maurice.'

'Kleist was dying anyway. He had cancer.'

'No, his girlfriend had cancer. So she got him to blow her brains out too.'

'You're being bloody.'

'Sorry.'

Laura left the piano and moved to some French windows which looked out on to the garden. There was a cold wind blowing, against which the daffodils stood up bravely.

She said 'Are you taking your lithium?'

'No.'

'Then no wonder you're in trouble.'

'As I said, I think the world's in trouble.'

'Then shouldn't you be different?'

'I've read that people are not in trouble in places where the world's in trouble. There are few depressed people in Belfast, Belgrade, Jerusalem.'

'And you got that from Maurice.'

'So the world organises itself to give people a chance who might otherwise be depressed. So thoughtful of it.'

'Maurice thought you could make use of that.'

'How.'

'You use your imagination. The world's always in trouble.'

'People ought to want to rescue it.'

'They do, but they usually make it worse. That's part of the trouble.'

Maisie sat up and put her feet down on the floor. She held her hands palm down underneath her and raised herself slightly into the air.

She said 'I want to go on a journey.'

'That's what people used to do. Go on a crusade, a pilgrimage. They thought that might be a way of rescuing things.'

'And were they wrong?'

'I don't know. I went on my journey.'

'But you didn't finish it. I don't think you saw what sort of thing those journeys are. Maurice tried to explain that sort of thing to me just before he went away.'

42

'Maurice tried to explain that to you?'

'Yes. He said one doesn't know what the outcome will be. He said people often made the most awful fools of themselves, but that it didn't matter, because something else might be coming out of it, and they could learn.'

'He said that to you when you were ten, eleven?'

'He was the first grown-up person I'd ever come across who seemed to make sense. Oh, you did sometimes I suppose.'

'He had that effect on people. What else did he say?'

'That people had the most strange and sometimes alarming desires, but that didn't matter either, because if you looked at these and understood them, you could turn them into something useful too.'

'He was talking about him and you?'

'Oh, I don't think so, was he? I thought he must be talking about you. Don't you suppose that was why he went away?'

'That's your imagination.'

'It may be.'

'Is that why you want to go away?'

'Well it would be some point to a journey, to go looking for him, wouldn't it?'

Maisie watched Laura's back as she stood at the window. Then she went to her and put an arm round her shoulders. She said 'I'm sorry. Thank you for putting up with me.'

Laura said 'You don't think he's dead?'

'No.'

'Why not? What about those bones?'

'Oh surely that was a story.'

Laura moved out into the garden. Maisie followed her. They began to walk round the walled garden as if it were the exercise yard of a prison.

Laura said 'If you think he's still alive, where would he be?'

'On a Himalayan mountain? Where did he talk about.'

'He talked about where in fact he went. To Beirut.'

'A trouble spot, you see! And you followed him.'

43

'Yes.'

'And then he just disappeared.'

'Yes.'

Maisie looked round at Laura's burgeoning flower beds and shrubs. She said 'Who was that man who was in prison for years and made a garden with pathways and features and a landscape so that when he walked he could imagine he was going round the world?'

Laura said 'Maurice said that you got to where you wanted to go in the mind.'

'But you still had to go. Exactly.'

'I thought he'd gone to Jerusalem. He had a wife and some sort of stepson there.'

'Maurice did? I didn't know that. Though this man Dario did say he sometimes imagines he might be his son.'

'He's joking.'

'I suppose so. He knows about Maurice. He's heard things on the Net.'

'There's been a lot recently on the Net.'

'Did Maurice himself write anything?'

'Not much.'

'Where's his stuff?'

'In the attic.'

'I think that's why Dario wants to see you. He wants you and him to write something.'

'To write what? What did he see on the Net?'

'Oh, that Maurice was held hostage because he had some secret information or something.'

'That's nonsense. Some information by which he might save or blow up the world?'

'It makes him sound like Christ.'

'People did that. And I suppose he liked it. But Maurice wasn't a scientist. He wasn't even a proper philosopher.'

'Then what was he?'

'Well he did want to change the way people see things. But mightn't he have been just a phoney?'

44

'You don't believe that.'

'No.'

'Then why don't you do something; write something; organise something. Stop going on about being hurt and thinking of yourself as a victim.'

# VI

In a courtyard of marble arcades and a fountain that was not playing, a thickset man with black hair and moustache sat beneath a canopy of embroidered silks on poles. He was on a chair like a throne which was wide enough for him to be toppling slightly sideways but to be kept from subsiding by cushions and shawls pressed round his back and sides. A man with a white turban squatted on the ground facing him and to one side of him; he held a cushion just off the ground and was gazing up at the thickset man as if waiting for instructions either to hand him the cushion or to smother him.

The scene was being picked up by satellite surveillance and was being relayed to a screen a thousand miles away. It was evident from shadows that the occasion was taking place in bright sunlight, but the representation on the screen was blurred. There were circles and lines at angles which made it seem that the courtyard was being targeted. Numbers flickered in rapid succession in a corner.

A third man appeared on a balcony above the courtyard; he was in military uniform and carried an automatic weapon. He looked down at the scene below: the squatting man made a slight gesture with his hand and the man on the balcony took the weapon from his shoulder and held it pointing over the balustrade. On the screen it could not be seen whether the eyes of the man in the chair were open or closed; it was as if the man with the cushion was uncertain of this too.

There were two men watching the surveillance screen. One was in tropical naval uniform with an open-necked shirt; the other was in a crumpled khaki-coloured jacket and wore a Panama hat. When he took the hat off to mop his forehead there was on his forehead the scar of a large wound. He said 'How long has this been going on?' The man in naval uniform said 'Not recorded.' The man with the hat said 'He might be a dummy.'

In the courtyard a figure in a white robe appeared, running. On the screen this seemed like a ghost, or an intrusion from another programme. It was in the form of a woman in flight from invisible pursuers. She ran towards the man in the chair and then stopped, and looked up at the man on the balcony with the weapon. Then she threw herself face down on the ground at the feet of the man in the chair.

The man with the wound on his forehead put his hat back on his head. He said 'She's the wife?'

The man in naval uniform said 'I thought he had dozens.'

'No, the other one's.'

'The eunuch's?'

'For God's sake, he's not a eunuch. And he's not come on yet.'

A fourth man was emerging from a door at the ground level of the courtyard. He was in dishevelled military uniform with the buttons of the jacket undone; he was carrying a bucket which appeared to contain water. He moved towards the fountain in the middle of the courtyard at the centrepiece of which was the figure of a dolphin plunging head first as if into a sea. But the basin of the fountain was empty. The man with the bucket paused by the prostrate woman and it seemed that he might be waiting for orders from the man in the chair to pour the contents of the bucket over her. Then he looked at the man with the white turban; but neither he nor the man in the chair showed any signs of noticing him.

The man in naval uniform said 'We need programme notes.'

The man with the hat said 'Ballet programmes are usually incomprehensible.'

'They haven't got any water? We've cut it off with the bombing?'

'And Jack if not Jill is being held responsible?'

In the courtyard the man carrying the bucket went to the edge of the basin of the fountain and held the bucket over the rim as if he would empty it there. Then he paused again as if waiting for instructions.

The man with the hat said 'How serious is it?'

The man in naval uniform said 'I don't think it's serious at all.'

'I mean the water.'

'Oh, the water. He's still got oil.'

'You mean it's oil in that bucket?'

'For God's sake, not in the bucket.'

The man with the automatic weapon was coming down steps from the balcony. The man with the white turban stood up and gestured towards the man with the bucket. This man pointed a finger of his free hand towards himself as if saying – Me? Then he climbed over the rim of the fountain and into the dry basin.

The man with the weapon had crossed the courtyard and come to the fountain. He stepped into the basin too. He stood behind the man with the bucket and prodded him with the muzzle of his weapon. The man put the bucket down and knelt, facing it. The woman who had been prostrate before the man in the chair lifted her head up to watch. The man with the Panama hat exclaimed as if he had seen the answer to a riddle – 'I know what they're going to do!'

The man in naval uniform said 'Well don't tell me, let me guess.'

The man kneeling in the basin of the fountain held his hands behind his back and put his head down into the bucket so that water overflowed from it. The woman turned her head and looked at the man in the chair. After a time the kneeling man took his head out of the bucket and drew deep breaths and gasped. The man with the weapon prodded him. The kneeling man put his head back in the bucket. The woman scuttled closer to the man in the chair and put her arms round his legs and her head against his knees. The man in naval uniform said 'He likes a threesome?'

The man with the weapon pressed its muzzle against the back of the kneeling man's head. After a time the kneeling man seemed to be trying to lift his head from the bucket but the man with the weapon held it down. After a time the man in the bucket was putting his arms back and trying to take hold of the weapon, but it was as if even then he was taking care not to upset the bucket. The woman who had gone to the man in the chair was pulling the rug on his knees over her head so that her face was on his lap. The man with his head in the bucket began to shuffle on his knees frantically. Suddenly it seemed that the bucket might tip over, and then the man with the weapon put it on the ground and took hold of the kneeling man's legs and lifted them so that he was held upside down with his head still jammed in the bucket. Then there began to be a lot of struggling and splashing and the man with the white turban jumped up and climbed into the fountain and held the bucket steady. Neither the man in the chair nor the woman with her head in his lap were showing signs of watching. The man in naval uniform said 'I know, he's the plunging dolphin!' The man with the hat said 'Oh for God's sake shoot him!'

# VII

The young man with the occasionally frenzied expression, Dario, sat opposite Andros in a café in which most of the other tables were occupied by people on their own. When Dario spoke he made faces as if to apologise for the ludicrousness of his words – perhaps of all words. Andros gazed down at the table top and made swirls in his coffee with his spoon as if he were conducting an experiment about which way water circulated before it went down a plughole. Dario was saying 'You mean we know that genetic engineering could change human nature, but we shouldn't use it?'

'Like the bomb.'

'But knowing that and not using it might in fact change human nature? That's what you're saying?'

'It's a sort of knowledge of empowerment. A trust.'

'Trust in what?'

'Whatever has given us the ability to make such choices.'

Dario looked round the café as if appealing to the people at the other tables to keep an eye out for him if the man sitting opposite him proved to be mad.

He said 'And this could be some sort of religion?'

'Things are connected. There are causes and effects. We can set up experiments and see what works. But knock-on effects go almost immediately outside the range of our knowledge.'

'But you say that your trust is, or can be, that if you do what seems right, then knock-on effects will be for the best.'

'If you've done your best to look for what seems right.'

'And how do you do that?'

'That's what I had hoped to talk about in my lecture.'

Andros stared into his coffee cup. Liquid went round in one direction in the northern hemisphere, and in the opposite direction in the southern. This was to do with gravity? The rotation of the earth? One took note of effects: did it matter if one could not remember causes?

Dario said 'You had begun to say that one might know this like an artist knows rightness in his work of art.'

'Yes.'

'But you would still be the judge of that.'

'There is still something that is art.'

Dario glanced round the room again as if to impart the message that things were not too mad at the moment, but he would like to know if people agreed.

He said 'You act as if this sort of religion were true, and then it is?'

'There seems to be that which makes it so.'

'How do you know this?'

'By what happens. But of course you never know the whole of it.'

'But what happens may be different from the sort of rubbish that would have happened anyway?'

'You would be different.'

'What if your religion requires the slaughter of infidels?'

'Then that would seem to be no good, wouldn't it.'

'But you might think it was.'

'Well you'd have to learn. You'd have to watch.'

'You'd have to know you might be wrong?'

'Of course.'

Dario did not look round the room again. He watched the

old man opposite him, who was obsessively stirring his coffee. He said 'Well thank you for seeing me.' He thought – I imagined he might be wanting to pick me up.

Andros said 'You wanted to talk about Maurice Rotblatt. He wasn't primarily concerned with telling you what was true and false, he wanted to suggest in what manner you could hope to make proper choices.'

'Could feel that they were proper –'

'Could reasonably trust. Of course you might see more of the effects later.'

'And still have a chance to put them right?'

'Quite.'

'I've seen some of the stuff about Maurice that's being put out on the Net. Not so much the stuff about living life as though it were an artwork, but of being involved in a conspiracy, a plot.'

'Well there are good and bad stories.'

'And that was a bad story? Yes.'

Andros looked up at Dario who was gazing at him across the table. Dario had a slightly crooked, crumpled mouth, as if pressed out of shape by a hot wind. Andros thought – People in the café will simply imagine we are picking each other up. Would that not be a commonplace story? That is why we are not?

He said 'Why does Maisie say she wants to kill herself?'

'She says she feels helpless. She's become obsessed by a writer called Heinrich von Kleist who killed himself in eighteen hundred and something because he thought he could never tell what was reality but only what his mind made up.'

'The best thing Kleist wrote was an essay on the Puppet Theatre in which he said that humans had lost their natural grace but could find it again if they went right round the world and into the Garden again by the back way.'

'Maisie wants to go on a journey.'

'Where does she want to go?'

'She wants to go looking for Maurice.'

'Good heavens, does she think she'll find him?'

'I don't think she thinks that's the point.'

'She would be living some myth? Some artwork?'

'Do you think Maurice is still alive?'

'He could be.'

'He didn't want to kill himself?'

'No. He might have wanted to take a gamble.'

Andros was looking down at the chequered tablecloth. He was thinking – I could go home with this boy: I could use him; he could use my money. Would I be corrupting him? There would be the release of tension like that of bowstrings with arrows thudding into bodies.

Andros said 'And what do you do about it?'

'About what? About Maisie? Oh sometimes she wants me around and sometimes she doesn't. That's how she gets her kicks.'

'But how do you get your kicks.'

'You mean I may not want either of us to change?'

'Well people don't, do they? They like other people being a mess.'

'I'm not seeing Maisie now.'

'You don't want yourself to change?'

'You mean my homosexuality? What's wrong with that?'

'Nothing.'

'I thought you might be interested.'

'Oh, I might be.'

'So what do you want to do?' Dario suddenly looked as though he might cry.

Andros, staring at the chequered tablecloth, was remembering the story of the wise man in China who had done the Emperor some service and was told he could have any reward he liked. He said he would like one grain of rice placed on the corner square of a chessboard, and then double the amount on the next square, and so on across and round the board until every square was covered. The Emperor thought he had got off lightly, but he found he had given away the entire rice crop of his kingdom.

Andros said 'Sorry, I asked for it.'

Dario said 'I thought you were trying to pick me up.'

'Perhaps I was.'

'But then you looked at the choices? The probable effects?'

'Some causes, as well as some effects, are more interesting than others.'

'Such as –'

'What were you doing in the basement of that house?'

Dario stared at him. He thought – There are too many connections here for me to work this out.

He said 'Trying to break in. Maisie wanted to pick up some things for her aunt.'

'Why don't you go and see her aunt? She's got most of Maurice's papers.'

'I've been trying to see her, but Maisie doesn't seem to want it.'

'Why should Maisie seem to want it? Anyway she's going on a journey.'

'She hasn't got any money.'

'And you don't want her to go? Well all this seems to be building into quite a good story.'

Dario stared at him. He thought – You mean a more interesting story than one about picking me up?

Andros said 'Look, you're interested in Maurice. Maurice was interested in the way things are connected – how they can be forming a reality which is different for instance from the patterns we expect or try to force them into – or indeed the virtual reality that is put out on the Net.'

'And the fact that you thought of picking me up might form some different connection?'

'You're clever. You could write something about Maurice.'

'Did I tell you that's what I want to do?'

'I don't know. Did you?'

'What was it about Maurice? He wanted to change the world. He got trapped.'

'He wanted to change the way people see the world, which may or may not be the same thing.'

'He had to cut his arm off to get free. Or that's the myth. The fairy story.'

'Then shouldn't someone have a go at the reality?' Andros looked round and waved for the bill.

Dario said 'I'm very fond of Maisie.'

'I'm sure you are.'

'Will you be seeing her?'

'I don't know.'

'If you ask her to meet you she'll say no.'

'Yes I'd thought of that.'

'So you'll just see what happens?'

'It's tricky.'

'She says she's trying to get her aunt Laurie to fix some sort of memorial service for Maurice.'

'You go. I won't.'

'Why not?'

'I'm not sure. Something about the timing?'

# VIII

Lisa became aware of an intense pain in her left arm and right leg. She was lying on her front with her left arm stretched out sideways; her right arm was pressed to her side by her injured leg. It was as if there were an enormous weight above her that was on the edge of crushing her. If she moved incautiously it would come down; but anyway she could not move. She was in a tomb, trapped: but alive, like that caterpillar that provided fresh food for the offspring of wasps.

She tried to remember what had happened. She had been on her way to her special place in the archaeological site; she had crawled through the fence; she had wanted to get to where she could be quiet, and dream. There had been music and someone dancing – or that was part of her dream? She had gone down the tunnel – why? Then something like a grenade had gone off: or had there just been a fall of rock? The pain in her left arm and right leg was becoming unbearable. What happened when pain became unbearable; did you faint, did you go mad? You did not die? Was it not the point of hell, that you stayed alive? If you could not move, you could not make yourself die.

She had been dreaming that she had been at an open-air concert at a kibbutz by the Sea of Galilee. A young pianist from Europe was playing one of Beethoven's last sonatas – Opus 111 was it? the one where notes seemed to tinkle down from the sky. The stars were bright and might be notations for a piece of music; music was the rainbow covenant that promised harmony between earth and heaven. Then there had been an explosion – a rocket had been fired from somewhere over the hills, aimed at where people were gathered so happily. Lisa had read about it in the papers: so she had not been at the concert herself? Dozens of people had been killed and injured. Bits of flesh and bone had rained down from the sky.

She was lying on her front with the weight of earth and rocks on top of her. If she tried to move her stretched-out arm the pain got worse. Or if she pulled hard enough perhaps her arm would come off, and then her blood would flow out, and eventually the pain with it, and then she could die. But there was no room for her arm to come off; there was nothing she could do except to make the pain worse. With her other hand that was pressed against her side she might reach for her leg where there was also the pain; perhaps she could dig with her nails and make a hole to try to get at the pain, but she would never be able to reach it. How was it that humans could hope for anything other than to be able to die.

She had imagined getting out of the train onto that platform; she would go up to the SS officer at the gate and say – I am not human; need I die? Was that really what she had been going to say? She could not remember. There were stones and dirt in her mouth; a jagged projection against her throat. She could not speak: she could not cry out. There had been the sound of footsteps above her; something like a stone, a grenade, falling; what had happened then? She had thought she could hide. You cannot hide from pain. She had wanted to look at the tunnel where they had been making excavations to discover – what? The unspeakable name of God? The whirlpool to hell?

Or they had been plotting to blow up the mosque. Then there might be war, in which humanity would blessedly be wiped out.

The pain was so bad that she was being forced to stop trying to remember. The pain was like a snake that had followed her and got its teeth into her bones. Was it true that you did not remember what happened just before you became unconscious? Could she not make herself again unconscious? Unconsciousness was a state of bliss: being alive was pain.

She could go up to the officer at the gate and say – Please, surely you intended us to die? But she could not get the words out. She might chew on the rubble that was in her mouth and try to swallow it, but her mouth was too dry. She might press on the sharp projection that was against her throat, but she did not seem able to make her muscles obey her: her brain had lost the ability to give instructions. If the pain seemed to lessen for a moment there was panic: the panic was that she would stay alive for ever without being able to move. This was an invasion by an awareness almost more terrible than pain; of the existence of eternal malevolence. At least she could make the pain come in again. Was this why people did not go to greater lengths to avoid suffering? Eternity with consciousness but no distraction was worse? She could say to the officer at the gate – You are trying to be God. You want to keep us alive for your experiments?

There had been times in previous years when Lisa had gone to stay with cousins in the country to help with the fruit harvest: this was at one of the settlements that were threatened with disbandment if there was peace. Lisa's cousins had said that they would rather die than move; they would fight their own troops if necessary. When Lisa talked about this with her uncle he had said – This is nothing new: people have seldom been frightened of war: what they can't bear is emptiness. Lisa had said – But can't we learn?

She became conscious of where she was again. It seemed she had fainted. There had been a boy whom she had been with at the fruit harvest; she had climbed into a tree and had thrown fruit down to him. He had smiled. How long would it be before she started screaming?

When she had been with her nursing class they had been taken to see a baby being born. The baby had become trapped half in and half out of the womb: it was being deprived of oxygen. It had seemed inanimate. She thought – Surely if I wait, I will become unconscious?

The previous year Lisa had gone with her family to the Western Wall in Jerusalem at the time of the Passover: here people had gathered from all over Israel for thanksgiving and celebration. The Passover was when the angel of death had flown over the rooftops in Egypt and had killed all the first-born of the Egyptians and had ensured that Jewish families would be spared; this was so that the Jews, who had been enslaved, could return to their Promised Land. But then things for Lisa had not worked out as she had planned. She had intended to break away from her family at the Wall and go herself to the mosque on Temple Mount; she wanted to put it to the angel of death that it had not been necessary to be so ruthless. But the way to the mosque had been barred; it was apparently thought that extremist Israelis on this day might perform some act of terrorism. So Lisa had made her way in the opposite direction through the crowds to where there was the Christian Church of the Holy Sepulchre. Here, she understood, there would be some celebration of Easter. Lisa had never been inside this church: her mother and father, though they nowadays had little regard for orthodox Judaism, had no tolerance of Christianity. Her father would say – How can you worship a God who gets himself strung up and put in a tomb? And why swap one God that at least doesn't contradict himself for three that do? Her mother said – You call it three! more like a dozen! they fight between themselves like cats and dogs, those Christians. Lisa had asked her uncle what he thought about Christians and he had been silent for a time and then had said – What is interesting about Christianity is that Jesus founded his church on the disciple that he knew would deny him.

Lisa was being crushed in the tunnel. She seemed to have

59

become semi-conscious again. Now she tried to move her injured arm and screamed. But there was no noise. Then she lay still until there might be a blessed darkness coming down. She thought – Perhaps after all I am dying.

In the Church of the Holy Sepulchre it was the evening of Easter Saturday which was when – so Lisa had learned from her uncle – Jesus, having been crucified and buried in a tomb, went down to hell or to limbo or whatever in order to free the souls of righteous unbelievers, before he returned to the tomb to be ready for the resurrection. Lisa had said – But how do the righteous deserve to be in hell? Her uncle had said – There is no need to imagine that the Christian Church makes sense.

Within the church there was a crowd that seemed to be waiting for an event: Lisa had wondered – They expect Jesus to pop out of that tomb? Indeed she could not make much sense of the church. She had come in at a side door and there were people bowing and murmuring in front of a stone slab; this was not so different from what Jews did at the Wall. She had thought – You mean, we all just feel better when we stop banging our heads against a wall? But beyond this entrance there was what seemed to be a central structure: was it over this that Christians fought like cats and dogs? where Jesus did not care if his disciples denied him? (What else had her uncle said – that they were at least sorry?) The church was dark and shadowy; more and more people were pressing in. She was wanting to say – Be careful, my arm and leg are broken! The crowd was trying to squeeze into the central structure. A priest with a tall hat was forcing his way through; Lisa got behind him, but it did not seem he was able to prevent her being crushed.

Her mouth was full of pebbles. There had been the noise like an explosion and the fall of rock. The sky had fallen, and little bits of humans had rained down. She was on her front in the tunnel. She had wanted to die, because she had thought she would never get out of this tomb.

60

She tried to remember – what happened to that baby who could get no oxygen?

There was no chance of anyone finding her. There were no attendants at the archaeological site; her family would not know where she was and would not miss her for some time. Whoever the footsteps had belonged to that she had thought she had heard at the top of the shaft – whoever had caused or witnessed the fall of rock – it would be in their interest presumably for her to remain buried. Her mother would say – How can God let such things happen! Her father would say – But you do not believe in God.

The baby had survived: but how?

Lisa managed to press her throat, hard, against the sharp projection of rock. This provided some distraction. She might find some jagged stone by her right hand and rub it against her wrist; but how could she find such a stone? How Jesus must have wanted to die! But something was keeping her alive?

Lisa had been pressed in the crush into the central enclosure of the church. Here were people sitting, crouching, crammed and perched on wooden seats or stalls: they seemed to be waiting for their miracle: but of course it would be a trick! What had seemed so objectionable about Christians was their delight in the trappings of death: their love of skulls and bones and their pictures of torment: no wonder they had treated people like cattle for the slaughter! So what could be their trick: wasn't it something about fire? The church had become almost totally dark. Lisa had tried to get her back against the inside wall of the enclosure but the press of people was too thick; she had begun to panic; she thought – I do not want to be dug up as a bag of bones! Then there seemed to be an insect, or snake, crawling up the inside of her leg; she began to struggle violently; she was in the tunnel; rocks were forcing their way down tighter against her shoulders; she tried to kick but she had no strength in her legs. She thought – Well I hope I will at least provide food all winter for something better than you, you old wasp, old God: how long does it take to be eaten by maggots?

She had managed to get some of the rubble out of her mouth. She seemed to have been in the tunnel, then in the church, then in the tunnel. She wanted to shout – Damn it, God, can't you make up your mind?

She felt some air against her legs. Or was it a hand? She thought – Can there be someone after all that is trying to rescue me?

Then – It's all right, God, I was only joking!

In the church someone behind her had put his hand on her shoulder. She had turned and seen a young man who was leaning against her in the crush perhaps to steady himself. In the tunnel in the course of her struggles a rock had come down even more firmly against her neck: there was, yes, cold air by her legs but there was still too much weight on her for anyone to rescue her: if they pulled at her her head would come off, her skin would come off, and only her guts would not be left behind. There had been a stirring in the church; beyond the central structure there was shouting and singing: Lisa had tried to say to the young man behind her – What's happening? – but her throat was too dry. Then it seemed that it was in the tunnel as well as the church that there was a clink of metal on stone, a spark of fire, a hot wind coming towards her. In the church, yes, in the dimness there had been an emanation of fire; then lighted candles were being passed over the heads of the crowd towards her. The young man had his hands on her shoulders. She thought – This is the trick?

Someone was pulling on her legs in the tunnel. It was this that was making her skin and flesh burn. She managed to scream. Then there was the jab of a needle in her leg; she thought – Like the sting of a wasp! Then – Oh thank you, thank you, old God! There was a fire coming up inside her veins, her arteries, into her mind. This was bringing cessation of pain. She was being rescued. She thought – But I expect it is still true that afterwards I will never know exactly what was happening at these moments.

# IX

Hafiz had taken to going to Richard Kahn's flat in the evenings. He was increasingly alarmed at stories that an experimental biological weapon was about to be tested – the one that was supposed to be able to distinguish genetically between races. He had heard that a village in the north had been chosen where there was a mixed population of Arabs and Kurds and to which Israeli prisoners held by Muslim extremists could be taken. Intelligence agencies in neighbouring countries might or might not have been made privy to this plan; but in any case knowledge, let alone any involvement, could be denied, as indeed could the whole plan until such a time as something could be seen to have happened; when information or misinformation could be leaked according to what effect was desired.

Joshua liked to come with Hafiz to Richard Kahn's on these evenings. He said 'But we've agreed that anything can be rumoured or denied. It's meaningless! For all anyone will know there might never have been even the prospect of such a weapon!' Hafiz said 'Biological weapons do exist.' 'But does that make a game of bluff more dangerous or potentially more profitable?'

Richard sat on the prayer mat in his living room with his plaster-encased leg stuck out like the needle of a compass. He said 'Well yes, but the question is, so far as trying to control events goes, what activity more than bluff do individuals have any access to?'

Hafiz said 'Well what do they?'

Joshua said 'They used to be able to pray.'

Hafiz said 'Fat lot of good that did.'

Richard said 'Well, you wouldn't know. Confidence can be effective.'

Richard's girlfriend Leila was usually there in the evenings before or after her work in the nightclub. She would move round the flat in a dressing gown or in her scanty working clothes that were aimed at projecting her as being sexually irresistible to men. She said 'Surely there's something more practical you could be doing than playing games with deceitful politicians and crazy scientists.'

Richard said 'Such as what.'

'I've asked someone to come round and mend your computer this evening.'

'My computer isn't broken.'

'I know. I met him at work. He's some sort of deputy head of police. But I don't think he's an ordinary policeman, I think he's one of those people who work for all sides or none.'

'You mean he's coming round here hoping to get off with you.'

'I've told him you're laid up with a broken leg.'

'And that encourages him?'

'We haven't got further than that yet.'

Hafiz looked displeased. He had fallen somewhat in love with Leila: he used to go to her nightclub in the evening and watch her dance. He was too nervous, or too loyal to Richard, to do anything further himself; but he recognised the extent of her power.

Richard said 'You mean he might help us?'

'He's no fool. He says he works with fools. He'd probably like to be part of something that makes sense.'

Richard closed his eyes and swayed to and fro on his prayer mat. After a time he said 'Well, Hafiz, you could go on a reconnaissance trip to the north, to where you say there's this village. You could see whether there's anything happening there or not.'

Hafiz said 'You mean actually go there?'

'Yes, actually go there. It would be a help that in the present climate of make-believe this would not be expected.'

'But I don't know where it is.'

'Well keep your ears open. Look.'

Joshua thought – You mean that might be a practical form of prayer?

Hafiz said 'But if people found out what I was doing –'

Richard said 'Well of course anything could happen or nothing.'

Joshua said 'Prayer was once felt as a means of making the individual effective?'

They were silent for a time. They imagined Hafiz being taken prisoner by security forces and chained to a radiator; information being extracted like teeth without an anaesthetic.

Hafiz thought – But I might thus impress Leila?

Joshua said 'But I do think we ought also to be trying to find out more about that man Maurice Rotblatt. He was supposed to be working for some intelligence organisation and to have known something about all this: and to have been held hostage for what information could be got out of him.'

Hafiz said 'That was a story.'

Leila said 'And years ago.'

Joshua said 'It's on the Net.'

Richard said 'I don't think Maurice had that sort of information.'

Hafiz said 'Did you make up that story?'

Joshua said 'But you've always said he was something special.'

Richard had closed his eyes and was swaying again on his prayer mat. The others watched him with some impatience.

They were never quite certain what might be one of Richard's tricks.

Sometimes when they were together in the flat in the evenings it was as if they were conspirators, members of a secret society in an upstairs room. Sometimes this seemed wildly pretentious; then sometimes not pretentious at all.

Richard said 'He had a girlfriend with him when he was here, did you know?'

Hafiz said 'Wasn't he supposed to be giving information to the Israelis?'

'His girlfriend was English. She went back to England.'

Leila said 'Someone must have interviewed her to find out what she knew.'

Joshua said 'I wouldn't mind going to England.'

Hafiz said 'You'd never get a visa!'

'Of course I would.'

Joshua wondered – Is he jealous? He might find that he still cared about me, if I went to England?

Then – Does Leila know he is in love with her?

Leila said 'My policeman might be able to help. He's rather nice. He says he wants to marry me.'

It seemed for a time that the others did not know how to respond to this.

Richard said 'When's he coming round?'

'Any moment.'

'Well it has seemed that something odd is happening.'

There was a ring on the doorbell. Hafiz and Joshua jumped. Richard had stopped swaying on his prayer mat, as if he were responsible for the summoning up of a spirit.

Leila went to the door. On her way she said to Richard 'I think I may have given him the impression that you work for the CIA.'

Richard said 'Oh yes, well that might seem like something practical.'

Leila opened the door. On the landing there was a large man with thick grey hair and a large scar on his chin. He held two bottles of champagne in his arms. When he saw Hafiz and Joshua he remained on the threshold. Leila moved back into the room and said 'Well here we all are, you've caught us red-handed.'

The policeman said 'That's all right, I've brought two bottles.'

Richard said 'Can one of you two get some glasses please?' Joshua went into the kitchen.

Leila said 'We were just discussing what on earth could be done if someone did decide to try out this biological weapon.'

The policeman came into the room slowly, as if he were testing the temperature of water.

Richard said 'Leila says you think the Americans wouldn't stand for it if the Israelis threatened to use their bomb in retaliation.'

The policeman said 'I said that?'

Leila said 'You might have done.' She smiled and put her hand on his arm.

The policeman said 'May I sit down?'

Richard said 'Please do.' Joshua came back from the kitchen with some glasses.

The policeman said 'So you are conspirators.'

'We'd like to be.'

'Or a prayer meeting? You'd rather be doing something than nothing?'

Hafiz said 'I work at the Biological Institute.'

The policeman said 'I know you do.'

Richard said 'We have our hopes, intentions. We don't know their effects.'

The policeman was opening one of the bottles of champagne. Leila held a glass for him. When it was full, she took the bottle from him and handed him the glass.

The policeman said to Hafiz 'Do you know where this village is that it's said they've chosen for their experiment?'

'I might be able to find out. I could look.'

'You wouldn't be very popular wandering around the country.'

'Or might it be another country?'

'Ah!'

The policeman nodded to Leila, who filled the other glasses and handed them round. Then she came back to the policeman and stared down at him. She said 'We hoped you might be able to help with some of that.'

The policeman laughed. He raised his glass to Leila. He said 'So it's not just for myself that you might love me!'

Leila said 'That would not be so interesting a form of love.'

The policeman said to Richard 'Do you agree about that?'

Richard said 'Oh I agree!'

The policeman drank some champagne. They all drank champagne. Then the policeman said 'Oh children children, this is serious.'

Richard said 'Yes we know.'

Leila said 'That's what makes us so curiously light-hearted.' She sat on the floor and rested her back against the policeman's legs and looked out on the others.

Hafiz said 'Are you getting anything from the satellite surveillance?'

The policeman said 'Not much.'

Joshua said 'The story about the biological weapon isn't a joke?'

Richard said 'One can make use of jokes.'

Leila said as if to no one in particular, 'Can you remember the name of the woman who was here with Maurice Rotblatt?'

The policeman said 'You take him seriously?'

Richard said 'Her name was Summers. Or Simmons. Laura Simmons.'

The policeman said 'I interviewed her at the time. It seemed she was withholding something.'

Joshua said 'I was hoping to go and talk to her.'

Hafiz said 'Didn't he have a wife who was an Israeli?'

The policeman looked from one to the other. Then he said 'Have either of you two any experience in this sort of thing?'

Richard said 'Official attitudes don't seem to be much good.'

The policeman said 'Are you a Sufi?'

Richard said nothing.

Joshua said 'Should I have trouble in getting a visa?'

The policeman said to Leila 'And what are you going to do?'

Leila said 'Well we'll see.'

'And that's all?'

Leila said 'That's enough, isn't it?'

Richard said 'As soon as I'm fit, which will be soon, I will be making a trip to Jerusalem.'

The policeman said 'And I called you children!'

# X

A line of vehicles was moving across a desert plain like ants. There was an armoured car at the front and one at the rear and in the middle a saloon car and a jeep. On satellite surveillance the column hardly seemed to be moving. On the ground, the people in the back of the saloon car were having to hold on to their seats as the rough track shook them like dice.

In the front seat there was a driver and a man in camouflage uniform; the two men in the back were in civilian clothes. One wore a Panama hat, and when the car went over a bump this became crushed against the roof. The man took it off and held it on his lap and began pressing and moulding it back into shape. There was the scar of an old wound on his bald head that glistened in the heat and looked as if it might just have been made by the movement of the car. The man beside him watched with increasing irritation as he smoothed and patted the hat. The man with the hat seemed aware of this, but continued with what he was doing, faintly smiling.

His companion said 'If they're genuine you're supposed to be able to put them under a steamroller.'

The man with the hat said 'It's not always easy to find a steamroller.'

'How did you get that head?'

'It came with the rest of me.'

The track was becoming increasingly indistinguishable from the unmarked surface of the desert. The leading armoured car veered off, and the other vehicles followed. The hatless man was unfolding a large map; then, having relinquished his hold on the seat, he hit his head on the roof. The man with the hat said 'A hat doesn't help much.' The man with the map called out to the people in front 'What's the reference?'

There were coming into view in the rocky desert some bumps or regular shapes that might be formed by the wind and the very occasional rain; or they could be man-made as archaeological remains or recent excavations. The man with the map said 'You're wasting our time.' The man in uniform in the front seat turned round and said 'Hittite.'

The man with the hat said 'Hittite shittite.'

The man in uniform said 'You do not want to see?'

'Oh just a peep, my good fellow, having come all this way.'

The convoy had come to a halt in front of the area which now seemed unmistakably that of an archaeological site. There was a notice board nailed to a post with writing on it in Arabic. The man in uniform leaned over the back of the front seat and said with a smile – 'Danger. Keep out. High explosives.'

The man with the map said 'You use high explosives for archaeological work?'

The man in uniform said 'Absolutely.' Then – 'To deter thieves.'

The man with the hat said 'Thieves could presumably do with a bit of high explosives.'

The man in uniform said 'Oh the English and Americans are the worst pillagers of our national treasures!'

The man with the map said 'Oh for goodness' sake!'

They climbed out of the car stiffly. The sun was hot overhead. The man with the hat put it on, took it off, made a new dent in it, put it on again. The man looking at the map was sweating so much that his spectacles fell off and he caught them with the map as if it were a safety net. Two men with automatic weapons had got out of the jeep; the man in camouflage uniform led the way round the half-excavated area towards a block-built shelter or storeroom just beyond. He gestured behind him with his hands as if to indicate to the others that they should follow carefully in his footsteps. The man with the map said 'For God's sake, mines?' The man with the hat said 'Well I suppose we are looking for explosives.'

The man in uniform stopped and the others stopped in a line behind him. The man in uniform said 'This is a World Heritage Site. We are ordered by the United Nations to protect it.'

'You protect it with landmines?'

'We have an exact plan where they are.'

The man with the hat said 'Very correct. Very impressive.'

The man with the map said 'And you think this sort of thing will end sanctions?'

The man in uniform set off again towards the concrete building. The door appeared to be locked. The man in uniform searched through a large bunch of keys. The man with the map said 'Look, we've got absolutely no interest in going into this building.' The man with the hat said 'For God's sake let's get out of the sun.' The man in uniform said 'I thought you wanted to see where they keep their explosives.'

One of the men with an automatic weapon went to the door and gave it a kick and it opened. Inside there was not much except a table and three chairs and a primus stove and a kettle and some mugs. The man with the hat said 'The English pillagers have got here first!'

The man with the map said 'And they seem to have taken all the archaeological equipment.'

The man in uniform said 'You want us to start digging?'

'No, we do not want you to start digging.'

The man with the hat said 'Have they left milk and sugar?'

He sat down and put his hat on the table and mopped his forehead. He said 'Well let's see if we can talk some sense.'

The man in uniform said 'I agree.' He sat down opposite him. The man with the map began prowling round the room looking at the walls and ceiling.

The man with the hat said to the man facing him 'There's no way we're going to find anything you don't want us to find, is there.'

'I don't believe so.'

'Is that what you want then – to keep the show going?'

'Until you're satisfied?'

'We won't be.'

'Why not?'

'Perhaps we don't want to be.'

'Then it's you who will be keeping the show going.'

'That's as may be.' Then – 'Look – would you mind if we had a word, as our policemen say in our movies when they mean they want to be on their own?'

The man in uniform spoke to the two men with weapons in a language that the others did not understand. After what seemed a brief argument the men with weapons left the building. The man with the map came and joined the two men at the table. After a time the man in uniform said 'This is more dangerous for me than for you.'

The man with the map said 'We know that.'

'Our children are suffering.'

The man with the hat said 'You make use of your children's suffering.'

'Have you equipment that can see this?'

'See the children? Isn't that your intention?'

'See what's going on here.'

The man with the map said 'Not inside the building.'

'You could be recording it.'

'For what purpose? To damage you? To upset the chessboard? Why should we want that!'

'How would you put it – for mutually assured destruction?'

73

The man in uniform seemed to be laughing. The others gazed at him.

The man with the map said 'Look we've agreed it may be in both our interests to keep the show going. But not to overdo it. Which would end it.'

The man with the hat said 'And we'll stay the villains. With respect to the children.'

The man with the map looked at him sharply. He said 'You're mad!'

'I did not say that!'

The man in uniform said 'Oh if there's a tape, we're all villains.'

The man with the hat said 'This is becoming a world in which people can make of it what they like. The perfect world for the artist.'

The man in uniform said 'We have always been good at that. You are the tradesmen.'

'Oh you're catching up fast.'

The man with the hat glanced at the man with the map, who appeared to be going to sleep. After a time he said to the man facing him across the table 'Would it be a help to you if we insisted on your doing some digging?'

'No not really.'

'You can swing it?'

'Swing it?'

'Say that this trip has been satisfactory.'

'You'll accept that?'

'And take us somewhere we can have a decent meal.'

The man in uniform laughed. The man with the map appeared to wake up suddenly. He said 'It can be quite dangerous for us too you know.'

'You mean our cooking?'

'I mean don't push us. There are people who would like to step up the bombing.'

'You think we three are the true patriots?'

74

The man with the hat said 'The last refuge of the scoundrel.'

The man in uniform said 'Aren't there others like you?'

'Good heavens; well one doesn't know.'

'Not know how many?'

'Look, there'll come a time when I'll suggest that just by going on like this, aren't we in fact getting somewhere?'

'And then the nonsense might stop?'

'It's possible.'

'The bombing? Sanctions?

'Oh, we all might have something else to worry about!'

'You do realise that?'

'That's not a threat?'

'I hope not.'

'No, I don't think so.'

The man with the map began folding it. He stood up. He said 'But we have very little influence you know.'

The man in uniform said 'Who does?'

The man with the hat thought – Has anyone understood a word of this conversation?

The man in uniform said 'It's the rogue elephant with a bomb or something worse that is the threat to all of us.'

The man with the map said 'We do realise that.'

The man with the hat said 'Do you know any Sufis?'

# XI

Laura Simmons stood in the pulpit of a church and faced a congregation of a few dozen people. She said –

'We are here to recognise the life of my old friend Maurice Rotblatt. It may seem strange to you that he should be commemorated in a church, because he made it clear that he had little time for socially organised religion; but he was looking for ways in which to talk about God, and he recognised that the Church did at least keep alive ways in which this had traditionally been attempted.

'The occasion of our coming here now, some seven years after Maurice disappeared, is the stories circulating about how some remains have been discovered in a cellar in Beirut. It is highly unlikely that these have anything to do with Maurice, and in fact there seems to be doubt that there were any bones at all; but the stories seem to have caught the public imagination, and Maurice would, I'm afraid, have been shamelessly amused at the parallels some media people have drawn between his own bodily disappearance and that of Jesus.

'Maurice had sympathy with those who felt that old ideas about God were dead; he felt especially that one could not talk about God with any certainty. Maurice was not by profession a scientist, but he believed in the efficacy of scientific techniques by which one made conjectures through observation and then tested their validity by experiment. But the scientists he admired were those who saw that even what could be put into words could not be said to be finally true, but was part of a process of uncovering what remained in its essence unknown.

'He became fascinated by the saying that if God did not exist it would be necessary to invent him. This has been taken for the most part to imply that God is a fantasy – one to provide comfort for humans helpless in a chaotic world and fearful at the prospect of dying. But if God is felt to be necessary – and if the presence of such a God seems to work for the purposes for which it was invented – then in what sense can God be said not to exist? What justification is there, for instance, for belief in the existence of gravity, except that it works? This argument of course depends on in what sense such a fitful invention as that of God can be said to 'work': a fantasy can at least for a time be said to work – to provide a sense of meaning and consolation. And to be sure there has been enough evidence in history that an allegiance to a God can also lead to horrific persecution.

'Maurice, as a would-be scientist, believed that the style of a belief was there to be tested: that what might truly seem to "work" – to be life-giving and enlightening – had to be subject to one's observation and experience. This did not mean that oneself alone was the arbiter; one was in partnership with what one had discovered; which had its own autonomy and which seemed to point to a further way. This is not dissimilar to the experience of a scientist.'

Laura paused. She looked down at her notes on the edge of the pulpit in front of her. She thought – This is where I come unstuck; where I do not know what I am talking about. Would it help to say that of course I cannot know what I am talking about?

There was a young man sitting on his own in a side aisle of the church who was smiling up at her as if to encourage her.

She went on – 'It was Maurice's contention that without a

77

sense of what he was still reluctant to call God, humans had no freedom and thus no autonomy – they were at the mercy of the environment, or of what constituted them, or of chance. But it was – or it could be – the experience of humans that they were not simply helpless like this: that they did have freedom and not just in a vacuum; they were in a context in which choices might be effective. Maurice claimed that the so-called invention of God was necessary in order to explain – and indeed to make possible – the human experience and exercise of freedom. God was not that which controlled humans, but that which guaranteed the conditions by which they had autonomy. God was also that by which enough information was available to make the exercise of choice seem reasonable. Without such a concept there was indeed no reason to believe that humans were not helpless.

'But in what manner, what style, might one exercise this partnership with a force beyond oneself; and not be plagued by fears of delusion?'

The young man at the side of the church was leaning forwards on the edge of his seat as if he were eager to add his own contribution to what she was saying.

Laura went on – 'It was Maurice's contention that one could see one's life as the creation of a work of art: that by painstaking care and patience, by observation and trial and error, one might make something that had meaning beyond what might be comic or tragic. The validity of an artwork cannot be judged in the same way as that which it depicts – that is, not simply morally. Artistic rightness and wrongness are known instinctively – both by the artist when he is form-ing a work, and the viewer or listener considering it. Many artists in fact have an impression of a partnership with God.'

Laura broke off again. She thought – Now this is the moment at which Maurice would tell me I should stop talking and start listening.

The young man in the side pew said quietly but audibly 'That's absolutely right.'

78

She said 'Thank you.'

'You knew Maurice well, didn't you?'

'Yes.'

People were turning, stretching their necks, to see who the speaker in the side pew might be. He was a rather wild-looking young man. Laura wondered – Do I know him?

She went on – 'To make of your life an artwork you see it as a story. The human brain naturally makes stories: it also has the ability to distinguish good stories from bad. Good stories are not arbitrary; they are more than a recognition of cause and effect; they are not of the triumph of either right or wrong, they are of the interplay between the two which conveys a meaning. They tell of coincidence, correlation, of the existence of various possibilities; of the style by which one possibility rather than another occurs. Such stories seem true. They are what make it natural for a human to be aware of the world of possibilities, and thus of an environment in which choice is valid. You can learn from your mistakes, but you do not choose mistakes because this would not be learning. You learn to choose, or perhaps that you are in league with choice, by recognising its existence. It is like a relationship with a loved one.'

Laura thought – If I have become unintelligible, might people think I am what was called speaking in tongues?

'Maurice used to say that one of the best stories invented was that at a certain stage God had handed over power on earth to humans, but humans could only make proper use of this in so far as they recognised it was God's empowerment. God does not instruct humans; but the world perhaps provides enough evidence for them to learn what they should or should not do. This seems to me a true story.

'Maurice saw this time as one of some absurdity and evil, but no more so than any other. Perhaps it even contained in it something unusually of good, because persons now had more chances to recognise absurdity and evil, and do something about them, at least within themselves. Maurice had an admiration for the Sufis, who are mystical Islamists, and from whom he got many such ideas.

'The stories that Maurice liked were of people who went on a journey; who wanted to move physically from stratified states of mind; not only to think, but to do. He liked myths in which protagonists embarked on adventures with no precise end in view – searchers in dark ages setting out across unknown seas; wise men in deserts or mountains moving from village to village –'

The young man in the side pew said 'Is that what you think he is doing?'

Laura said 'I don't know.'

'You don't think he's dead?'

'I don't know.'

Laura thought – This is the first time I've said that. So what are we doing in this church? Something, as Maurice would say, quite different? She felt faint. She had to get down from the pulpit.

She said in the direction of the young man 'So what do you think?'

'I think he's up to something.'

'Yes.'

'I'm sorry if I've interrupted you.'

'No, I've finished.'

As she began to move down from the pulpit she staggered a little. The vicar came to help her. She thought – Perhaps I should stumble and fall: then people can think I am overcome with emotion. But what do I want people to think? What on earth is happening in this strange story?

More people came to help her at the bottom of the steps. She said 'It's all right, thank you, I just need a little fresh air.' She hoped – The young man will come out and talk to me. The vicar was saying 'We will now sing our last hymn.'

In the graveyard there was a cold wind blowing that rustled the new leaves as if it might be autumn. A man was standing in the long grass by a gravestone. As Laura came out of the church he began to watch her intently. Laura thought – But he is not the young man from the church. Who are all these people suddenly popping up in this story?

This young man waited for her to come to him. Then he said 'Mrs Summers?'

'No, Miss Simmons.'

'Oh I'm sorry!'

'That's all right.'

'You must think I have not done my homework!'

'No.'

'I am afraid I got here too late for the service.'

'I see.'

'I wonder if I could talk to you about Professor Rotblatt.'

'He wasn't a professor.'

'Oh dear! Soon you will not want to talk to me at all!'

He spoke rather affectedly, with a slight foreign accent. Laura wondered – He is homosexual?

She said 'No, I mean I will talk. It's just that I'm waiting for someone to come out of the church.'

There were the noises of the hymn coming from the church. She wanted to catch the other young man before he disappeared. Maurice had disappeared: nothing had been heard about Maurice for years, and now a rush of things was happening. She did in fact feel faint. She propped herself against a gravestone.

The man said 'Perhaps I could come and see you at your home.'

'Yes that would be nice.'

'I come from Beirut.'

'Beirut! Then you know Richard Kahn?'

'Yes it was he who suggested I come and talk to you.'

'How is Richard? I hear he broke his leg.'

'He feels he has perhaps put the cat among the pigeons.'

Laura laughed. 'Did he make up that story?'

'I don't know. But can there not be a virtue in stories?' He laughed.

The other young man had come darting out of the church. When he saw Laura and the man by the gravestone, he stopped. Laura thought – He came running out to find me, and now he will think I am tied up with this young man and he will go.

The man she was with said 'My name is Joshua.'

'What a good name.'

'Oh he was a mass murderer!'

'So they say.'

'But no one minded in those days.'

'No.'

The man she was with was staring at the young man by the church. Laura said 'Excuse me a moment.' She began to move towards the young man by the church. She thought – And now this other young man will believe I do not approve of him and will go.

Then as she approached the young man by the church she saw that his attention was directed not at her, but at the man she had just left by the gravestone. She thought – They know each other? This is some pick-up between homosexuals?

So what an absurd story!

When she reached the young man by the church he said rather aggressively 'Do you know where Maisie is?'

'No. She was here the other day.'

'Yes I know. I drove her down from London.'

'Oh I see. Yes, she told me. Don't you want to talk about Maurice?'

'Yes. Who is that person you were talking with, do you know?'

'No.'

'You don't?'

'No. He says he's called Joshua. He too wants to talk about Maurice.'

'Ah. Then perhaps I'll meet him.'

'Perhaps you will. Or do you want to talk about Maisie?'

'Why does she want to kill herself, do you know?'

82

'No. She says she wants to go on a journey.'

'Yes. She wants to go to Beirut.'

'That man I was talking to comes from Beirut.'

'Does he?' The young man's eyes seemed to glitter. He was still gazing over Laura's shoulder at the man by the tombstone. The man by the tombstone was gazing back at him.

Laura thought – Well perhaps all this is so that I can go and lie down, which is what I want to do. She said 'Well I've got to go now.'

'Can I come and talk to you some time?'

'Yes.'

She began to move away. Neither the young man by the church nor the man by the tombstone made any move to follow her. She thought – Why did I think I might have any control over this story?

People were emerging from the church. The vicar was trying to talk to the young man. The young man and the man by the tombstone remained intent on one another.

Laura thought – Didn't Maurice say it was all like gravity?

# XII

What made Maisie want to die was the feel of herself as part of a mechanism in which everything in order to live had to devour something else. This was what life was: every atom, molecule, cell that made up her body and her brain – let alone everything alive in the outside world – was occupied in surviving at the expense of everything else. She, Maisie, was a battlefield on which there was savagery and the stench of death: she was a representation of the world in which animals and insects tore at each other and munched like crabs; in which the painted faces and sickly perfumes of plants nurtured insects that bred worms and maggots. Only in death were things restored to the peace of nothingness. For the planet this might not take place for billions of years: in the meantime she, Maisie, was a paralysed caterpillar providing a living for grubs and beetles. But what could she do to make an end of this that would not itself be an act of destruction? She could at least stop eating. She would have made some protest and in the end she would die; but the things which fed off her would also die. Or would they all remain conscious as if under ice for ever, as in those ghastly pictures and stories of hell?

Andros sat in front of his computer and checked his e-mail. There had recently been a craze for hackers or jokers to flood sites at random with offers of virulent pornography; once accepted, these were programmed to spread like a virus from computer to computer and cause jamming and destruction of software. Busy people were said to fall for this, since they had little time to search for pornography on their own. Recently there had been a spate of offerings purporting to show punishment for anorexic schoolgirls.

There came into Andros's mind the image of the young girl Maisie whom he had met with Dario when they had been on the way to his lecture. He should have recognised Maisie, because she was the niece of his old friend Laura Simmons; but he had not seen her since she was a child and she had grown so thin and waif-like; also pretty. But then before the lecture she had run off; perhaps because she had been upset by his not knowing her. But she had seemed interested in what he had said to her, and she had told him that she hoped she would see him again. Andros was at an age when he could still dream of young girls though he could not sensibly do much about this. But he had told Dario that, yes, he hoped to see her again.

Maisie had taken to walking at night in a part of the town where troubled people felt at home; where predators and scavengers would at least not scorn or pity them. Also there was the chance, the excitement, of being offered dope or other drugs. Maisie had not indulged much in drugs but she liked to know they were there; and she had a fantasy about getting hold of a suicide pill which might at least be a comfort to keep by her. In these streets she could wander for a time without pain while imagining she might find, if things worked out like that, a corner in which to lie down and wait to die. This would be better than being strapped in a hospital room with people looking down on her and forcing tubes down her throat, as if through the ice.

Andros sometimes was drawn to this part of the town at night. He was a tall, ascetic-looking man in his sixties, he worked hard at his writing and lecturing and research, he had drifted apart from two wives and several mistresses, and he did not want to be involved with such relationships again. But he became lonely in the evenings, and was sickened by the pornography on the Net with its offer of a quick climax like a glass of poured beer spilling over. Better was the non-consummation of wandering through streets which at least had the texture of sound and sight and smell. The windows of massage parlours and strip joints were like the blossoms on trees that Adam and Eve must have wandered around.

Maisie was thinking – The reason why I do not take drugs is because I do not want to lose control – unless, that is, I lose it for ever. My dislike of eating is an exercise in control – of a body whose mechanisms are almost entirely unknown to me; but at least by starving it I can show my contempt for it. But then – will I not be behaving in the same destructive way as everyone else? She saw this, but did not know what to do about it. She imagined she might come to a part of the town where women have no more responsibility because they are murdered.

Andros had been wondering if he should ring up Laura Simmons and ask what was happening to Maisie: if she was in trouble, should he get in touch with her? Laura would not think he was simply running after her: or if she did – or if he was – did it matter? Maurice Rotblatt had been fond of Maisie as a child: Laura would know that it was through such attraction that genuine care could flourish. But still, it was probably better if this occurred naturally rather than by manipulation.

Maisie had thought once or twice of Professor Andros since their meeting on the way to the lecture, and of their both saying that they hoped they would meet again. Andros had a way of seeming to make awkward things acceptable: this was what she had felt, as a child, about her mother's lover Maurice Rotblatt. She regretted now not having stayed for Andros's lecture: she had wanted to get away from Dario: but she was so proud and impulsive! How could she now get in touch with Andros without this seeming to be running after him?

Andros saw Maisie standing with her back to him looking at a window the glass of which was opaque. He did not at first believe it could be her – it was too unlikely! – then he went back to being interested in the question that had been exercising him just before – how much are coincidences that seem unlikely or even miraculous the result of oneself being in a receptive state of mind through which quite natural coincidences are more likely to be noticed: or might there be some faculty in the outside world by which coincidences are facilitated? Psychologists and even a few rogue physicists speculated about this but of course had no way of coming to a rational conclusion. Andros had stopped in his walk: he hoped that the girl he had imagined might be Maisie would turn so that he could see her face. Then when she did – yes – he was sure it was Maisie! Then it was too late to lose his nerve. He said 'I was just thinking about you!' She said 'Well we did say we were going to meet, didn't we?' He said 'Do you think these coincidences happen if you expect them to or if you don't?' She said 'Well, that's the sort of thing I was going to ask you.' He thought – Well, this is happening: and she has become more thin and waif-like than ever. Then – Such people are needy, but dangerous; they seem to invite, but then reject, care and protection.

There was a doorman at the entrance next to the opaque-glass window who said 'Well are you coming in or aren't you?' Andros said 'Perhaps another time.' Maisie said 'Oh I've always wanted to go to one of these places!' Andros said 'Well let's go in then.' He paid at a counter and they went through a curtain into a half-dark room with tables and chairs and nondescript music and a stage jutting out with a pole that went up from it to the ceiling. A naked woman was wrapping herself round the pole like a snake. Andros thought – I am like Dante taking Beatrice on a quick trip to hell: or to purgatory, on the way to heaven?

He and Maisie sat at a table. Maisie said 'Weren't you saying that interesting things happen if you trust them?'

Andros said 'Oh yes I suppose I was.'

'And you weren't following me?'

'No.'

'I wouldn't have minded if you were.'

'That's very nice of you to say so.'

'Or perhaps you were, in a way. Do you think so? You like this part of town? I do.'

'That's a way of putting it.'

'But you don't think one can say very much more about coincidences.'

'Not really.'

A waiter came up for their orders. Andros said he would like a beer. Maisie said she would like a glass of champagne. The waiter said that champagne was seventy pounds a bottle. Maisie asked how much was the beer. The waiter said it was eight pounds a glass. Maisie said she would like water. The waiter said that water was seven pounds a bottle. Andros ordered two beers. Maisie said 'Why don't they make these places nice?' Andros said 'Because they're not nice. People like them being horrible.'

Maisie watched the woman writhing round the pole. She thought – That's the sort of pole that firemen used to slide down in old movies. She said 'So what happens now?'

Andros said 'Would you like to eat?'

'No.'

'You don't eat much.'

'No.'

'Why not.'

'It rots inside you.'

'I'll take you to a very good restaurant.'

'I quite like this place. Yes, it's so obviously horrible.'

'I'm going to Paris tomorrow. You could come with me. To a restaurant.'

'Why are you going to Paris?'

'Business.'

'What sort?'

'Official.'

'Laura thinks you're a spy.'

'Maybe.'

'Why are you asking me?'

'If you don't eat you get ill.'

'I want to go on a journey.'

'This could be a first step then.'

'Were you thinking of coming to this place anyway?'

The woman on the stage had got herself upside down on the pole. Her legs were slowly toppling over so that her behind was sticking out like something being skinned.

Andros said 'No. But I quite like being on the outside and knowing this sort of thing is going on.'

'Why?'

'Because it's what a lot of life is like. As you say, rotting.'

'And you don't mind that.'

'No.'

'Why not?'

'You have digestion. Shit. Shit has its uses.'

The waiter came back with the beers and said there was a fifty per cent service charge. Andros said 'Twenty-five.' The waiter said 'Fifty.' Andros handed him twenty pounds in settlement of the bill. The waiter moved away. Maisie said 'What would you have done if he'd threatened to beat you up?' Andros said 'I didn't think he was that good at maths.'

They sipped their beer. Andros thought – We are in a casino with a little white ball clattering round a wheel.

Maisie said 'You mean a place like this digests a lot of stuff that would otherwise get stuck and make you ill.'

'Yes.'

'But does it come out in shit?'

'If you don't let yourself get too constipated.'

'You're sure you wouldn't rather I was like that woman wrapping myself round a pole?'

89

'Well that would be pleasant, but it would probably be preventing other and nicer things happening.'

'Such as what.'

'Such as your going off on a journey.'

'That's the sort thing my uncle Maurice used to say.'

'You call him your uncle?'

'Wasn't he?'

'If you want him to be, yes.'

The woman on the pole remained for a time as if suspended from a meat hook; then she flopped down and began to pick up various bits of discarded clothing from the floor.

Maisie said 'You don't think that by coming to this place you might be blackmailed?'

'What if I was.'

'You could lose your official business?'

'That might be a mercy.'

The music suddenly ceased. In the cavernous silence Maisie said 'I thought you might be going to lecture me.'

'You seem to know most of it anyway.'

'Most of what?' Then – 'Do you believe in God?'

'I believe, as we were saying, that if you believe, then things can happen for you.'

'And you can risk saying that?'

'Oh, at a strip joint. With the music playing.'

'The music's stopped playing.'

'Oh yes, so it has.'

'Music stops you listening?'

The waiter came back to take away their glasses. Maisie hung on to hers which still had some beer in it. The waiter went away. Andros said 'As you get older, the best music's anyway mostly in your head.'

Maisie said 'Where did you get all this stuff?'

Andros said 'A lot of it, like you, from my old friend Maurice.'

'I think he was a bit in love with me.'

'Possibly.'
'I'm apt to think that sort of thing.'
'I see.'
'Is that why he went away?'
'Good heavens no!'
'Is that why I can't eat?'
'I shouldn't think so.'
'It's a sort of defence.'
'Yes.'
'What shall I do?'
'I thought you were going on a journey.'
'Yes. Can I come to Paris tomorrow?'

# XIII

Lisa had been aware on and off that she was being moved, carried, from where she had been trapped in the tunnel: from where she had wanted to die, where she had tried to die, because being unable to move and with the weight of rock on top of her, living was not bearable. But she had had no access to death; so this was hell; this was the eternal torment that seemed to be justice to moralists and gave satisfaction to traditional Christians. But then she had been rescued. Someone had dug their way up the tunnel behind her and stuck a needle in her leg; it had been like the sting of a wasp, and the torment had gone; in its place had come oblivion, with the momentary impression of herself setting out on a journey. Whatever was left of her waved goodbye to this part of herself: but what part was it? She was being lifted, carried, but roughly, not on a stretcher; her consciousness kept stopping and starting; it caught up with itself, tripped over itself; pain hovered like a vulture. But who had rescued her and given her the drug? Not her own people, surely, for they did not speak to her and so she found she did not speak to them. In whose interests was it to try to blow up the mosque – or to try to prevent it? She had tried to work this out before: her grasp of it, like her consciousness, kept slipping away. There was confusion between the people who wanted peace and those who wanted war; who might want to find her and yet not to be found with her? Questions floated to and fro in her mind like flotsam on the tide in an estuary: but it was not the confusion, chaos, that was hell. She thought – I am that baby that was stuck half in and half out of the womb; or am I now out and just do not know what is happening?

She was gaining no clear memory of what had happened: how could she, as a new-born baby lying on the edge of a bed? She was being kept drugged probably just in order that she would have no memory; no means of knowing who her rescuers or captors might be. If they were Israelis why did they not question her? Might they be Palestinians self-appointed to guard the mosque? She had impressions of being in a dingy room with quiet arguments going on around her. When the pain came in again she cried out, and hoped that she might be made unconscious again. A man with a smooth round face came up and did something to her leg and she screamed and he gave her another shot of the drug. She wanted to say to him – Are you God? Do you know the Jewish joke about the Jew who came across a party of Arabs in the desert, and was told what could be worse – a party of Jews? She would say to God – Do you think that's funny?

She had a dream in which she had been liberated from hell; but she had to go back to rescue lost souls in limbo. This was a setting like an enormous open-cast mine in which people were digging for rare chemicals or gold; there were guards with guns standing on the edge of the crater. The people who dug could not make use of the drugs or the gold themselves but only hand them over; but they were laughing, because the people on the rim of the crater could not get down to dig. Lisa was slightly apart from this and was looking down as if at a book of illustrations. Her father was saying – You don't believe any of this do you? Her mother was saying – How can God let it happen! Lisa was thinking – You have to take your chances.

She was lying on the floor in a dark room. She felt she

could move, but she did not want to. She was now in a place from which dead bodies are taken to be thrown into a pit: if you are alive then you have to stay very still, then people might not notice you. She gently tested the muscles in her arm, her leg; this did not seem after all to be broken. The man with the smooth round face had gone, and in his place was a fierce dark man with what her father used to call a towel round his head. She thought – But it is a devil perhaps who might help me out of here.

Some time later the pain was coming back and she was leaning up on an elbow trying to drag herself away; but it was in her neck, ribs, heart; everywhere in the world around her. She cried out loudly again. She remembered a film in which a man was tied on his back and was being tortured and to stop him making any sound molten metal was poured down his throat; then the torturers could proceed peacefully. The fierce dark man had come in and had stared down at her. He had a wound on his cheek like the young soldier she had wanted to go up to at the gate and say – It is all right, there is nothing wrong with me, I am not human. She remembered the story of a man who had been handcuffed to a wall in a cellar and to get himself free he had cut off his arm; but was this possible? There was a joke that he had afterwards explained – But it was a false arm, you see: I had the old one cut off some time ago because I thought this one might come in useful. She could say to the fierce dark man – Don't you think that's funny?

She was being carried at night and placed in the back of a truck where there were other bodies because she could hear them muttering and groaning. She was on her way to be thrown into the pit: if you were still alive you had to try to fall in such a way that there was a small space round your head where you could breathe, and your mouth would not fill with detritus. They had come to give her another injection but it seemed they had thought she did not need it. Did this mean they thought her dead? alive?

94

When she emerged eventually into something unmistakably like consciousness she did not know for how long she had been drugged: she had been in a truck going over rough ground and was being bounced as if someone was shaking her violently to rouse her. Her limbs were flung about but she seemed to be in one piece; she now needed to get somewhere quiet where they could no longer torment her. She thought – That poor baby! The truck had stopped. To whatever had been trying to rouse her she wanted to say – All right, I'm coming! I've been down to hell, you can't rush these things: now what is the next stage: can't I remember?

She was feeling very thirsty. She thought – That baby needed a drink. In the desert people sometimes skinned and chewed snakes to get moisture. She thought – Kind snakes! But I would like to slip out of my own dry skin.

# XIV

Laura Simmons reclined on the sofa in her sitting room where in the vase on the grand piano there were now the flowers of a slightly later time of the year. Opposite her Joshua sat straight-backed on an upright chair. Laura thought – I imagined him as homosexual; but more to the point is that he is learning how to handle it.

Joshua was saying in his precise, faintly foreign voice – 'I'm sorry I could not come to you after the service. I imagined there were many people queuing to see you.'

Laura said 'I thought you were after that boy.'

After a pause Joshua said 'Who is he, do you know?'

'You didn't talk to him?'

'No.'

'Do you want me to find his address?'

'I generally find that no good comes of that sort of thing.'

Laura found she was blushing. After a time she said 'I see. I apologise.'

'You are very perceptive. It is good of you to say you will talk to me.'

Laura thought – He watches his words. He is like a mountain climber with crampons taking care not to make a slip.

She said 'You want to talk about Maurice?'

'I have friends in Beirut who have a story that he may have possessed some specialist scientific information, to extract which he was taken prisoner; if indeed he was.'

'Yes I've heard that story.'

'Do you think it is true?'

'No. He wasn't a scientist. He wanted to get away.'

'To get away from what?'

'Well from me, mostly. Or from himself.'

'You are very honest.'

She thought – No, it is you who are honest. It is catching. I have not talked about this to anyone for years. It is you who have no charm, no slipperiness: but a kind of graceful stillness that is like someone posing for a painter.

He said 'My friend in Beirut who is engaged in scientific business doesn't believe that story either. But where did Doctor Rotblatt want to get away to?'

Laura thought – He has learned that Maurice can be called Doctor. She said 'Wherever it was, the question is did he get there.'

'There are stories that he might have gone to one of the villages in the mountains in eastern Turkey. There are Kurds there, and Armenians, who manage to have a certain autonomy. People do not intrude on them except for occasional persecutions. They have their own forms of religion, which I believe Doctor Rotblatt was interested in.'

'And you are interested?'

'His is an odd story. It has caught people's imagination.'

'There were some people in the hills called Alevis. Do you know them?'

'I know of them.'

'They believe in angels.'

'It is not exactly angels. It is perhaps a system of connections which, if you recognise it, has influence.'

'Maurice would have liked that. You think he might have gone to these people?'

'That's what I was going to ask you.'

Laura stood up and moved around the room. She thought of doing her stage act of rearranging flowers, but with Joshua watching this seemed ridiculous. She said 'I always found the spiritual stuff difficult.'

'It is difficult to put into words.'

'You think Maurice may be becoming a sort of legend?'

'In my part of the world we are closer to legends because we are closer to violence and fear.'

'Legends haven't done much good in the past.'

'That you don't know.'

Laura came and stood in front of him. She said 'I didn't expect a conversation quite like this.'

'Neither did I.'

'People need legends?'

'To accommodate wonder. Not necessarily to believe or obey.'

Laura sat down opposite him again. She said 'What work do you do?'

'I am an anthropologist. I would like to write books.'

'About people who wonder but do not necessarily obey?'

'Yes.'

She stared at him. She said 'Maurice was kidnapped, held hostage, chained in a cellar, then miraculously escaped. That's the story?'

'I don't think people exactly believe it.'

'But people do believe that sort of thing. With Jesus.'

'But they should believe it in the way of it being a story.'

'And that's effective?'

'It's a good story. It's telling you something. But you have to listen. To think. To go on from there. To be responsible.'

'Yes that's what I was saying in the church. But it's telling you what?'

'About such an attitude of mind. Didn't Doctor Rotblatt say he wanted to change people's attitude of mind?'

'To an attitude of wonder?'

'Yes.'

Laura stared at him. She thought – But it is I who am losing my old attitude. It is somewhere out there, and I do not need to find it again.

After a time Joshua said 'And it is true that after Doctor Rotblatt disappeared there have been no more hostages.'

'After Richard's story of the bones?'

'Oh well, no. Before. That was a confirmation.'

'A confirmation of not even the story being the point? The story might be impossible: but what happens after it?'

Joshua said nothing.

Then Laura said 'Don't you think Maurice and Richard together might have made the whole thing up?'

'Oh well that wouldn't have worked, surely.'

'You think this has worked?'

Joshua smiled and said 'Well here we are, aren't we?'

Laura felt excited; as if she were almost out of her depth. She said – 'You mean, that's why you didn't pick up that boy?'

Joshua seemed to consider this gravely. Then he said 'It's true I was much struck by that boy. But there seemed other things more important. Though I am perhaps now regretting that I did not have the temerity to go after him.'

'But as you say, here we are.'

'Yes.'

'You can't do everything all at once.'

Joshua seemed suddenly exhausted. He closed his eyes. She wondered – Or is he praying?

He said 'Is that what was happening between you and Maurice? Forgive me for asking.'

'No, that's all right. You mean sex? Which doesn't easily mix with other things?'

'Yes. The genome and the phenome.'

'What?'

'I'm sorry. So you had to get away.'

'You talk as if it might still be going on.'

99

'Well isn't it? Or you wouldn't be interested in writing about him.'

'Me write about him?'

'I'm sorry. I understood that's what we were saying.'

'About a legend? But I'm a publisher. I handle academic books.'

'So what do you make of this story: of your own story?'

She said 'That boy you're keen on – he wanted to talk about Maurice.'

'He did? A good story is one that one would not have total control over.'

'That boy had a story that he might be some sort of adopted son of Maurice.'

'That's a fantasy?'

'I suppose so.'

Laura, watching Joshua, thought – But it is amazing we have got as far as we have in this conversation. Can we now rest awhile?

She said 'You have this friend in Beirut? The one who knows about the scientific information?'

'He's heterosexual.'

'Oh I see.' Then – 'I've got a niece called Maisie who wants to go to Beirut.'

'I was wondering if you knew someone called Professor Andros, whom Richard said I should get in touch with.'

'Yes indeed I know Andros. But your interest in all this has led you to that boy?' She laughed.

Joshua said 'I'm afraid I'm feeling rather exhausted at the moment. Would you mind if I went and lay down for a time in your garden?'

'No I wouldn't mind.'

'It's the style that's exhausting. Trying to cut out what's irrelevant.'

'Yes.'

'Why does your niece Maisie want to go to Beirut?'

'I think she wanted to look for Maurice.'

'Perhaps she will be led to something different.'
'That's possible.'
'Do you think Doctor Rotblatt is dead? Alive?'
'But you're saying that's not really the point; is it?'

# XV

In the Tuileries gardens in Paris the sun shone brightly and young rollerblade skaters with coloured helmets floated about like fishes. Occasionally a parent of an even younger child would object, and a park-keeper would appear and the skaters would dart off, as fishes do; and then after a while would be there again, languidly rolling.

The man with the Panama hat stood by the basin of a large fountain and looked down into the water. He was recalling the scene he had witnessed on a satellite surveillance screen some time ago when a disgraced senior official in a Middle Eastern country had been held upside down with his head in a bucket as a punishment, so it was thought, for his responsibility for a water shortage. The man with the hat was remembering a song that men in the army used to sing, which went – There's a hole in the old oaken bucket, fuck fuck fuck it – which had seemed to have a numinous significance. Why did some catches, phrases, stick and then pop up in the mind: something to do with rhythm? rhyme? esoteric sexual connections?

A voice behind him said 'I spotted your hat.'

'Everyone goes on about my hat.'

'It guarantees your probity. Too transparent to be a double agent.'

'Probity being the last refuge of the scoundrel.'

The man who had arrived at the fountain was Andros. He shook the other man's hand and said 'It's good to see you. Can we talk here, or have they got equipment that can hear up to half a mile?'

'We can talk, but they've probably got the equipment.'

'I'm getting rather deaf.'

'Useful in our profession.'

'What, you can't hear, or can say you have misheard?'

'What's that?'

'Both?'

'I did not say that!'

They moved away, smiling, from the fountain towards a patch of grass where there were two green-painted metal chairs side by side on their own that looked as if they might be there to lure people to have indiscreet conversations. Andros said 'We saw you on the telly. You were going into that hut. Guy Fawkes and his mob.'

'A fine put-up job.'

'We don't have to worry?'

'Not much about that. Not unless we want to. The game can go on – of problems that are necessarily insoluble.'

'These chairs look as though they're going to collapse.'

'But still, they're not the only things that may.'

'A hazard of the omnipresence of market forces? But not for the big brands that will survive?'

'Well even for them, if someone powerful enough decides not to play the game: to upset the whole chessboard.'

They balanced precariously on the two chairs. Andros thought – We might be seen as two old queens come to ogle the children balanced on their skates.

He said 'Did he concede that?'

'In so many exquisitely chosen non-words.'

'Do you trust him?'

'Good Lord no!'

'Are the oil people happy?'

'Do oil people ever say they're happy?'

'And did you tell him we quite need them to go on being a threat on account of the rottenness at the core of our body politic?'

'My dear fellow!'

'I bet you did.'

'He knows that. I didn't know which way you'd jump.'

'Neither do I.

'So that's all right.'

The chairs were so uncomfortable that they had to tilt them and hold their legs in oddly contorted positions.

Andros said 'So who does run the show?'

'Who cuts the crap?'

'Who are the seven good men and true who, according to conspiracy theory, or is it the Kabbalah, keep the whole show on the road?'

'The ones who don't know each other and often don't even know who they are themselves?'

'They're the boys.'

'Well there's a good deal of the left hand not knowing what the right hand is doing. Catching Allah in a compromising position.'

'And that works?'

'But what a metaphor!'

Andros thought – One day people like us will be talking to each other and we really won't have the slightest idea what we're talking about.

He said 'But in fact nothing much has happened for ten, eleven years.'

'Things here and there have happened, or we'd be tearing up the paving stones.'

'No nervous breakdowns in Macedonia.'

'Quite. Perhaps politicians should be naturally seen as therapists as well as comics.'

'But too many children dying?'

'But probably not as many as if there was war or civil war.'

'He knows that? But also that it might be harder for us to be successful hypocrites.'

'Really? Not so many chances to be witty?'

'Keeps the world going round.'

'The aspidistra flying.'

They watched a young girl in tight jeans bending forwards to adjust her skates. She was like a pony harnessed to a trap.

Andros said 'But we don't really get away with anything. Not lies, not truth, not even the family silver.'

'There's always schadenfreude. The feel-good factor.'

'The dominant gene?'

'I don't see why you science fellows shouldn't do something about that.'

The man with the hat had been balancing so far back on his chair that he was suddenly over the point of tipping backwards, and he had to fling his arms and legs about wildly. He said 'Mayday, Mayday.' Then – 'Let's have some lunch.'

Andros said 'Look I'm sorry, I can't today.'

'A previous engagement?'

'Something like that.'

'About sixteen, wears black stockings, and a short black skirt?'

'You've had your voyeurs on me!'

'Quite by chance. At the Gare du Nord.'

'She's eighteen and she's my god-daughter. She's not what's nowadays called my niece.'

'No offence. Envy. Why should it not be your god-daughter that makes the world go round?'

He stood up. He took off his hat, mopped his forehead, put his hat on again. He said 'But look, before you go, you don't know anything more about this absurd weapon?'

'No, do you?'

'They're supposed to be testing.'

'It would be a laugh if it worked.'

'Something like mad cow disease? That's what's going to

land on us, you know. Mad fundamentalist disease. One man with a bag of chemicals like a poisoned udder.'

'Look, why don't you come and have some lunch? She's the niece of that man Maurice Rotblatt.'

'Oh yes. Do we know what happened to him?'

'He wasn't ever working for you?'

'Not that I know of. Wasn't he supposed to be holier than thou or me or you?'

'My god-daughter, Maisie, wants to go to Beirut. Looking for him.'

'Why?'

'I don't really know. But that's what the young do, isn't it? Not knowing why they're doing anything, just looking and travelling.'

'Backpacking as a spiritual exercise? I understand that.'

'You do? She's been anorexic. Suicidal.'

'Wasn't it Rotblatt who got into trouble for saying – No Bulimia in Belsen?'

'Not Belsen, Belgrade. He's being turned into quite a guru on the Net.'

The two of them had begun to walk out of the gardens towards the bridge over the river. The man with the hat said 'And that's not your doing?'

'No. Do you think it should be? I don't know if Maurice would have liked it.'

'I should have thought he would have. No one in control. Things just happening.'

'But too much talking. No one listens. Tower of Babel.'

'Oh well, yes. But gives you the chance to be choosy.'

# XVI

Hafiz had been travelling for two days in the truck which had been provided for him by Leon, the police officer in Beirut. His story was that he was taking supplies to a medical team investigating an unidentified epidemic in a village in the north, somewhere near the border with Syria. If such an investigation had existed it would of course be being kept secret, so if Hafiz was stopped and questioned he would hardly be expected to give plausible answers. He had an idea about where he should be heading, because he had found papers in the laboratory office that gave the location of a village to which it was suggested that supplies might have to be taken. Hafiz had asked his immediate superiors for a few days off to pursue an enquiry of his own: he had put this unusual request in such a way that they had suspected that he must be under confidential orders from some higher authority. Hafiz thought – The real biological or psychological weapon being tested at this time is the readiness to carry out and accept any sort of bluff, so that soon no one will have any contact with reality.

However when he set off on his journey it struck him that it might be himself he had bluffed out of any form of sanity. Why did he think that in fact there might be anything to discover; and what could he do about it if there was? Might there in fact be an epidemic in the north? And yet, was there anything better he might be doing than going off into the desert on his own like a would-be hermit to get away from the inanities of his work in Beirut. It was true he might never be able to get back if it was found he had been deceiving the people he had been working with; but he might still be able to explain to himself that he was escaping in a traditional way from the frustration of his feelings for Leila; from the increasing tensions of his relationship with Joshua.

The documents he had seen in the laboratory office had given the reference of a location which on the map seemed to be empty desert; but once more this might mean anything or nothing. He had started off on his journey in a state of some excitement: did anyone embarking on a voyage of discovery ever know just what they would find? The people who had discovered the North Pole, for instance, had they an exact idea of its nature and location – or indeed of their own motivation. But was not this the point? However by the end of the first day Hafiz seemed to be losing both his confidence and his bearings. The map reference might have been disinformation; and was it not true that as you approached the Pole compasses ceased to work?

The area to which he was heading was in fact over the border of Lebanon and not far from the Syrian border with Turkey. It had been assumed by those half in the know that authorities in Syria would have had to have been made privy to the testing of any weapon, though such involvement would of course be denied. Also, speculation about funding from Iraq had had to remain largely unspoken. But it was common knowledge that around the borders of Syria with Turkey, and even in the north of Lebanon itself, there were scattered villages with populations of Kurds, either indigenous or as refugees; and Kurds had for generations been seen by the authorities in the countries in which they had settled as outcasts, anarchists, almost a different species. And every so often there were what were said to be spontaneous local uprisings against Kurds: so could there not be something to be looked into about what was said to be a mysterious epidemic? The use of such a village for the purpose of the experiment that was supposed to have been planned at least in theory made sense; and presumably potential victims of other so-called racial types could be found and brought in as required. It was Leila's police-officer friend who had mentioned some Israeli prisoners who might be held by Muslim extremists.

It was even conceivable that Israeli intelligence might know about this, but be willing at the moment to turn a blind eye because valuable information might be gained by all sides if the experiment were carried out.

After a night without sleep Hafiz felt more than ever disorientated. He had crossed one frontier with the help of the documents that Leila's policeman had obtained for him; but now, in a strange country, the possibilities for intrigue and self-deception that were available in Beirut were drying up. Hafiz had learned from Richard of the Muslim so-called heretics who as well as the Kurds lived in the hills to the north; who had formed their own communities and whose concern it was to avoid interference. Hafiz had even thought that if his plans went wrong, and it was not these villages that had been harmed, he might take refuge with them.

By the late afternoon of the second day he was approaching the location of the map reference he had come across in the office. He had been crossing a rocky plain in which it had seemed unlikely there would be a village – unless it was one built partly underground both because of ease of construction, and in order to be protected from heat and dust and any attackers. Also, if necessary, could not such a village now be bulldozed and filled in so that it would be as if it had never existed?

Then there did appear in front of him in a dip in the ground a low wall with what seemed to be dwellings beyond it; not quite underground, but makeshift like a shanty town for the homeless. And in front of the wall there were two official-looking trucks drawn up – of a different type from his own, but they could be those of some reconnaissance party. He realised that he had been hoping and even expecting to come across nothing; then he could turn round and go home, with the feeling he had at least made an effort. But had he not at the same time been hoping for a reason not to go home; for something to turn up that would give him a change of direction and release from duplicity? And now here was this village and these trucks drawn up and he had a choice – to go home, or if he stayed and things went wrong, perhaps never to be able to go home.

And supposing these trucks outside the village did belong to people engaged in putting a biological agent into, say, the well or water supply – this had been one of the suggested plans – would not any unauthorised witness have to be eliminated? Of course all this had once seemed to him to be moonshine. But here were two trucks and a desolate village.

Hafiz drew up behind and to one side of the trucks and tried to consider his options. There was no sign of life that he could see in the village. The experiment might already have occurred, with men in protective clothing within the walls sorting out bodies: or everyone in the village might be dead – including, with luck, the people who had come to kill the inhabitants. But then if he went on, would not Hafiz himself be in danger? Or perhaps nothing was happening – this was not even the right village, and the trucks were just those of any local officials. But Hafiz still did not want to turn round and go back: if he did, would he not be acknowledging what he had suspected – that he and his friends were being half-witted? Of course he could make up a story – Oh yes, there was definitely something happening, but I think I was spotted and I had to get out quick. But then how could he bear the imagination of his own lying voice? He decided that he should at least get out of his truck and walk to the gap in the wall that was the entrance to the village. The place might have become deserted for any number of reasons. He would just have to see. He could take a few steps through the wall, and then possibilities should become clearer. If anyone challenged him he could say – I was just passing and I happened to see your trucks and I was curious.

To himself he was saying – I know I am doing this without being conscious of any good reason, but isn't this normally the case with any voyage of discovery? And this is not to say that a reason may not become apparent.

He left his truck and went to the gap in the wall. Beyond it there was a path that ran between low-built mud and brick shacks: there was still no sign of life. There might indeed have been a plague; but where were the bodies? Then at some distance there was what looked like a telegraph pole with the figure of a man in overalls halfway up it. So what was he doing – establishing communications? Raising a flag? Fixing the device that would distribute the biological agent?

Hafiz stepped out of sight into the shelter of a doorway. It seemed that he should stay there for enough time to make sure he had not been seen; then he could withdraw with some justification and dignity. But still, after that, where might he go?

To ensure that he would stick it out long enough in the doorway – long enough, that is, to satisfy what was becoming a battle against an increasing sense that he was mad – he thought he should hold his breath as if he were under water. How long could an inexperienced diver hold his breath – a minute? A minute and a half – before he passed out? Did he want to pass out? When Hafiz let his breath out it came with a whoosh, so that he thought the man up the telegraph pole must have heard him.

He set off back towards his truck urgently, without bothering now about concealment. Then when he got to the edge of the village he saw that there was a figure slithering out of the back of one of the two parked trucks and making its way stumbling to the back of his own truck: the figure was dressed in a dirty white robe like that of a hospital patient. Hafiz thought – So something in our speculation might be true after all? The figure appeared to be trying to get into the back of his truck through the canvas canopy. Hafiz did not want to call out nor to move hurriedly because this might attract attention: he had to make out that all this was quite normal; he was anyway leaving. He walked to the back of his truck as if he might be going to the assistance of whoever was fumbling with the straps of the canvas; his best chance of getting away would be to see that the person was concealed with the minimum of fuss. He reached his truck and took hold of the figure in its dishevelled white robe by its elbow; not to deter it, but to encourage it; to give it the message – It is all right but do not make a sound, people may be watching. The arm through the material of the robe was thin as if it might belong to someone who had been starved. He thought – Oh my God, does this indeed make sense? The figure had become still; he held his arms on either side of it as he took over the unfastening of the straps of the canvas. When there was enough of a gap between the canvas and the tailboard of the truck the figure began to slither through: he helped by lifting and pushing; its body through the cloth seemed brittle as if there were no flesh on it. He thought – Hurry, we must hurry. Then – This is some visitation? When the figure had gone head first into the truck he began to refasten the straps; then a hand came through the gap as if it were wanting him to acknowledge it. He took the hand and held it briefly. Then it withdrew. He went to sit in the driving seat of his truck. He thought – Could one not make out that this is normal? Like picking up a child from school?

He found that he was trembling. As he drove away a man in overalls appeared at the entrance to the village and watched him. Hafiz thought – Well you'd better not say anything about this, you bugger, or it may be you who'll be shot.

# XVII

Maisie was in a train travelling through wooded country in central Europe. The trees were dying or dead, they had lost their foliage, they stuck up from the earth like bones in a desecrated graveyard. Chemicals had blown on the wind and skeletons had been left exposed. There had been some burning as if to get rid of smell and bacteria, but the ground would have to wait for a flood if there was to be any cleansing, after which there would be just mud, rock, rubble.

Maisie saw herself as a traveller without a context; it was hardly relevant where she had come from or where she was going. She had had dinner with Andros in Paris at a grand restaurant; she had managed to eat much of what he had ordered for her. Then he had got a room for her in a hotel close to where he was staying. She had said 'But tell me again why are you doing this.' He had said 'Sexual sublimation, which Freud suggested is the basis of civilisation.' The next day they had had lunch with a man who wore a hat and rolled his eyes and said 'Sublimation is the blessed refuge of the scoundrel.'

Maisie had been travelling in the train all night. It was as if Andros had sent her off into space after a celebration at the launching pad; now she was in the capsule or whatever it was called with no objective reference points to give information about her location or direction. The train shook: it might be stationary with just the landscape being rolled back past it.

Andros had said – I do understand what you're doing. Nowadays we have to make our own stories out of adventure.

She had slept fitfully on the hard seat of her compartment. She had woken to this harsh and anonymous landscape. She thought – I am in one of those films in which you have been made insubstantial and are on a voyage to your own inside: this forest is my brain which has been polluted, it is not known if it will ever put forth shoots again.

The only other occupant of the compartment was a man who must have got in during the night; he was wearing a huge military overcoat buttoned up to his chin. He was hollow-cheeked and unshaven; he might be a deserter or a murderer, or a saint. He had been staring at her quite openly for some time; and when she glanced at him he did not look away. According to a conventional feminist way of thinking it would be only a matter of time before he advanced on her and tried to rape her; and now she did not even have the knife with which, in line again with convention, she might defend herself; Dario had taken it off her and then she had said she no longer needed it. Why had she said this? Because she had felt that to be human she had to have the confidence to defy convention? Might victims collude in rape by expecting it?

But what was it that Andros had been suggesting – that you go into adventure in order to learn not to be a victim?

The man in the compartment was smiling at her. She remembered a film in which a woman confronted by an alarming man had kept talking, talking; and the man had seemed to become incapacitated by watching her mouth.

After a time she said looking out of the window – 'What killed the trees?'

The man said nothing. She thought – Of course he does not understand English. But does that matter?

She turned to him so that he could watch her face and she

enunciated her words carefully. She said, frowning – 'I suppose you were all trying to control things. But instead you got radioactivity, pollution. I know about that, it's like what I've been doing to myself. I've been refusing to eat. But you can't control things. Or rather you control them only by killing them.'

She was staring at the man intently. She thought – I am trying to control him? But I have read about things like this, in which men like to be controlled, and collude in it.

The man was holding his mouth open like a fish just under the surface of water.

Maisie went on as if sternly – 'But aren't you supposed to be getting over that sort of thing? I mean, become a responsible member of the community of nations? Like us, and that sort of thing? Except that we're not, we're ravaged by greeds and diseases; we feed cattle and pigs with their own minced-up brains. And then we eat the cattle and pigs, so our brains become polluted. And soon the worms will be eating us, so there will be mad worm disease, which will spread through the soil, everywhere.'

The man was making adjustments to his large military overcoat. It seemed strange how he had kept this on now the morning was becoming hot. He was pulling at the cuff of one sleeve and getting the arm up inside it so that it would be free to move within the heavy folds. She thought – Perhaps he has nothing on underneath and will suddenly flash open his wings like an angel.

She went on – 'Sometimes when there's a plague or a forest fire people isolate villages and leave other people to die there; what else is there to do? You make rides or open spaces by burning areas where the fire has not yet come; you hope that the sparks or bacteria will not leap over them. But they do. Contamination learns. But you have to learn tricks too. Do you understand what I'm saying? Do you think you can manage to do this?'

He was watching her mouth. She herself had become

conscious of the movements of her mouth, as if it might be a rat gnawing at the folds of his overcoat.

She said 'Well that's the problem. There are these predicaments, drives, and we don't know what to do with them. Or we're so disgusted that we want to wipe them out, or wipe ourselves out, or the whole human race. But there should be a better way of dealing with them. Perhaps we can look after them. Don't you think so?'

The man had succeeded in getting his other arm up and out of its sleeve and inside his overcoat: it was as if he were struggling out of a straitjacket. She wondered – Do you need both hands?

She said 'I mean there are all these people in the streets firing guns and throwing stones and I suggest they could be at home watching a video. One can get some quite good videos, I believe, with all sorts of oddities. But perhaps you want love? But then how do you think you get it?'

The man had opened his mouth wider and was rolling his eyes towards the ceiling as if he were seeing a vision. His hands within his greatcoat were scrabbling like mice. She thought – He is taking the bait. Is he imagining that he is doing something to me, or I to him?

The man made a groaning noise and seemed to be clutching himself inside his greatcoat as if he had been stabbed in the stomach.

She thought – Sex is a sort of medical problem, yes, like anorexia or bulimia.

When she had been with Andros in the grand restaurant in Paris with its candles and cut glass and waiters like servers at an altar, Andros had said – You have to learn to put up with things bit by bit. She had said – Put up with what? He had said – Not being guilty.

In the train she had begun to feel extraordinarily hungry. She wondered if the man in the greatcoat opposite her had any food in the haversack that was in the rack above his head.

She tried to remember more of what Andros had said:

something about – What is difficult to deal with is not when things are bad, but when they're good.

– Why?

– Because it's as if you had been specially favoured.

The man in the compartment had begun to relax. But he was still seeming to be guarding himself within his overcoat. Maisie thought – He may not feel free to reach for his haversack for some time.

She smiled at him encouragingly.

The man was managing to get a hand out of the front of his overcoat. He looked at her slyly. He pointed with a finger to his mouth.

She thought – But we've already done that, haven't we?

Then the man stood and freed his other hand and was getting his haversack down from the rack.

She watched him while he unfastened the straps. He was glancing at her and nodding and smiling. She thought – What on earth will he produce: a rabbit, a string of flags, a flock of pigeons?

He enunciated carefully – 'Cho–co–late.'

She said 'I don't believe it! You are an angel!'

He produced two bars of milk chocolate from the haversack and handed one to her. He seemed to be concentrating again on trying to understand what she was saying. Then his face lit up and he said 'No you angel!'

She said 'Oh I don't know! I didn't do anything really.'

He said 'You very beautiful. I like your body.'

'Well that's very good of you to say so! But I was starving!'

'I get out at next station.'

'Well perhaps that's just as well!' She laughed.

'You come with me?'

'Oh no, I don't think so.'

'I like introduce you to my mother.'

They ate their chocolate bars sitting opposite one another. Maisie thought – Well I do see what Andros calls sublimation. She had come across in her aunt Laura's house some

Indian prints like this – of a man and a woman facing each other and not touching but looking pleased and satisfied. She thought – Perhaps they were just licking their own fingers.

She said 'That's very sweet of you. But I must get on.'

He said 'Me virgin.'

She said 'Me virgin too.' She laughed. She thought – What on earth is the world coming to!

When they said goodbye at the next station she thought she might put out a hand and touch his cheek, but she decided against it.

# XVIII

Dario had gone back to London after the service in the church without having talked any more with Laura Simmons. He had come out of the church and had seen Laura in conversation with a young man by a tombstone: he had thought the young man the most beautiful person he had ever seen: this was not just aesthetic; he had been gripped by the throat, heart, balls; he had felt helpless. He had seen the man watching him and had felt sure that the man felt something for him; but then Laura had come over to him and he had had to wait for Laura to go; they had become involved in talking about Maisie, in whom he could not imagine ever having been interested. Laura had gone, but then the vicar had come out from the church and had talked to him, and the man by the tombstone had waited for a time but then had seemed to give up, and had walked away. Dario had not gone after him: it was as if he was still paralysed – they had been attracted but forced apart as if by some switch in magnetic poles. The attraction had been sexual but then was the avoidance natural too? Could one not make assignations in a country churchyard? He had watched the love of his life disappear like a ghost back into a grave. Dario felt he had to get back to London quickly, where he might find a practical way of getting over such misfortune. The ache in his guts, heart, groin, was like the gnawing of a rat.

After almost sleepless nights during which he had taken refuge in both sleeping pills and pornography, which had fought against each other and left him in the morning as if half dead on their battlefield, he set out in the afternoon of the third day for Hampstead Heath where, he had read, there was a well-known homosexual pick-up area. His reluctance to do this before had not been (so he told himself) because of a reluctance to face up to his homosexuality, but because he had come to feel that all sex was an enemy. When he became invaded, as he now was, he craved not for straightforward love or relief or indulgence but for something dark and violent: he dreamed of being ravaged, beaten up, raped. It was also not just that he was ashamed of this – he had read enough pornography to know that such obsessions were not rare – but to indulge them was, for obvious reasons, difficult with friends and dangerous with strangers. He had read stories of men who had seemed to invite their own murder. His desire was for things to be out of his control, but he was frightened. Faced with the man in the graveyard he had felt ready to prostrate himself; but the man had seemed like a god, stern and pure and incorruptible.

Dario set off for Hampstead Heath as if for some ritual blood-letting – leeches applied to the skin; vacuums in heated glass jars. Until this happened he was a fish with a hook through his balls, brain; the sooner he was gaffed and gutted and laid out on the floor of a boat the better. Then he might have peace. He had read of men who put paper bags over their heads and hanged themselves and thus emulated the struggles of fishes out of water. So he went off somewhat grimly, as both the fisherman and the fish, longing for what he feared might destroy him. Humans were animals that could see their own grotesque predicaments: they were both spiders needing to devour the legs of flies, and flies needing to abase themselves to the great god-spider.

He was approaching across a patch of open grass the part of the Heath he had read about: in front of him was an area of woodland that might be like that in which Dante found himself before his journey to hell. As soon as Dario entered it he became aware of a limbo of shadowy figures standing or quietly moving amongst the trees: many had mobile phones held to their ears: it was as if they were keeping in touch with old loved ones while waiting to pick up new; having to keep some line with a hook open by which they could be gutted. As Dario moved into the trees one or two men broke off from their murmuring to watch him; but he kept his eyes down: when it came to the point, would he funk it? Would he just rather creep back to his magazines? But he needed some more dramatic cure to what was happening to his guts, balls, brain.

There was a young boy sitting on the fallen branch of a tree who was looking at him brightly. The boy was clothed roughly and somewhat dirtily; but was not this just what was required? Dario felt his insides being spilled out on to the ground. He stopped by the boy. He was, yes, frightened.

The boy said 'Got a match?'

Dario heard himself saying 'You're too young to be smoking.'

'I'm not smoking am I?'

'No.'

'Well then.'

The boy's mouth, lips, were like those against which poisonous fruit had been crushed. Where did this image come from – Antony and Cleopatra? Swinburne?

– From the succulent fungus on a tree that you did not know if it would be an elixir or would kill you?

The boy said 'Aren't you going to offer me a cigarette?'

'I don't smoke.'

'But I can say you offered me one, can't I?'

Dario did not know what was happening. He was pleased that he was not simply being subservient. Might he not even have a good relationship with this boy, with a bit of raillery and teasing?

He said 'Why should you say that?'

'How much were you going to give me?'

'I haven't said I was going to give you anything.'

'Fifty? Double it.'

'Double nothing's still nothing.'

The boy suddenly said loudly 'Help! Get off me you fucking perv! I don't do that!'

Dario suddenly realised that he was in the presence of evil. Also that evil was not, after all, attractive.

A few of the shadowy figures among the trees had turned to watch. But they did not come closer. Perhaps they knew the boy was poison? But like scavengers they might wait till after the kill.

Dario said 'All right, fifty.'

'Too late now.'

'Why?'

'I don't trust you.'

'Why not –'

'Why should I?'

'You said fifty.'

'No I didn't. You did.'

Dario felt himself once more paralysed. The poison that had been in his veins was now out in the world, all-powerful: he had lost the ability to choose: he would have to accept whatever happened to him. Had he ever really imagined he had wanted this?

It struck him that the boy in fact was not so much dishevelled and dirty as made up to seem so. He was what was called jailbait?

Dario said 'All right forget it.'

'Are you deaf?'

'Go home.'

'I've got a knife. I can say I had to fight to get it off you.'

The shadowy figures that had been hovering like vultures

among the trees were now hurrying off. Dario thought –
Does this presage the approach of the killer-predator?

He said to the boy 'Someone one day may kill you.'

The boy said loudly 'You heard that? He threatened to kill
me!'

He was looking over Dario's shoulder to where a group of
several men and one woman were now coming towards them
like a sheriff's posse through the trees. They were led by a
stocky round-faced man with a small Hitler moustache. For a
moment Dario thought – Well that must be a joke! As he
came up the man said, looking first at Dario and then at the
boy 'Is this man threatening you?'

Dario said 'I'm the one being threatened.'

'I'm not talking to you.'

The boy said 'He said if I didn't do it for free he'd cut me.'

The man said to Dario 'You'd better come along with us.'

Dario said 'Who are you?'

'We look after this neck of the woods.'

'I offered him money.'

'You admit that.'

'For doing nothing. To go home.'

'This is going to cost you a lot more than what you
offered.'

'I haven't got more.'

'You've got cards haven't you? This boy's thirteen. We've
got witnesses.'

Dario thought – So this is abasement, humiliation? But
what an absurd business! They've learned their lines from a
soap opera.

There was then another man approaching, running across
the stretch of grass to the side of the area of trees. Dario
recognised him, but did not believe this. The man was
waving an arm and shouting – 'Don't cut! Keep it running!'
He came up to the man with the Hitler moustache and said
'And who the hell are you? We didn't hire you.'

The man with the moustache said 'What?'

The man who had turned up in such a bizarre manner was the man who had been talking to Laura in the graveyard. Dario felt as if his consciousness might burst; he might hold his arms out to try to contain it; might shout to the sky – But I do believe this! The man who had turned up then started laughing and doubling up and moving around with his hands dangling towards the ground: he was saying 'Fantastic! I don't believe this!' Then he straightened and said as if to the sky – 'Blackmail with menaces! Extortion! And using children!' He turned as if to some people out of sight beyond the patch of grass and shouted 'You're getting this?'

The boy quickly ducked under the branch of the tree he had been sitting on and ran away into the wood.

The man with the moustache said 'We are members of a citizens watchdog committee democratically appointed –'

The man who had turned up said 'Like shit you are, bonzo.'

The man with the moustache said to Dario 'You bastard.' Then the woman in the group pulled at his sleeve and whispered, and they all moved off through the trees.

The man who had turned up said to Dario 'You do remember me?'

Dario said 'You know I do!'

'My name's Joshua.'

'How did you know where I was?'

'Look, we'd better keep up appearances a bit longer.'

'You're not really filming?'

'There are some tricks you learn where I come from.'

They walked back across the patch of open grass towards a road. Dario said 'Were you following me?'

'Miss Simmons seemed to think she might know where you were staying.'

'How did she know?'

'I don't know.'

'Can we go back to where I'm staying now?'

'Oh sometime. Yes. I'm so glad I found you!'

'But in what a mess!'

'No. We've been so lucky.'

'I think I'm going to cry.'

Joshua said 'You do that. We've got all the time. We needn't rush things.'

Dario said 'That's one of the tricks you've learned where you come from?'

# XIX

Hafiz had been driving for so long while struggling against sleep that when he did eventually succumb it appeared that for a time he had just carried on driving: he had gone off the road into the desert and there had been nothing at first to stop him. He had dreamed; but it was now hardly clear to him what had been a dream and what had not: he had been at a village where official-looking cars were parked outside, he had had to get away, had he been spotted? were there people after him? A hand had reached out to him through the canvas at the back of the truck; that was surely a dream! He had gone bumping over stony ground, had been hurled from side to side in the cabin, when this had woken him he had stopped. But where was he now, in what direction was he facing? How could he get back onto the road; wasn't it anyway hardly more than a track; had he ever known where it was leading? He had had to get away from the village and someone had climbed into the back of the truck but that had not been a dream! So should he not now get out and have a look? He could not just proceed without knowing what was behind him. His head hurt from where it had banged against the side of the truck: when he breathed his throat was so dry that it made a rattling noise.

Some way ahead in the shimmering heat of what must be

late afternoon there was a structure in the desert like an old-fashioned oil drill, or the skeleton of a dinosaur. It had a curved arm or back, a massive ribcage, and a large snout or tail resting on the ground. Had it been on its way to find water when a giant meteor had struck and dust had blocked out the life-giving properties of the sun? And now it had been dug up and again abandoned. But if it was man-made, might it not be sheltering some form of life? He could investigate: he could circle round it. He was swinging the truck round in what he imagined was the direction of the track when he looked at the apparition again and it was then clear that it was a large bulldozer or excavating machine, with an arm and a scoop at the tail or head. Hafiz stopped again. So might this not in fact be something to do with what he had come to find out about – some sort of disposal area for bodies from the village where an experiment had been carried out? Of course he should look. It was easier to decide this than to think of whether there still might be the mysterious figure in the back of the truck.

He turned again and pulled up just short of the bulldozer. Beyond it were a series of bumps on the ground like a massive heat rash: this was where the dinosaur had been laying its eggs – and ensuring that its young would have something to feed off all winter? He was of course not making sense. But beyond the bumps was a mound of earth at the side of a pit that had been excavated and partly filled in. He tried to work out – Do humans survive catastrophes in evolution?

He climbed out of the truck. He walked stiffly towards the mound of earth and the pit. He did not want to turn to see if anyone was getting out of the truck behind him. If they were, might it happen that he would be in some quite different construct of reality?

Then when he did turn he saw the figure in the dirty white robe that he had helped to climb in earlier emerging head first from the back of the truck, as if it were performing an unusual birth. It seemed obvious that he should help again. He went back to the truck and took hold of her arms below the shoulders; it was now also evident, yes, that the figure was that of a young girl: how awkward and bony she was! indeed like a new-born calf. She was also trembling as if with some input or output of energy. The scraping of her body against the tailboard of the truck seemed to cause her pain; he pulled her clear and her legs flopped down but they did not seem immediately able to support her; she sat in a heap and he stood over her. He said 'Who are you?' After a time she said in English with a faint foreign accent – 'That was what I was going to ask you.' Then with a half laugh – 'I mean who am I, not who are you.' He said 'You don't know?' She said 'No.'

She tried to stand up but her legs seemed uncoordinated, and her garment kept getting in their way, like afterbirth. She said 'I mean, it seemed you must know me when you helped me into your truck.' He said 'No, I just wanted to get away quick.'

'I see.'

'I thought perhaps you did too.'

'Yes I did.'

She had got herself upright, and steady. He thought – We really must get her a new garment.

She said 'Have you got a drink of water?'

He said 'Yes.' He went to the truck and got his water bottle.

She drank. She said 'Thank you.' She looked round. She said 'So where are we?'

He said 'Well that is what I don't exactly know.'

'I mean what is this place? What have they been doing here?'

She set off towards where the ground was pock-marked with bumps. She walked with her arms out sideways as if to keep her balance. He thought – She learns quickly. Then – She is like a child wading into the sea.

He called out 'Be careful, the ground might be mined!'

'You think so?'

'Look, you must know who you are!'

'Why? I've lost my memory.' She said this composedly.
Hafiz thought – She's acting. Why should she not be acting?

Then she turned and faced him and said 'Anyway, that's
what I'm saying.'

'I see.'

'You needn't mind.'

'No.'

She had dark curly hair and a round face and eyes that
gazed at him sternly. He thought – You mean, we can make
of things what we like, if we say we've lost our memory?

She said 'And who are you?'

He said 'Well we needn't mind that, need we?'

'No.'

She turned back to the bumps in the ground and she went
round them towards the mound and the pit. He followed as
if keeping to her footsteps. She said 'They've been excavating
something.' He said 'Or burying it.' She turned to him again.
She said 'Is that the sort of thing you're looking for?' He said
'Why do you say that?' She said 'I don't know. I don't know
anything.' He said 'It's perhaps what I've been looking for,
it's not what I do.' He thought – She is like a painting of
someone having risen from a grave.

He remembered Richard Kahn saying – A state of
enlightenment is when you know you don't know what is
happening, not when you do –

– But you see things as if they were in a painting.

He was walking behind her again. He said 'Can you
remember what was going on in that village?'

'No.'

'But you were taken there? You were going to be held
there?'

'I never got out of their truck.'

'Till you got into mine.'

'Yes.'

'Why did you do that?'

'Where else was there for me to go?'

'Yes I see.'

'Thank you.'

'You're very lucky.'

'That I know.'

'Were you drugged?'

'I suppose so.'

'I mean lucky to be alive.'

'Yes.'

She had gone round the bumps and was coming to the mound that looked as if it might have come from a structure that had been bulldozed. To one side of it was the half-filled-in pit. There was a smell, but not quite strong enough. Hafiz thought – What do I mean, not strong enough for what? Not enough to make us have to worry?

He said 'Be careful. Don't touch.'

'I wasn't going to.'

'Come away. We don't want to be found here.'

'No.'

She had gone to the edge of the almost-filled-in pit. He came and stood by her. They both looked down. There were some bits of wood, or furnishings, or plaster, projecting from the rubble. Some of the bits had shapes which might be those of limbs covered in dust.

He said 'Let's go.'

'Is this what you were looking for?'

'Maybe. But it's done. It doesn't matter.'

'You'd have done something about it if you'd had the chance?'

'But I haven't.'

'I'm trying to understand why you helped me into your truck.'

'Yes I see.'

They began to move back towards the truck. On the way she said 'I think those were bodies.'

'There was no smell.'

'They might have had that dust put on them?'

'I don't think that works so effectively.'

'They might have been bits of statues? They've been smashing a lot of artworks recently.'

'Yes I believe so.'

When they were back by the excavating machine they saw propped against it, which they had not noticed before, the body of a man. He was evidently dead. There had begun to be a smell.

'Should we just leave him?'

'Yes.'

'What do you think killed him?'

'I don't know.'

'And we don't tell anyone?'

'Not unless there seems to be some point.'

They went back to Hafiz's truck. He opened the door of the front passenger seat for her and she climbed in. They sat side by side gazing through the windscreen at the desert. After a time he said 'Where do you want to go?'

'Where were you heading?'

'Anywhere. I don't think I can go back to where I came from.'

'Why not?'

'They'll think I've betrayed them.'

'Who's "they"?'

'That doesn't matter. Anyway, I don't want to go back.'

They sat side by side. Hafiz thought – Well it doesn't really seem we have a choice.

She said 'I can't go back either. I mean, to where I originally came from.'

'Would they shoot you?'

'No, they'd just keep on talking.'

They were silent for a time. Then Hafiz said 'Well you'd better come along with me.'

She said 'Yes I think so. Thank you.'

# XX

Leila returned from her work in the nightclub to Richard Kahn's apartment in the early hours of the morning and found that he had waited up for her but had fallen asleep in front of his computer as he quite often did. He was on his mat on the floor and was wearing only a loincloth; one leg was tucked up in the lotus position and the other leg in plaster was stretched out in front of him. His head was bowed over it so that he was in the attitude of a hurdler.

Leila went into the bedroom and undressed and stood facing a mirror. She took a pair of scissors and made as if to cut the ends of some strands of hair. From her image in the mirror she found it difficult to tell by instinct which way to move her hand to adjust the scissors. She could do this if she worked it out.

She put on a dressing gown and went back into the sitting room where Richard was sitting up. She said 'Have you heard from Hafiz?' Richard said 'No.' 'Or from Joshua?' 'No.' Leila said 'Things are breaking up.' Richard said 'They're scattering.'

'What's happening in Jerusalem?'

'Don't you get that from your policeman?'

'He's called Leon. He thinks there may be full-scale war. That'll be their only way of keeping things together.'

'We're not programmed for peace.'

'Well, you keep trying.'

'Does he still want to marry you?'

'All that's been quite useful for you while you've been laid up.'

'Don't you see I suffer?'

Leila took off her dressing gown and came and stood in front of him and straddled his stretched-out leg. Richard began to sway and groan as if he were having an ecstatic vision.

She said 'You like it.'

'It takes practice.'

'Do you picture him and me?'

'No.'

'I bet you do.'

'It's a matter of working things out.'

Leila lowered herself on to Richard's lap. She faced him with her legs on either side of him. She began kissing him. He became impassive.

She said 'Practice to be detached?'

'Or to heighten orgasm.'

'And does it work?'

'Don't you think so?'

She began to adjust his loincloth which was underneath her. She said 'He says people need enemies.'

'If only to come to terms with them.'

'Jews and Arabs?'

'Oh, they choose orgasm.'

'Well someone has to.'

'To keep things going?'

'As well as the other thing.'

'What?'

'Prayer. Detachment.'

'Everything is either a conspiracy to save the world or to destroy it.'

'Except politics.'

'Oh, not politics. Politics are about oneself and money.'

'So everyone gets what they want.'

'Which is alarming.'

Leila had succeeded in removing his loincloth underneath her. She settled herself again; they both became still. They were still for so long that it was as if with effort and concentration they were making of themselves a statue.

Then it was as if the statue were glowing and rising slightly from the ground.

Then Richard lay back slowly, and Leila, with a sudden athletic movement, swung her legs back and balanced herself on her hands and hovered over Richard with her face a few inches above his so that it was as if she were a bird feeding a fledgling in a nest. Then she laughed, pushed herself back, and got to her feet. She said 'You're an old fraud! You get it both ways! I bet you do see visions!' Then she put her dressing gown on and went into the kitchen.

Richard called after her – 'But you have enjoyed these weeks?'

'I've never been happier.'

'I didn't know you were so clever when I picked you.'

'You picked me?'

'Well, I lusted after you.'

'It was your mystical stuff I didn't know about.'

'And now you do?'

'Oh, it's all quite unknowable.'

She came back from the kitchen carrying the pair of scissors. She said 'Do you want it off now? It's getting crumbly.'

He said 'Has it come to this? It's my age!'

'Oh do shut up.'

Leila knelt by him and began to try to cut the plaster from his leg. She did not have much success. Richard lay back and breathed deeply. Leila said 'Why do they geld horses but not humans?'

'Because of the mystical stuff.'

'Do you know the story of the man who had to have an amputation so he arranged beforehand to have a wooden leg?'

'Yes I told that in one of my classes.'

'Yes I know you did.'

'Oh I see.'

'As a matter of fact I think we're the perfect couple.' She stood up and went into the kitchen and returned with a large serrated knife. Richard watched her.

He said 'So what will you do when I get my leg back?'

'What will you do?'

'I may have to go to Jerusalem.'

'Why? Oh no, you don't know why.'

'Ask your policeman.'

'I'm fed up with being a dancer.'

'What would you rather do? Blow up a synagogue? a mosque?'

'I want to do good.'

'Help! Have mercy!'

'Stay still!' She hacked at the plaster with the knife. Richard acted gritting his teeth. She said 'It was you who taught me.'

'What.'

'To throw bread on the water.'

'But you will be sad?'

Richard began to feel immeasurably sad. He thought – But sadness is quite a formidable emotion, it opens one up in all directions.

Leila said 'But anyway, why shouldn't this part of the world blow itself up? It's old and decadent. That's what you say, isn't it?'

'You can blow up what deserves to be blown up in your mind.'

'You say everything's in the mind. Practical things are just a ritual, a peacock's tail –'

'But it helps if you're beautiful.'

135

She sawed away at the plaster. Richard thought – She's like a goddess come to reconstruct heroes on a battlefield.

She said 'So what are those places that you and Hafiz and Joshua talk about? That place in the mountains?'

'That doesn't exist.'

'How do you know?'

'I don't. It may do.'

'But in the mind –'

'Oh we have to look. To try to find it.'

'To go there?'

'Each in his own way.'

'Then it does exist.'

'Of course it exists!'

'But you said it didn't.'

'Whatever you like.'

Leila managed to get the plaster off Richard's leg. They stared at the pale soft skin that was like that of something that has emerged from being a long time under water.

Leila said 'It's like a baby.'

'Did you want a baby?'

'I don't know. The world's so horrible.'

'Oh but it's not. You've said so. Or have a monstrous baby that will defeat it.'

'You'll soon be able to choose what sort of baby?'

'You wouldn't choose a monster.'

'But any baby might be a monster.'

'So you'll have to risk it.'

'Should I? You wouldn't mind? I'm frightened.'

'Don't be.'

'Do you have to go to Jerusalem?'

'You can come with me.'

'You know I can't. They wouldn't let me in. And I don't think Leon would quite fix that for me.'

'Then you know I'll be coming back.'

'And we'll be floating like bread on the waters again?'

'You want to settle down?'

Richard was struggling to his feet. Leila put out a hand to help him. He shook his head. She withdrew her hand. Then Richard tottered and half fell, and Leila caught him. He said 'You should settle. That will be all right!'

'But what about you?'

'You've been so extraordinarily good to me!'

'You think that counts?'

'Of course it does! You've made yourself adorable!'

They remained for some time with their arms wrapped round each other like an illustration of a perfect couple.

# XXI

Hafiz and Lisa, who it was whom he had rescued, sat in the small patch of shade cast by their stationary truck and looked across the dried bed of a river. They were eating biscuits and cheese that Hafiz had been carrying in the back of the truck. Lisa said 'But what were you looking for?'

Hafiz said 'I'd been involved with an experiment with a biological weapon they wanted to test. At least they said they wanted this.'

'Who are "they"?'

'The people I worked with.'

'And what was special about this weapon?'

'It was designed to discover and make use of any genetic distinction between races.'

'So that some people would be killed and not others?'

'Yes.'

'Israelis but not Arabs.'

'And they hoped that by this it would be established once and for all that there are fundamental differences between races.'

'And so a reason for enmity would be established.'

'Yes.'

'And what was your part in this experiment?'

'I was trying to keep track of it. I didn't think it was

possible. I mean I didn't think there were such genetic distinctions between races. And so this was what might finally be established.'

'Because if such a weapon were tested and worked but not as expected, it might wipe out everyone?'

'Exactly.'

'But that mightn't be a bad thing?'

'Well the threat of it. The fear.'

'But what if people would rather die –'

'That's always possible.'

Across the dried bed of the river a bit of tumbleweed was blowing hither and thither like a demented cannonball. Hafiz thought – Our imaginations are running after it like players with hockey sticks.

Lisa said 'But if the differences between peoples are not important, then what is?'

'Seeing how things fit in with each other. It's called symbiosis.'

'You think that can happen?'

'Are you an Israeli?'

'I'm saying I can't remember.'

'Is that why you can't go back?'

'What if I don't want to.'

'They wouldn't shoot you.'

'No, but they could make something bad and dangerous out of it.'

They watched the tumbleweed blowing about on the far side of the dried river. Hafiz thought – Could we see this sort of thing as essentially comic?

Lisa said 'And you can't go back because they'd think you'd betrayed them? Especially now, if you were found with me?'

'Yes. But isn't life in the wilderness a sort of death?'

'I don't know, is it?'

'You could go back and try to explain.'

'Explain what –'

'What you believe. What you've discovered.'
'You say you couldn't explain what you've discovered.'
'No.'
'But we've got so far!'
'Yes.'
'We should do something about it.'

The sun was getting close to being directly overhead so that there was less and less shade. Lisa pulled her feet up to get them away from the heat. The two of them had spent the night in the truck, Lisa in the back and Hafiz at the front, and they were tired.

Hafiz said 'Don't you know how you came to be at that village?'

'No.'
'You can't remember or don't want to?'
'Both. It's better if I don't try.'
'You could make up a story.'
'I want a story to be true.'
'Well you must want to live, or you wouldn't be here.'

Lisa looked out across the dried bed of the river. She thought – That is the Red Sea and I am one of the children of Israel: what did we think would be the Promised Land when we grew up?

She said 'I suppose we both want to live. But there must be a number of us who don't want to go on living with the old hatreds and fears: trapped in the old stories.'

'Then we can change. Tell new stories.'
'Oh I think I've changed! I'm a mutant.'
'Then you're looking for a suitable environment.'

She looked at him quickly. She said 'You know about that?'

'I'm a biologist.'

'Oh yes so you are. But doesn't biology tell us it's all a matter of luck?'

'Well you seem to be having the most incredible luck!'

'You mean I bumped into you? But then you're not only a biologist. Where do you get this stuff?'

'Life depends on luck.'

'Oh yes so it does.' She seemed to quote – 'Life is the result of an infinity of unlikely chances.'

Lisa was looking out over her imagined Red Sea. She thought – We have at times tried to settle in various wildernesses and transform them.

She said 'But if loyalty to a race doesn't make sense, and you don't want to be alone in the wilderness, what do you give allegiance to?'

'Well both our peoples used to say it was God.'

'But it wasn't God if we each thought we could own him.'

'But now here we are. Having been taken so far.'

'But you know you shouldn't stay with me.'

'No I can't. But where will you go?'

'Will you drive me as far as the border?'

'It's just another border. There's nothing beyond.'

'That's what we don't know.'

The amount of shade had now got so small that Lisa had had to turn with her knees almost pressing against Hafiz. She thought – Perhaps he is the man in my dream who was standing behind me in that church.

He said 'All right, it might be in the mind. It could be.'

'What could be?'

'Your Promised Land. Beyond the wilderness. But I'd still have to leave you.'

'Yes.'

'It's possible I might go back to my friends. After all, the only thing I've done is to bump into you.'

'But that has made a difference?'

'Of course.'

'How much?'

'Total. The odds against that are surely almost infinite.'

He thought – It might have to be in another universe that I stay with her.

He too had swung his legs round so that they would be in the shade. He and Lisa now faced each other with their knees up, their hands round their knees, the backs of their hands just touching.

He said 'There are in fact some villages over the border, in the mountains. Where they might take you in.'

'Do you know them?'

'I've heard of them. That's where I get some of what you call my "stuff".'

'I'd like it to be me who rescues you!'

'I've told you, you have!'

'What have I done?'

'You've given me meaning.'

'All right, when you go back tell a story about God. All good stories are about God – but God who can be discovered, not possessed.'

'Do you mean that then they will or won't shoot me?'

'Now you're laughing at me!'

'No I'm not. Yes I am. Of course I'm laughing!'

'Because you're happy?'

'Yes.'

She put her head down against her knees. He put his head down on his knees, so that the tops of their heads were touching.

She said 'You think we can manage this?'

'Yes.'

'You think we won't be on our own? Who are these people in the mountains?'

'They say they believe in angels.'

'What are angels?'

'They're the almost infinitely unlikely coincidences from which life comes. It's useful to believe in them.'

'As if they were true?'

'Well they happen, don't they?'

'Like you?'

'Or you.'

'But if they're infinite, they'll come round, won't they, so that we bump into each other again?'

# XXII

Laura Simmons sat at her desk in her study with her fingers poised over the keyboard of her computer. She had wanted to find out what was happening to her niece Maisie, but she realised she had no means of doing this either by e-mail or by telephone. She had not heard from Maisie since her announcement she was setting off on a journey; she had seemed to say she was going to hitch-hike to Beirut, and Laura had at first not taken this seriously. Recently however it had seemed to her that this was just the sort of thing that Maisie might do, both because of her obsession about risking self-destruction and the theories she had adopted from Maurice Rotblatt about dealing with this. Maurice used to say – but Laura realised she didn't want to remember what Maurice used to say, though she had begun to feel guilty about her attitude towards Maurice. It was Maisie who had told her that she, Laura, was still angry and resentful about his disappearance, and it had struck her this was true. She had arranged the memorial service, but what she had said in it was mainly taken from things that Andros had written; she had never quite settled what she felt in her own mind about Maurice's ideas. Could it be that Maisie in fact understood or accepted more about Maurice's view of what could be called God, for instance, than she had ever done herself? What was this – that God was both creator and created, creating humans to stand on their own, but operating thus through what humans had the courage to recognise and do? So was it with guilt about not thinking about this that Maisie had confronted her? And now Maisie was out of touch. She had no computer, no e-mail address; she refused to carry a mobile phone and the last ordinary telephone number that Laura had had for her was said to be out of order. Laura would have liked to ring the young man Dario, but she did not know how to find him. She thought of ringing Andros, but she was shy of becoming involved with Andros again. She thought – In this age of information, I have no means of finding what I want.

There intruded on this trail of indecision the sound of her own mobile phone ringing. She went through her usual routine in relation to this – she wouldn't answer it; she'd better answer it, for it might convey some vital news, for instance, now, about Maisie. But where was it anyway? It made an absurdly insistent noise like a baby crying: hadn't crying evolved to be so annoying that one had to respond to it? She found her mobile in her bag, but then became momentarily confused about the buttons. Of course Maisie was right: mobiles were like the bells that summoned servants in old-fashioned country houses.

'Hello –'

'Laura, can you help me.'

'Oh Melissa, hello.'

'You know Maurice.'

'Yes I know Maurice.'

'You remember the sort of things he used to say –'

'I mostly try to forget them.'

'You know my son Ben –'

'Yes I know your son Ben.'

'He's not been well. He's got this girlfriend.'

'That must be a terrible worry for you.'

Laura tried to tilt her chair into a more comfortable

position. Melissa was one of her oldest friends. She thought –
I mustn't be bitchy! I'm probably jealous that Melissa has a
son.

'Well, he was going to join his father to recuperate by the
Red Sea, but at the last minute his girlfriend joined him, and
they never got as far as his father, who's out there doing some
filming.'

'Yes I think you told me about that.'

'And now it appears that the girlfriend's having a baby. And
they don't want to come home. They want to have it
somewhere out there.'

'Where?'

'They don't say. The aeroplane was diverted. I can't make
any sense of it. I think they just want to get away.'

'They sound like my niece Maisie.'

'Is Maisie having a baby?'

'Not that I know of. I wouldn't be surprised.'

'I think it's to do with the girlfriend. She's Irish. She wants
the baby to be born as far away as possible from any family
influence.'

'Well I do see that.'

'And Harry and I have been getting on rather badly lately.
But it's not the genes they want to get away from, it's what
nowadays are called the vibrations.'

'Oh the vibrations.'

'I don't blame them really. And you know what the young
are like. Everything's a con, everything's an ad, everything's
a brand to do with money. And Ben has been coming across
some things of Maurice's on the Net. Who's been putting out
that stuff, do you know?'

'No. Perhaps it's Andros.'

'So what were those places that Maurice was on about?
That's what I wanted to ask you. In the Middle East, in the
mountains. The sort of place people went on pilgrimages to.'

'I expect that's where Maisie is going.'

'But you know the places I mean?'

'I don't know what they're called. I could look it up. But I expect the young just want to get away from their families.'

'But you can't have a baby on top of Mount Ararat. Or is that just where you can? Is that what Maurice was on about?'

'Why don't you go and join them?'

'They don't want us there. Not till after the baby.'

'Well that does sound reasonable. Maybe you'd be one of the people due to be drowned.'

'Oh fuck off Laura. Just fuck off.'

The telephone made one of its unintelligible bleeping sounds. Laura, who had taken it from her ear, observed its small window. She thought – That's the sort of porthole through which you view strange creatures at some unimaginable depth of the sea.

'Are you still there?'

'Yes.'

'Sorry, we got cut off. But you know how maddening you can be.'

'Yes. But what I meant was, you know about grandparents and babies. And it's because families have done their job well that children want to be free of them.'

'Yes I know all that. But of course I still feel anxious and guilty. Do you think you can just look up those places Maurice talked about?'

'Yes I'll try. I was thinking of doing something about Maurice's papers anyway.'

'Oh that's good Laura. Thank you.'

'I do sometimes think we're strange creatures at the bottom of the sea.'

'I don't. I think everyone else is.'

'Oh well, yes, I think that really.'

Laura pressed a button and the small window went blank. One could always make out one had pushed a button by mistake. She put the telephone down and leaned over the keyboard of her computer. She thought – But Maurice never had an e-mail address. Then – But that's somewhere I might have gone, to a place in the mountains, if I had been going to have a baby.

– In fact that's where Maurice might be? Though he never said he wanted a baby.

– But that's the part of the world, yes, where Noah's Ark was said to have come down, where there was supposed to have been the Garden of Eden, where that tower was being built up to heaven before it was Babel.

After a time she found herself climbing up the stairs and then a ladder into the attic. Here there were boxes of papers stored from the time when she had lived with Maurice. Because her break with him had been so unexplained – though not wholly unexpected, she had had to admit to herself – she had for some time after it not been able to believe that she would not be with him again: he would turn up as he had gone, wandering in the night. She had kept his papers as he had left them, with the feeling that they were waiting for the story of her and him to be resumed; that to intrude on them might disturb a course of events that would otherwise happen. But then the expectation and indeed the desire for his return had faded; she had begun to resent that he had gone; also not that he might be dead but that he might have wanted her to think him dead. And then she did not want to disturb the boxes because to do so might stir up grief and anger.

Recently however there had been the revival of interest in Maurice, not only because of Richard Kahn's lurid story about what might have been his ordeal, but because pieces about Maurice's life and writings had been published on the Net and had gained a small cult following. This was not so much to do with the possibility of his having been a secret intelligence agent as had once been rumoured, but rather with reports of his blend of science-with-mysticism that had been ignored or criticised by a majority of professional scientists, but which had been taken up by others because it confronted questions that were indeed coming more into vogue, even with some professionals. On the question of how life on earth, and in particular conscious human life, had begun – which, scientists admitted, had been scientifically almost infinitely unlikely – Maurice proposed that it had to be faced that, yes, there was mingling here of the finite with the infinite that could well be called God if the word had not become so devalued – not a simple creator god nor a day-to-day power-exercising god, but one which enabled and gave deference to the creative consciousness of humans. This idea became known, after Maurice had disappeared, as the Creator/Created Synthesis. Laura had thought – How he would have hated that! No wonder poor Maurice wanted to disappear.

She sat on a broken-down armchair in the attic and surveyed the cardboard boxes as if they might contain Maurice's ashes or murdered remains. She was succeeding in giving up anger and resentment; but then, did not grief get a hold? Maurice had once said to her – 'When someone dies, it is not the people who depended on that person who feel let down, but the people on whom that person depended.' She had said 'You mean, if I died, you'd feel let down?' He had said 'No, if I died, you'd feel let down.'

She put out a hand to open one of the boxes. What if it contained his John-the-Baptist-like head?

She and Maurice had gone walking one day round the damp edges of fields. Laura had said 'All right, humans create their histories. But someone some time has to know what is an artificial story and what is not: what is true. Or some part of everyone has to.'

Maurice had said 'Yes, but you find out. You check it against the reality. Truth is what happens.'

'Even if it can't be explained?'

'Can anything ever quite be explained.'

'But you say you have choices about what happens.'

148

'You have a choice to turn your attention to what is happening; to what appears to be happening, or what could happen.'

'And that affects it?'

'Well, yes, it may be just one of the almost infinite things that affect it.'

'But you can believe you've had a hand in it?'

'Yes.'

'But is that true?'

'Well, if it happens.'

The fields were muddy. Laura and Maurice floundered slightly. She had thought – We are bogged down in talk. He has always said that people get bogged down in talk, but there is a strange connection between us and the outside world, like gravity, by which we may keep our balance.

She had said 'You want to start a new religion.'

'I want individuals to feel that they have some use and responsibility.'

'What if you give your attention to something that doesn't happen?'

'What you give your attention to are possibilities.'

'One of which will happen?'

'Possibly.'

'So you can't lose.'

'That's right.' Then – 'It's an old religion, it's the basis of all religions. It's acknowledging that things are all right. It's when you look back that you may understand how you have had a hand in them.'

'And thus you can have a trust in looking forward?'

'Yes.'

'And that's what you call having use and responsibility?'

'Yes.'

'And that's all you can say about it?'

'Well you can tell stories about what the experience is like.'

It had begun to rain. They had turned up their collars as if they were being bombarded with particles.

149

She had said 'And the stories are what matter? Stories which other people can judge?'

'Well, either appreciate or not.'

'No dogmas, creeds, rituals –'

'But they are stories.'

'And how would you learn what to appreciate and what not to?'

'You'd put it up, as I say, against your experience.'

'Which is fashioned by what you appreciate.'

'Yes.'

'You go round and round.'

'Yes. It's what is called learning.'

'And by this you know God.'

'You may do. You don't prove God. You experience and appreciate.'

There was a ringing noise from somewhere downstairs. Laura jumped. It was not the telephone; not her mobile phone; it was the doorbell. But the door was unlocked. No one usually used the doorbell.

She said quietly 'Just a minute.'

Maurice could be coming back from the dead, mutilated, as in that horror story?

That day in the rain she had said 'But how do you know that things are all right?'

She couldn't remember what Maurice had said. You either do or you don't – ? He had seemed not to want to go on talking.

There was another ring. Laura got up and stumbled towards the ladder. She said 'I'm coming!' She thought – I will fall, and people will think I have been struck down by a thunderbolt.

She could hear rain on the windows, the roof. She thought – But I do need now to write a story.

When she got to the front door there was a young man outside in the rain who was familiar to her but for a moment she could not place him, he was so damp and bedraggled, like a new-born calf. She said 'Oh hullo.' He said 'Do you remember me? I'm Dario, Maisie's friend. I spoke to you that day at the church.' She said 'Oh yes, of course. Did that man find you?' He said 'What man?' Then – 'Oh Joshua, yes, that's an extraordinary story!' Laura said 'I'm sure it is.' Dario had his jacket draped over his head to protect it from the rain: he also, Laura thought, looked like a pilgrim or a novice monk. She said 'But do come in.' Dario said 'Thank you.' Laura thought – I think what Maurice said was that one knows things are all right by what happens. Dario said 'Joshua and I thought you might like some help with sorting those papers.'

# XXIII

Maisie waited at the side of a long straight road across a stony plain in southern Turkey. She sat straight-backed on her haversack and tried to bring back in memory the expressions on the faces of the ruefully smiling figures that she had seen on the walls of some of the local churches – to imagine their states of mind; what they might have been feeling.

She had sat like this for much of the late afternoon. A few trucks had gone past: one had stopped with a squeal of brakes and a driver with a huge black moustache had beckoned to her; she had picked up her haversack and had retreated into the desert. She had been surprised at her wariness. She had thought – I must want not to die?

She had been given a lift in the morning by some fruit farmers who were returning from the local market town in their van. They had been friendly; they had joked with her and shown an interest in her journey. She and they had shared little common language, but it was because of a feeling of unstated warmth that she had begun, it seemed, to lose the impression of herself at enmity with a hostile world. It was this that had carried her across Europe and into Asia Minor – the image of herself as a knight in armour not afraid of death and getting confidence and indeed identity through confronting fear. But it was as if she had in the last day come to the edge of a different world: the people in the van were benign and humorous: they did not talk much even among themselves. She had thought – They communicate like those figures on the walls of their churches.

They had suggested (or so she had understood) that she could come back with them to their village where she could be accommodated, though this would mean turning off her planned route and going into the mountains. She had at first instinctively seen such an invitation as a trap: but then when the suggestion had not been pressed she had almost at once regretted her lack of response to it: her new friends had seemed to respect her refusal without resentment, and this had made her feel even more that she had something to recognise and learn. When they had come to their turning into the hills she had hoped that they might once more issue their invitation, but after a brief murmuring among themselves they had driven off, waving goodbye cheerfully. She had been left by the side of the road with her rucksack and sleeping bag. She had thought – So all right, I am on my own again and in the middle of an empty plain: what am I learning?

The road into the hills where she might have found refuge would have taken her to the north. Her planned route took her east and then south: this was the route by which crusaders had come to the Holy Land: not many had travelled by boat, because that would not have provided them with killing and pillaging. But on this long and mostly featureless stretch of road she felt it more and more absurd to stick rigidly to her plan; might she not somehow speed it up? Could she not have gone for a rest into the hills? She should pay more attention to what turned up. Was that not what Andros, and indeed Maurice, had been saying?

In the evening she walked along the road for an hour or two, coming only to a cluster of ruined houses. She decided to stay by these: if no suitable vehicle came along by nightfall, she would have some shelter within which to set out her sleeping bag. She had her water bottle, and cheese and biscuits in her haversack. But then what? What was the point of trusting to chances if she did not take them?

Andros had encouraged her to go on her journey: why had he not preferred to set her up in a flat in Paris or London? When she had explained to him her plans and how she felt as she did, he had just raised his eyebrows and pursed his lips and said – Well, go your own way, but remember to look for the figures of saints and animals on the churches in eastern Turkey. Andros was like the people in the van in that he respected her and had not tried to stop her. He had even bought her a train ticket! But how alarming. How did one know what one was, what was right, if there was nothing to fight against?

She tried to remember how she had imagined the end of her journey – though in fact she had hardly thought about an end. She would be in Beirut, and she would go to see Richard Kahn – both Laura and Andros had talked of Richard Kahn, who had been a pupil of Maurice's. And then recently Richard was said to have found Maurice's bones, and although people said they did not believe this story, in some manner it seemed they did, because they liked repeating it – perhaps just because it was a good story. No one seemed much interested in finding out what was in fact true. Laura had said – But how could it be! Maisie had thought – But if it was, would it make such an interesting story?

So she had set off like a crusader in search of the truth – or if truth was not available, then at least she might have seemed to behave like a hero. But now she was stuck on a lonely road in the desert. This was truth? She would be here till nightfall when with luck she would fall asleep. She would then have learned – some humility? She curled up behind a low wall with her head on her haversack: at least like this she could dream: she would be like an animal in its lair.

Why had she not gone off with those friendly people into the hills? They would have looked after her. But it had seemed that they had felt that this would not have been right for her.

What was happening to Dario? He had wanted to help her, she had wanted to help him, but he had wanted them to be lovers. But he had also said he was homosexual, and she had said – So what is the point of that? He had said – Can't we still help each other?

They had tried to break into Maurice's old flat in London which Laura was supposed to be looking after: Laura had mentioned she wanted some of her things. And Dario had said he'd like to see where Maurice had lived. Maisie had wondered if he would try to make love to her there, but anyway they had not been able to get into the flat; however while they were trying they had come across Andros. Dario had told some story about how he had known Maurice in Jerusalem, but Maisie had not known whether to believe this. But then she had bumped into Andros again, and he had helped to start her on her journey. So had in fact she and Dario helped each other?

When she emerged from what seemed to have been a dream it was dark except for a thin crescent moon. This was like a curve of bright metal: why should it not come swinging down to earth like a giant scimitar to chop off the heads of infidels and crusaders. Was it possible that just when she wanted not to die, she might die? Surely this was not what was meant by a possibility?

Then later in the night there was a roaring noise, and a whoosh, and a thump on the ground not far from her. She thought – But was I still dreaming? Was God pointing a finger at me, as if I were someone available being chosen in a brothel?

Or was it just a meteor?

She did not want to move from her own curled-up ball to look. The night had become very cold. But she imagined there had been a faint warmth in the air: a pattering sound; a hissing.

She thought – Wolves? Snakes? A devil's spittle? She wanted to get back to her dream about God who might have some task for her.

Then in the half-light of just before dawn she did sit up because she was so uncomfortable, she was in pain; and then she saw not far from the low wall under which she was sheltering small bits of debris scattered on the stony ground like an outcrop of petals; they were fragments of metal, it seemed, to which were attached pieces of fabric which swayed slightly in the breeze. And further off there was a larger shape sticking up from the ground like the beak of a bird – but broken off, as if in the act of pecking. Well something had made the whoosh and thump: were these fragments of a plane; a satellite; a decrepit space station?

Carrying her haversack she set off across the desert. Or perhaps the object sticking up was the fossilised wing of a giant dinosaur; perhaps it was the slab of stone which in that film symbolised the possibility of harmony between the universe and humans. As she got close to the object there seemed to be heat coming from it; this might be her imagination, but she could hold out her cold hands to it. It was a construction of metal with a covering not so much of fabric as of thin shiny foil; yes indeed it could be part of the tail-fin of a plane; or indeed a piece of that ancient Russian space station that was always said to be cracking up. Such bits were supposed to burn up in the atmosphere? Well this one was providing warmth for her. Maisie sat on her haversack and held her hands out gratefully.

Then she must have dozed again, because she was startled by a great clatter as of more objects falling from the sky and this time also a mighty rushing wind. She thought – Oh God, really! Then there was a helicopter overhead; it was coming down to land: she wanted to joke – The cavalry are coming! And this did seem funny. Then when the wind had lessened and the huge sword blades were only languidly whirling two men jumped down from the helicopter and one of them went to the object sticking up from the ground and peered at it gingerly and the other came up to Maisie and said 'Who the hell are you?' and then – 'Do you understand English?' Maisie thought she might say – I fell out of the sky too, but I bounced, fortunately. She said 'I was just sitting here having a snooze when whoosh! this happened!' The man said 'But did you see just what?' Then – 'And what are you doing here?' Maisie said 'Well that's a long story.' Then there was another roaring noise in the distance and growing stronger and another helicopter was approaching. Maisie thought – There should be the music of the Ride of the Valkyries. The man with Maisie said 'My God those buggers haven't wasted much time!' Then to Maisie – 'You'd better come along with us. You don't want that lot to get hold of you.' Maisie said 'No.' She picked up her haversack and moved towards the first helicopter. The man said 'Quick, in you go. And you can tell us on the way what you know.' Maisie said 'Do you happen to be going anywhere near Beirut?' The man stopped for a moment and looked at her with a quizzical expression like that on the face of a figure on one of the churches. Maisie said 'That's where I was on my way to.' The second helicopter had landed and men were getting out and were moving quickly to the object on the ground; they were calling out to the man who was already there in a language that Maisie did not understand but which she imagined might be Russian. The man who was ushering her into the first helicopter said with his amused smile 'Oh I expect we can accommodate you, darling!'

# PART II

# XXIV

In a valley of fruit trees surrounded by snow-capped mountains a village lodged on a slope above a swiftly flowing river. A track ran alongside the river and into the village and there ended; the line of the river continued upwards with the water tumbling down until in the immensity of the mountains all movement ceased.

The air was cool, and there were not many people about in the village. A man walked beside a donkey carrying brushwood; a group with a ladder were repairing a roof. The stillness was like that enshrined in a painting: the faint movements like the tinkling of cow bells.

A young man sat on the steps of the verandah of a wooden-built house set back from the road, a short distance from the village. He held his hands round his knees and rocked slightly backwards and forwards as if at the centre of a see-saw. The voice of a woman from inside the house called – 'I don't mean what I said you know!' The man said 'Yes I know.' The voice of the woman declaimed – 'Oh what are we doing here, we shouldn't be here!' Then in an ordinary voice – 'I'm placating the demons. Oh beautiful, useful demons!'

The man went into the house, which consisted of one large room serving as sitting room and bedroom and workroom and kitchen. At one end there was a bed on which a woman lay propped half naked with her legs apart: she was evidently in the early stages of labour. She was being tended by a young girl in a local dress of quilted smock and baggy trousers. The woman said to the man as if she were once more acting lines from a script – 'Oh how can I have got you into this terrible predicament! cut off from family and friends! and all I can do is to moan!' The man said 'Well if it helps.' The woman said 'And all that rubbish.'

The young girl smiled. She went to a stove by the far wall on which there was a pan of water boiling. She took a cloth from it with two sticks like tongs and put the cloth into a bucket of cold water on the floor. Then she rinsed it and squeezed it and wrung it out and hung it on a line stretched between the stove and the wall. She took another cloth from a basket and put it in the pan of boiling water. She squatted on her haunches with her back against the wall.

The woman, watching her, said 'Lily of the Valley, Rose of Sharon, whoever you are, what shall we call you? Who have come like a thief in the night to help rescue us from our inheritance, what would we do without you? We would be more than ever like sounding brass and a tinkling cymbal.'

The man said 'Symbol – '

'That's what I said.'

'The women of the village have set up a prayer meeting for you, with a lot of bells and horns and lutes and dancing.'

'Have you told them how terribly grateful we are –'

'Yes.'

'And we hope to join in later.'

The woman appeared to suffer another spasm of pain; and then she half sang, half declaimed, as if in opera – 'Oh the lot of women is a hard and cruel one, tra la, we bring forth in travail and sorrow, tra la.' Then in her ordinary voice – 'Do you think the women help with the demons?'

'They think they do.'

'And that's why we came here?'

The young man and the young woman, Ben and Julie, had

162

come to this village after they had been working for some months at an archaeological site some miles away. They had intended to stay in their accommodation there until the baby was born, but the people in charge of the site had become so alarmed at the prospect of what might be seen as their responsibility for a birth without up-to-date safeguards that they had insisted that Ben and Julie should move to where there were doctors and a hospital, or else they would have to inform the authorities, who would doubtless get in touch with Julie's family. Julie had said 'My family are dead.' The woman in charge had said 'Where do you come from?' Julie had said 'Ireland.' The woman had said 'Oh I see.' Julie had said to Ben 'What does she see? That the Irish are used to dropping their babies in bogs?' So Ben and Julie had made up a story that they had in fact got in touch with Ben's family, and Ben's mother was coming out and would meet them at a town on the coast.

The people in charge of the site had then been apologetic, but had explained that Ben and Julie might have been able to sue them for damages if things went wrong. Julie had said to Ben 'So it's right that we don't want to be with these people when the baby's born, they'd be worse than what we've tried to get away from, they'd be envious as witches with claws.' So Ben and Julie had gone off one morning in a car provided by one of the local dignitaries who did not like the people at the site: he indicated to Ben and Julie that he knew just the place for them to have the baby – the village of his ancestors, some distance over the hills, where they would be looked after. It seemed that he had heard of, but had discounted, the story that they were going to meet Ben's mother.

Ben said 'He's a holy man. He's like one of those figures on the walls of their churches.'

Julie said 'Ask him what's so special about where he's taking us.'

'I did, but I couldn't really understand. I think he just wants us to trust him.'

163

'Which we do, don't we?'

'Yes. It seems the thing to do.'

So Julie and Ben were taken by their friend to an inn in the village at the far side of a mountain, where they settled in while he explained about them to the people in the village who treated them with great kindness and courtesy. Julie said 'What on earth do you think he told them?' Ben said 'Perhaps just that we are nice.' Julie said 'I sometimes get frightened.' Ben said 'Don't. These people believe in angels.'

While they were waiting for the baby to be born Julie went out on foot each day to some caves where there were wall paintings done probably in the twelfth century AD: the colours were still striking due to the dryness of the atmosphere. Julie made drawings, which she later coloured. At the archaeological site the task had been mainly to rescue and preserve some first-century Roman mosaics which depicted the sybaritic life of the time – men reclining on couches being tended by elegant women; wild animals being hunted with spears. In contrast to this, the cave paintings by their new village were unworldly and sometimes hard to decipher: there were saints with their feet off the ground and their faces scratched out: or they might, yes, be angels. While Julie was doing her drawings Ben took lessons in the local language from one of the elders of the village; he learned something of their beliefs and traditions, and their ways of seeing the world.

He said to Julie, 'But like all truly religious people they're better at saying what things are not rather than what they are. They are Muslims, but not orthodox; in some ways they're more like Christians. They believe in a universal Spirit which is served by angels; but this Spirit's chief incarnation is not Mohammed, but his son-in-law Ali, who should have been his rightful heir, and was gentle and spiritual and did not believe in militarism. But he was murdered. They don't have creeds or dogmas or mosques or churches; they feel they have personal contact with the Spirit by music and dancing; and by – oh yes – hanging prayer offerings in the form of strips of material on the branches of trees.' Julie said 'So we have come to the right place.'

The people of the village had from the first been strikingly hospitable; they brought provisions for Ben and Julie, they invited them into their homes. Then when they realised that life at the inn might be tiring for Julie and that she and Ben might like to be more on their own, they had suggested that they move to a guesthouse on the outskirts of the village which at the moment was unused and which would be quieter, but where an eye could still be kept on them. Julie said 'It's difficult to believe this!' Ben said 'It's happening.'

Then one day when Julie had been on her way to the caves with her drawing materials and stool, a girl had turned up and had offered to carry these. This was a girl they had become aware of as a new arrival in the village: apparently she had turned up one day on a bus from the coast; she had been dressed in a black robe down to the ground so that she was like some novice in a religious order. She could not or did not choose to speak: she might have suffered some trauma, or taken a vow of silence. She made it known that she would undertake any work if she was allowed to stay for a while in the village: she could for instance work as a nurse in the clinic, for which it seemed she had had training. It was of course rare for a young girl to be on her own in this country, but the village had the reputation for being a place of some sanctity to which pilgrims came; and thus the villagers were accustomed, as they had shown with Julie and Ben, to strangers turning up and staying for a while. And the girl did prove to be of help to the women in the clinic.

When she had helped to carry Julie's drawing-board to the cave she had waited till Julie was set up on her stool and then had left her, indicating that she intended to come back when required. Julie had found her eyes suffused with tears. The blinded figures on the walls seemed to smile down on her encouragingly.

Then when Julie and Ben moved to the house on the outskirts of the village the girl came with them; this again seemed just to happen, or perhaps the women in the clinic had arranged it. Julie said to Ben 'Isn't it right to be frightened when good things happen?' Ben said 'Well, all birth is a miracle.' Julie said 'No wonder it's so difficult to stand it.' And then to the girl – 'Rose of Sharon, Lily of the Valley, you will stay with us till we move on, won't you?'

The girl had discarded her dark robe and now wore brightly coloured local clothes that Julie and Ben had found for her. She cooked and cleaned and collected provisions: she would not take money, but accepted any presents that were given to her. She had black curly hair and a round clear-skinned face and eyes that were sad and cautious but sometimes amused. She was very thin, and walked with a slight limp. She gave to no one, not even to Ben and Julie, any information about her history.

Julie said 'But she knows about delivering babies. I expect she's the archangel Gabriel.'

Ben said 'Julie, we've got to be careful!'

'I shall call her Gaby.'

'Well, we'll be here till we've had the baby, then we'll have to move on. That's what we decided wasn't it?'

'Yes that's what we wanted.'

In the evenings Julie would sometimes draw Gaby – as she worked at the stove, as she sat on the floor with her arms round her knees and her back against a wall. Sometimes Julie would transform the figure she had drawn into something else – a mountain, a tree, a landscape. She would say 'Gaby, you're a spirit, no wonder you have come to this place! Did you see a star? Did you leave your own people in a distant country?' When Julie was tired and her back ached she would lie on the bed and Gaby would sit by her on the floor with a hand just resting on her. Ben would sit on the verandah while the light lasted and write in a notebook.

Ben and Gaby were shy with one another. Julie would say

– 'Ben, you ought to be married to Gaby! Perhaps you were in another existence.'

To Gaby Julie would say – 'Gaby, isn't it a mercy you don't talk, or we'd have to ask you questions – where do you come from, where were you going. And we would have to try to tell you about us, why we are here, what may happen to us, which we don't really know, so what's the point of talking. But we know we don't know, so that's all right. We can all live in the present, this beautiful present, and watch what happens, which is so extraordinary if you watch it. I mean why does one thing happen rather than another? why does anything happen rather than nothing? And everyone here is so nice. That's what's frightening.

'What happened to you, Gaby, did they torture you, did they try to cut your tongue out? I'm only asking because perhaps in the end nothing is too terrible to know. Talking should be like singing; and perhaps a song doesn't need an answer. Do you ever sing to yourself, Gaby? They would be such sad songs, but you would be smiling. Are you just grateful to be alive? Where I come from they still torture people; they break their legs and arms because of nothing. And they talk and talk – about the past, about the future; they have a hatred for the present.

'Do you believe in God, Gaby: how did you get here; where will you be going? I expect you come from an age-old people who talk and talk and you are trying to get away, you wanted to change your nature like a dragonfly, but then to live for more than a day. Do you feel there are things watching over you, Gaby? Will you help me and the baby to live? And if I die, will you look after Ben? We are so grateful, Gaby, for all you are doing for us: and I hope that one day we will have been able to do things for you.'

# XXV

Dario sat on the floor in front of a large cardboard box which he had that morning carried down to Laura's sitting room from the attic. He closed his eyes and put his hand into the box as if he were picking a gift from a bran tub. He pulled out a loose-leaf notebook with pages covered in handwriting. He opened it and propped himself against the sofa and read –

Towards the end of the twentieth century when it was realised that many of the old certainties and ideals were blowing away and people were groping after them like children with gas balloons gone on the wind –

– no more communism, no more fascism, no more God as an old retainer in the sky whom one could tell what to tell one to do –

– towers built up towards heaven coming crashing down and each person talking, talking, complaining in a different language and putting the blame on others –

– then the best that could be done, it seemed, was just for everyone to point out what they perceived to be wrong and demand that someone else should put it right. And with nothing to be learned from the past, and with no vision of hope for the future, could not almost everything be seen as wrong? Indeed what could there be to make it seem anything else? Complaint, resentment, were taking the place of the style once provided by religion.

In a free-for-all world it has to be said – Let the best man win. But those who win are likely to be those who bluff and deceive and get away with it: and with no truth, there need not be guilt. There is only a network, a web, like that of a spider; in which people are not identities but words: where meaning has been sucked out by the spider. The spider is the rule of Nietzsche's 'last man' – whose power is exercised by resentment.

Dario broke off. He thought – Oh I knew Nietzsche would get in somewhere! No one understands Nietzsche. And most people use him, as he knew they would, to shit on him.

He continued reading –

But wait! Is not this a propitious state of affairs for anyone who wishes to explore and discover life: when flies and spiders are occupied on their web? Humans are no different from plants and animals in the necessary struggle for existence; all matter is at the mercy of needs, of cause and effect. But humans have the added capacity to see this. And through this they can be free.

Dario thought – Yes, but then what? You have a nice aesthetic view of the ruins; the rubble? He leaned forwards to where he could see out of the French windows to where Laura was tending to her rose bushes. He thought – All right, one can cultivate one's garden.

He read –

But in an age in which politics and business are quite openly matters of playing games; in which those who wish to disrupt the fields of play are called anarchists, terrorists; but who can without too much difficulty be absorbed and fought in what can be taken as a greater and more exciting game –

– What activity can there be in fact for the person who with at least part of him or her chooses not to play these games: who wishes to look in the unknown areas beyond the fields of play – for truth, for meaning? Of course they will be mocked, ignored: but more to the point here, they will still be human. And so they may find themselves involved in their own games; and thus may feel defeated.

Perhaps it was because of this that the philosopher Wittgenstein suggested that such aspirants should stay silent; for they do have a valid field of play, which is to question and even gently mock themselves. But having said this the philosopher was not silent – perhaps this was his joke! – he found he could ruminate on art, religion, morals: it was just that the game had to be one of questions rather than answers.

Dario thought – Oh damn, Wittgenstein! Anyone can make what they like of Wittgenstein.

He put the notebook down on the floor, where it lay beside other papers he had taken from the box. He lay with his head resting against the seat of the sofa and closed his eyes.

When he had arrived the evening before, Laura had welcomed him out of the rain almost as if she had been expecting him. He had said 'I'm sorry I had to hurry away the last time!' She had said 'Oh I know about that.' She had produced dry clothes for him – he supposed these might have been Maurice's – and they had sat in the kitchen and she had cooked for him sausages and eggs. He had said 'Andros seemed to think you might like something written about Maurice.' She had said 'It was Maisie who thinks I should write something about Maurice.' Then – 'Have you heard from Maisie?'

'No.'

'There are suddenly all you people turning up.'

The next morning Laura had gone out early and he had got

170

his own breakfast and then had carried the first box down from the attic. Laura had returned later but she had not come into the sitting room, she had gone straight to the garden where he could see her from time to time among the roses. He had thought – She still wants to make it known that she is not at home with this business.

Now, in the later morning, when he had gone through some press cuttings and articles that were not by Maurice, and had put aside the handwritten notebook which he was not certain whether or not was Maurice's, he went out into the garden where Laura was like a disconsolate earth-goddess still not quite reconciled to the prospect of being frustrated by winter.

He said 'This box is a bit of a muddle. It's mostly notes, reviews. How much is original?'

'Maurice didn't write much down. He had this terrible mistrust of language.'

'But this notebook's original?'

'It seems to be.'

'He did lecture; teach.'

'He thought if other people wrote it down it wouldn't be so much his imposition.'

'And he didn't want that?'

'No. He thought people should find their own ways.'

'But this only made sense if there were maps provided by what might be called God?'

Laura made her way out of the flower bed. She trod delicately, removing thorns that got caught on her clothes; turning and smoothing her footprints in the soil with her toes.

She said 'Yes, I suppose so. But he was a bit mad.'

'And that got on your nerves?'

'No.'

'Something must have done.'

'He said one couldn't talk about God, but then he did. He said this was no contradiction. So long, that is, as one knew that it was. And so on.'

'And that was godlike behaviour?'

'Yes, that's clever. – Omnipotence is what makes all possibilities; it's we who make one thing happen rather than another –'

'That's a quote?'

'Yes.'

Dario squatted on the lawn and pulled out a notebook of his own and wrote in it. Laura sat down beside him and stretched her bare legs out and crossed her ankles. Dario watched her out of the corner of an eye. He thought – Perhaps I could make love to an older woman: she is not my mother.

Laura said 'I'm sorry if I seem a bit stand-offish. I've asked you to look at the papers after all.'

'You're not stand-offish.'

'A lot of what you'll find was written by other people. Pupils. Andros, Richard Kahn.'

'He kept it all?'

'He wanted everything kept. So that it could have a chance to sort itself out.' She laughed.

'That's the sort of thing Andros says.'

'You see?'

'And then someone like me comes along.' He laughed.

Laura lay back and put her hands behind her head. She was aware of Dario watching her. She said 'You've done your homework.'

'I sat up last night.'

'Of course, yes, what he meant was that God sorts things out. Making use of all our muddles; but things do get sorted.'

Dario pulled a piece of paper from his pocket and read –

'The possibility of performing a right rather than wrong act depends on one's ability to be aware both of it and of oneself doing it. It is by this recognition of such connectedness that one becomes part of a larger whole.' He looked up and said 'That's how oneself becomes godlike? That's Zen? Sufi?'

'He didn't claim to be original. He didn't think there was all that much original.'

'Anyway that bit wasn't Maurice, it was me.'

Laura laughed. 'But you got it through Maurice.'

'I suppose so, yes.'

Laura lay back and pulled her knees up so that her skirt fell back on her thighs. She thought – Well, something should be made of this lonely house, this lovely house and garden; it is summer and there are seeds coming in.

Dario was thinking – I am being taken up into a more elaborate existence in this house and garden. Laura should be the abbess of a semi-religious order; or perhaps the madame of a psycho-spiritual brothel, because she could allow anything in that turns up. She might have seen Maurice as a devil: he might have been frightened of her power.

He said 'If you want me to sort this stuff out, do you also want me to write it up, edit it?'

'You write what you like. Everyone should write what they like.'

'There may be things about people that we don't yet know about.'

'Indeed.'

'I wish we knew about Maisie.'

'Why aren't you with Joshua?'

'I was. But we thought you needed help with these papers.'

'I see. Do I see? Well somewhere in those boxes you'll find things I've written about me and Maurice.'

# XXVI

At night in the village in the valley of fruit trees surrounded by snow-capped mountains the silence was pervasive as if it consisted of the particles that hold the universe together. On this night there was an occasional cry like a snatch of wild song that came from the house set back from the road. A light inside the house cast shadows against the thin curtain that covered the doorway, as if it were a screen on which might be projected a hidden drama. People from the village sat on the ground at some distance from the house like an audience playing their own part in the ritual. At the front there was a row of children, still and attentive.

Inside the house the young man called Ben knelt at the bottom of the bed with his body bent over it and his hands holding the feet of the young woman, Julie, who was propped on cushions at the far end of the bed giving birth. The girl whom they called Gaby was by Julie's head and was holding a cloth with which from time to time she wiped Julie's face. Julie uttered another cry, which she managed to shape at the end into almost a melody. She said 'Oh I do think opera's ridiculous!'

Ben said 'I'll hold you.'

Julie declaimed 'We sing unto the Lord an old song – You're such a bastard, God!'

Ben climbed onto the bed behind her and sat with his legs on either side of her and with his arms around her body. Gaby went to the end of the bed and watched between her legs.

There was an old woman in the room who seemed to be overseeing what happened, but was allowing Gaby to do things in her own way.

Julie said 'Adam and Eve got it right – how terrible not to be able to have a baby! God was jealous when he made humans infertile, but we were clever and learned how to do the trick. So God threw a fit, and we were able to escape from the garden. But how thoughtful of God! He must have known what would happen.'

Julie had another spasm and arched her back. Ben held on to her as if he were surfing in a high wind. Gaby held her hands out as if to catch the baby.

Julie said 'Can you see its head, Gaby? Is it like the sun? Does it have two arms two legs and one in between? Surely God was not jealous! It was easier for us if we could blame him. Do you think that one day we shall hear his song?'

She stretched her arms back and clasped her hands behind Ben's neck. She spoke with her face turned to the ceiling.

'Who did you think you were kidding, old God, when you said we'd bring forth in sorrow? Didn't you know we'd get a taste for it? Oh beautiful sorrow, from which the best poems are made and to which the best songs are sung! Didn't you have to find out what it was like yourself, God?'

It was as if Julie's body was riding on the crests and troughs of waves. Then there was a huge breaker which seemed to hold her poised on top of it and she shouted between clenched teeth 'Damn it, God, you did nothing wrong!'

Outside in the night there was a murmuring as if of ghostly presences approaching the door.

Julie uttered a loud cry – 'Oh fucking hell!' – and then quietly as if it were quotation – 'And so she split from arse to tit.'

The baby came with a whoosh, with Ben holding on to

Julie as if she herself were a breaker and Gaby catching the baby as if it were a fish leaping up a waterfall. Gaby held the baby up and watched it until it breathed; then she severed the cord and fastened it, and wrapped the baby in a cloth, and handed it to Julie. Julie said 'Oh thank you, thank you, God, for all your unspeakable wonder!'

Ben let go of her and laid her back on the pillows. The old woman came to the foot of the bed and attended to the afterbirth. Ben went to the door and pulled the curtain back and looked out into the night.

Julie said, looking at her baby – 'This is a chance which does redeem all sorrows.'

Ben turned to her and said 'Can they come in now?'

'Yes.'

Ben gestured to the watchers outside. The old lady was wrapping the afterbirth in one of the cloths that Gaby had prepared. Ben wondered – Do they plant it beneath a tree? There began to come into the room in twos and threes more women, a few men, and the children wide-eyed and attentive. Julie smiled at them as they gathered and stood round her bed. Then after a time both she and the baby went to sleep.

The old woman ushered the others out of the room, giving to one of the women the afterbirth. Then she indicated to Ben that she would stay and keep watch if he wanted to go out into the night. Ben stood looking down at Julie and his baby and he wondered if he should pick the baby up in his arms as he supposed he might be expected to do, but both the baby and Julie looked so peaceful! Then he noticed that Gaby had left the room; and he seemed to know what he should be doing.

He went out under the cold sky and saw that Gaby had gone down towards the river. He thought – Perhaps she feels that she has done what she came to do, and can now disappear to where she came from.

He went up to her where she was sitting beneath a tree and

176

he sat down beside her. He said 'Gaby, we're so grateful, you know that, and you can stay with us if you like. I don't know what you would like, but we could arrange for you to come with us when we leave here, if we go home. That's what we would like.'

It was beginning to get light in the east. He could see the darkness of Gaby's hair, but her face was turned away from him.

He said 'Gaby, you may have to be on your own, but you mustn't die, even if you may sometimes want to. We all have to learn. You could help bring up the baby, Julie would like that, and so would the baby. A baby needs all the help it can get. And you needn't talk, Gaby. But I think you can talk if you like, can't you?'

After a time Gaby turned her face towards him and he saw that she had been crying. She said 'Yes I can talk.'

He said 'Gaby, what happened to you? One day you will tell us.'

'Yes one day I'll tell you.'

'Oh Gaby, did you want to save the world? All proper people want to save the world!'

'I wanted to get away.'

'Then you have. Don't cry, Gaby.'

'I have been so lucky.'

Ben looked out across the grey world where the dawn sky had extinguished all the stars except one.

He said 'In time we'll be going down to the coast, where we'll meet my mother and father. We wanted to get away too, you see, for the birth of the baby, but now we can all join up again. You understand that? We can't change the world, but we can change the way we look at the world. As if it were a baby. Then it may smile at us.'

'Yes I understand that.'

'So will you come with us?'

'I met a man on my way here. He was such a good man. He helped me.'

'As you've helped us.'

'Perhaps someone else will help him.'

'Yes, surely, they will, Gaby.'

'I should like to know. It is something that is not in our scriptures.'

# XXVII

When Maisie arrived in Beirut she went to the apartment
building in which there was Richard Kahn's flat, the address
of which had been given to her by Andros. She rang the bell
of the outside door and when there was no reply she went
and sat in a café across the road and waited to see who might
arrive and go into the building. She knew that Richard Kahn
was supposed to have broken his leg, so she could look out
for someone on crutches.

The impetus for her journey had been given her initially by
her memories of her godfather Maurice Rotblatt, whom she
had known as a child. After the angry divorce of her parents
she had gone to live with her aunt Laura, and had seen
Maurice as a father-figure. After he had gone her feelings
about him had become imbued with legend; but had he
himself not said that legends were what people lived by? She
wanted to become part of a legend herself: could she not find
out what had happened to him? She saw Maurice as a godlike
figure who gave the impression that there were matters of
huge importance to be attended to, the outcome of which
might depend on one's own efforts. What these might be was
not clear: hence after his disappearance it had been easy after
a time to sink into a fashionable despair. However her
meetings with Andros had revived her memories of Maurice:

of course one could choose not to despair! It just required some jump in the dark. The last time she had seen Maurice he had been leaving her aunt Laura to set out on a journey; he had come up to her room to say goodbye. She had had a fantasy that he might be leaving with her some expectation to follow him when she was old enough; to some Promised Land, some Shangri-La.

When, years later, she had become besieged by depression, she had felt this was due to some haunting by Maurice; by not having done what he had suggested. Then it had occurred to her that of course she should set off on a journey – not so much to find him or follow him, as simply to get herself moving. Was this not what he had advocated? Maisie imagined that on a journey she might come across some pattern to her life, some pointers – like the vast configurations in Peru she had read about which cannot be seen from the ground but might have been designed by the ancient Peruvians if they had gone up in a balloon. But historically how was this possible! So had these lines, shapes, patterns, fallen from the air by chance? Or been imposed from another planet? Or was it a metaphor? Anyway, why should not Maisie as it were go up in a balloon?

She sat in the café in Beirut opposite the apartment building and thought – What strange occurrences have in fact happened on my journey! why should there not be further sightings as if I were an old Peruvian? There had been her chance meetings with Andros in London, their celebration in Paris, her encounter with the soldier on the train which had seemed likely to be frightening but then had turned out almost like a blessing; her time with the cheerful people from a village in the hills and then finally her lift with the man in the helicopter who had indeed taken her up as if in a balloon. He had flown her at first to a base in Cyprus and then, after questioning her, had sent her on her way, still with some amusement, to Beirut. The man had said – That's what you call yourselves nowadays, isn't it, travellers?

A car drew up outside the building across the road in which there was Richard Kahn's flat. Two men got out and rang Richard Kahn's bell. When there was no reply they went to their car and one of them spoke on a mobile telephone. Then they got into the car and drove a short way up the street and stopped by the kerb and waited.

Maisie intoned in her mind as if it were a mantra – They look like policemen, they behave like policemen, but don't be taken in by that, they really are policemen.

– Richard is in trouble? He is about to be arrested?

– Or I am imagining these patterns? But can I warn Richard?

The flow of people each way along the street was like the current in a river in which an eddy suddenly changes direction and goes back and bits of flotsam go round and round until eventually out of the flux something breaks free, and goes on its way again.

After a time a young man in rumpled tropical-kit clothes approached the building from the opposite direction to that in which the parked car was facing. He was acting as if he were nonchalant and aimless, but in such an obvious manner that to Maisie at least it seemed that he was not. He was approaching the door of the apartment building: then he stopped and bent down as if to tie up the lace of a shoe. Maisie thought – But there is nothing wrong with his shoe, he has seen the parked car and has registered that it contains policemen. So now what will he do? He is too young to be Richard Kahn. But he is the best-looking man I have ever seen! He retraced his steps some way on the pavement and then crossed the road, not looking out for traffic but keeping his face turned away from the parked car. Maisie intoned to herself – Please let him come and sit in the café: in that way he can keep an eye both on the entrance to the building and the parked car. He came to the café and sat at a table further back from the window than where Maisie was sitting. Maisie thought – But that is all right: he was on his way to visit

Richard, so of course has to keep to the shadows: but how will he be able to warn Richard about the policemen, without both him and Richard being seen?

– I could volunteer to warn Richard when he comes but I do not know what he looks like; but that is what I can ask the young man –

– What an amazing set of patterns!

The young man had an olive-coloured skin and was slightly unshaven; he might indeed be involved in some underground activity. She could just make it known to him that she was there to help him or Richard, and then she could wait for Richard on the other side of the road. One thing she had been learning was that one should not miss making use of such opportunities. She went over to the young man at his table and said – 'Are you waiting for Richard?' He looked up at her as if he were amazed. She thought – But even if he has nothing to do with Richard I will have spoken to him and this might be the point of my journey. She said 'I thought you might be waiting for Richard Kahn.' He said 'Do you know Richard?' She sat down at his table. She said 'I wanted to get in touch with him.' He said 'Why?' She thought she might say – In order that I might meet you. She said 'I think there are men waiting for him on the other side of the road.'

When the young man looked at her he seemed too exhausted to stay for long amazed: she thought – He has been through some ordeal. He said 'Are you one of his pupils?' She said 'No.' He said 'How long have the men been waiting?' She said 'About ten minutes. I think they rang the bell of his flat, but he doesn't answer.' She thought – Or does this person always look as if he wants to fall across the table and put his arms round one's neck? He said 'You haven't got a key?' She said 'No.' He said 'I want to get somewhere to lie down.' She said 'I wouldn't mind that.'

After a time in which he went on staring at her he said 'Did one of the men have a scar on his chin?'

'I'm not sure.'

'Because if so, he's all right. He's some sort of policeman.'

'I thought they were all policemen.'

'Yes. But he's in with Richard.'

'What do mean, in with Richard?'

'He's a friend of his girlfriend.'

'Oh I see.'

Maisie thought – What on earth do I see? That his girl-friend is not your girlfriend?

One of the men had got out of the parked car and was coming down the pavement to the door of the apartment building. He was speaking into his mobile phone and was looking up at the windows at the top level of the building. Maisie thought – We might still just find somewhere to lie down together; also of course a way to warn Richard.

The young man said 'Look, if I have to disappear quickly, can you give a message to Richard?'

Maisie said 'Yes.'

'Will you tell him that you saw me, and I think it's all a bluff, but it may not be, or they may be making out that it's not, and so anyone can believe what they like, and so it may matter what we tell them.'

Maisie said 'And so it may matter what we tell them.'

'Yes.'

'I see that.'

'Do you?' The young man stared at her.

'It's just the way I see things.'

She thought – He is like some dark god: what were those people called: Aztecs, Incas?

The young man said 'I mean, that's the message.'

'Yes.'

'And if those men question you, don't tell them that you've seen me.'

'Unless it's one with a scar on his chin.'

'Oh yes, that's right.'

'It's not you they're after?'

'It may be. I don't know.'

'But more likely Richard.'

'Who are you?'

'Well who are you?'

'You seemed to know me.'

'Yes it did seem as if I did.'

'Well Richard might be in danger. He might be in danger through me. But I don't want to involve you.'

'Oh that's all right.'

On the other side of the road there was a woman approaching the door of the apartment building from the direction of the parked car. She passed the car without appearing to notice it and was coming up to the man who was talking on the mobile phone. She slowed down and the man lowered his phone, and he put a hand on her arm. The young man who was with Maisie said 'Oh fuck!' Maisie said 'Who's that?' The young man said 'That's Richard's girlfriend Leila.'

'The one who's friendly with the policeman?'

'Yes.'

'Is that the one she's talking to?'

'No.'

'Has she got a key?'

The young man had turned from watching what was happening across the road and was staring at Maisie again. He said 'Oh yes, she's got a key.'

'Then she might be able to let us in. I mean let me in, and then I can wave to you from a window, and can let you in when they've gone.'

'But why should you do that? I mean why should she do that?'

'I can say I'm one of Richard's pupils.'

'But aren't you? Oh no, you said you're not.'

'I've come from England.'

'Why have you come from England?'

'It's a long story. But look, we've got to hurry.'

The man who was like a policeman and the woman who had come walking up the street were still talking outside the

184

door of the apartment building. The young man in the café was still as if transfixed by Maisie. He said 'But Richard might be inside.'

'Then I can give him your message.'

'But they might find him.'

'But they might find him anyway, if she's got a key.'

'Yes that's true.'

'But then we can tell them what we think is best. That's the message.'

'Oh yes that's the message.'

'It's as if we can see things from a balloon.'

'What?'

'There does seem to be some pattern.'

# XXVIII

Andros and Joshua sat in the smoking room of Andros's London club. They were not quite facing one another in deep leather armchairs which seemed to protect them like the armour plating of tanks. Andros said 'You live in Beirut? You're a colleague of Richard Kahn's?'

'I'm a friend of Richard's, yes.'

'And you've talked with Laura?'

'I met her after Maurice Rotblatt's commemoration service.'

'I said I wouldn't go. She's a difficult woman, Laura.'

'I saw her again later. She seems a bit on the defensive.'

'What exactly is it you want to know about Maurice?'

A waiter came to take orders for drinks. Joshua thought – He is like a stretcher-bearer moving among the wounded old men on a battlefield.

Joshua said 'Well the whole business has come up again. Did Rotblatt have special information that other people would have wanted to get hold of?'

'I thought Richard made up that story.'

'He probably made up the bit about the bones.'

'I don't think Maurice had specialist information. He wasn't a scientist. You mean about possible genetic distinctions between races?'

'You know about that?'

'He'd have thought it conceivable; but the situation would be on such a knife-edge that it couldn't be used.'

'Richard says he had the idea that you could influence things by making up stories –'

'That's what every politician and newspaperman now thinks.'

'– but you have to put them up against reality, or you come down to earth with a bang.'

'Well I suppose that's what Maurice did?'

'But there may be something in that story, even if nothing to do with Maurice?'

The waiter came with their drinks. Joshua thought – He doesn't even think he has to listen in to our conversation.

Andros said 'You think someone may go ahead with this absurd weapon?'

'It would almost certainly be a matter of bluff. But might not anything seem possible in this climate of deception and self-deception?'

'You mean someone might get bored of the game of who blinks first?'

'Or just make a miscalculation.'

'And justify it by saying they didn't know it would work.'

'And then we all might suffer.'

'About which prospect no one seems particularly appalled.'

They sipped their drinks. Joshua thought – But why should not old men in a place like this seem to be waiting to be given a coup de grâce on a battlefield?

Andros said 'The story I heard was that Maurice insulted nearly everyone in Beirut, so there could have been any number of people who would have wanted to get rid of him.'

'What was it you heard?'

'Arabs, Jews, what-have-you. He got drunk at the club. Of course he might have been doing one of his experiments.'

'At the Commodore Hotel.'

'Yes the Commodore Hotel. He insulted them all equally. So who was it who put a fatwa on him? It would make a good detective story.'

'What was Maurice supposed to have said?'

'Oh, just that all sacred cows spread mad cow disease.'

'Why did he want to risk things?'

'Oh, he wanted to be a hero. He thought it terrible that there were no more heroes, only tradesmen. Who said that: Carlyle? Heidegger?'

Joshua looked round the room. He thought – People think they are immune in these armour-plated chairs. He said 'He thought there should be an elite?'

'Of the unfashionable, the powerless. Not the usual.'

'Did he believe that or did he just say it?'

'He believed it in the way that he said one should believe things.'

'Which was what –'

'Try it and see.'

'You make him sound like Christ.'

'Oh, he'd have been quite pleased to hear you say that!'

Joshua watched Andros as he sipped his whisky. He thought – He is an amused and attractive old man who is coming to the end of his life and who can afford to be amusing since there is not much longer to go.

Joshua said 'But what do you think of the idea that it's a proper religious activity to make up stories? That that's how one understands God?'

'Well that's what people have always done. But they have to be good stories.'

'What do you mean "good"?'

'Aesthetically good.'

'And what's that?'

'What seems to illuminate what one knows one doesn't quite know.'

'And then one does?'

Joshua drank his whisky. He thought – But perhaps all

anyone in fact needs are shots of morphia on a battlefield. He said 'But what did Maurice not quite know?'

Andros said 'Maurice felt he was being defeated by what he was learning about himself. No, not defeated, because he felt that all learning was some sort of victory. If you want to alter the way people see the world then you have to imagine that you're different: and in the end Maurice was too clever to have delusions about that. But he probably thought that in demonstrating not having delusions he might yet alter the way people see the world. Ask Laura.'

'I did.'

'And what did she say?'

'She didn't. But there's a young man now helping her to go through Maurice's papers.'

'Oh yes, Dario.'

'You know Dario?'

'The beautiful Dario. What does he say?'

'That Laura said —' Joshua stopped and looked round the room.

Andros said 'It's all right. We're all fully paid-up members of the "life is more interesting if all secrets are revealed" club.'

'Well it's not really anything Laura said. It's just that Dario seems to have gathered that Maurice saw instincts in himself that he didn't like.'

'Well, indeed, shouldn't we all. But does he suggest that Laura didn't like them?'

'But might these instincts have been instrumental in his getting himself taken prisoner, or being beaten up, or killed, or whatever?'

'You mean there might be a masochistic explanation for all our carry-ons?'

'Well didn't he see himself like Christ?'

'But that was a good story.'

'Yes, indeed.'

Andros gazed round the room. He thought — It was old

men like us who thought war might be fun: that we all should be home by Christmas.

He said 'What impression did you get of Laura?'

'There were things I didn't understand.'

'You're not the only one. She didn't talk about herself and Maurice?'

'No.'

'What did Richard say about them?'

'I don't think Richard liked her.'

'Indeed. And now Dario's editing the papers.'

'But you knew Maurice and Laura.'

'Oh I can make up stories!' He signalled for a waiter. 'We need another drink.'

While they waited Andros was frowning and looking down at his knees as if he were studying a map. Joshua was thinking – He is trying to work out not so much what will be true about what he is going to tell me, because he's not sure what this means, but rather what purpose he will be trying to serve.

When more drinks had arrived Andros said –

'Maurice was obsessed about Laura. This gave him energy and courage to say and write things he wouldn't otherwise have risked, but it also maddened him, because he felt he was not in control – for all his cleverness, his wit, his ability to manipulate stories.'

'His obsession was sexual?'

'Laura was very beautiful. Perhaps you don't see this now. She too seems to have become dissatisfied with her powers.'

'Maurice became dissatisfied?'

'I suppose he saw Laura as someone who could defeat him.'

'But that became the nature of his obsession?'

'I suppose you could say that.'

'And she went along with it?'

'She needed to feel she could defeat him.'

'And he liked that?'

'She could bring him down to earth. Then he wouldn't be godlike.'

'And that was the way he could feel human – by her being godlike?'

'That's clever, yes. But she could be both godlike and human, because she was a woman.'

Andros watched Joshua as he took time to consider this. He thought – He is in love with Dario: perhaps he has the intuition of a woman.

Joshua said 'You don't like Laura.'

Andros said 'I adore Laura! I always have done! I always will.'

'I see.' Then – 'So how did you survive?'

'You mean, am I bisexual? Well perhaps Laura needed someone with whom to make Maurice jealous. You yourself know something of this?'

Joshua said after a time 'My friend in Beirut is hetero-sexual.'

'Ah.'

'So I see destruction in sexual patterns, yes.'

'You haven't come to terms with that?'

'Perhaps by keeping clear.'

'And so you deal in stories. About how to save the world.'

'Which you say Maurice got tired of doing.'

'I suppose what he came to terms with was more simple and yet bizarre.'

'He needed to be a victim? He didn't want to hurt Laura?'

'Oh no, he didn't want to hurt Laura.'

'But she treated him like shit?'

'Oh well, I suppose you could say that's how she treated him.'

'In order to achieve ordinary human contact –'

'Well that's what people do, isn't it?'

'Dear God.'

'And what no one talks about. Because it's too difficult. But if they did, it might alter the way people see the world?'

# XXIX

Dario was reading –

I, Laura Simmons, had only a vague idea about what Beirut was like before the war – the civil war, that is, which by the time I arrived in the 1990s was being taken as part of the natural order of things. Before this, Beirut's reputation had been of a place where hedonism and commercialism ruled; where money proliferated and pleasures could be bought. When customary delights became boring exotic ones were made available; then as a last resort there could be the fun and excitement of war. By the 1990s the war had been going on for some years but in spite of the savagery and increasing devastation it maintained a businesslike air. On certain days there seemed to be a tacit agreement on all sides that there should be a respite: shops that were still intact took down their shutters and made brisk sales, not only of everyday necessities but of luxury goods which were sought and appreciated as rarities: restaurants became crowded and families emerged onto the beach with their sun-mattresses and umbrellas like crabs after a storm. Then after a day or two there would have been enough of this, and shells would start coming over again; there was the distant clatter of machine-gun fire and sunbathers would move off as crabs do at the sight of a human. The return to war was accepted without much demur: it was understood that if peace lasted too long, petty jealousies and resentments would take over again.

Maurice went to Beirut in response to an invitation from his old pupil Richard Kahn to lecture to his students. Maurice had by this time gained some notoriety in England as a pundit who spoke out against what were thought to be conventionally correct attitudes. He had been in demand for a time on television; then when he began to suggest what might be right instead of what was wrong, he began to be ignored. This was partly a common reaction to anyone not dealing in mockery, but it also dawned on people that Maurice was unfashionably mystical. He assumed as obvious that social injustice and violence could not adequately be dealt with by political means; there had to be recognition of deeper forces than those susceptible to social manipulation.

Richard Kahn had written to him – But what will you find here? The Director of our Hospital for Mental and Nervous Disorders has just published a paper in which he notes that at times of shelling and gunfire the condition of most of his patients noticeably improves.

I, Laura Simmons, had been living for some months with Maurice in England. He was in his early sixties: I was in my twenties. He had an ex-wife who had gone back to her family home in Israel: she was said to have adopted a child. Maurice did not talk much about his own family background: his parents had come to England when he was young as victims of Middle Eastern persecution. Maurice had trained and qualified as an academic psychologist.

He was a large man with greying hair and a face that was craggy and rock-like but which could frequently and rapidly change expression. He had the sort of looks that might have made him vain except that he took no trouble with his appearance: he wore the sort of clothes that he must have got used to when he was young – cotton or corduroy trousers and open-necked shirts with denim or cotton jackets. Admirers occasionally described him as Christ-like, but it seemed to me there was too much uncertainty about him: he was like someone in the dark, finding his way.

When the time came for him to go to Beirut he did not want me to go with him: he said he did not wish to expose me to danger. But I knew that also he simply wanted to be on his own. There was something in him that troubled him at that time: I think he'd seen that the ills of the world had a breeding ground in himself. And if one could not hope to alter the world by either the force of will or the example of one's personality, then what could one do? He had a vision of it being an instinctive part of their nature that drove humans to war – for just as there was an instinct, as it were, to scatter and nurture seed, so also there was a need to grab and clear ground on which seeds could grow. The latter impulse as well as the first was represented in sexuality, though humans exhausted and wasted themselves in denying this. They could not hope to modify instincts, he thought, if they did not recognise what these were.

When I first met Maurice it had been me who wanted to claim and possess him: but as soon as I had to some extent achieved this he became an obsessive and as it were haunted lover. It was as if he had to find out what gave me my power over him that he had not expected; to crawl over me like a geologist exploring rock; to delve into me, dissect me, in order to find what was inside me.

He said – Of course there is a battle! Life is to do with power. So what if I realise you have the ability to hurt me?

I said – Why bother? What does it matter?

– Because what you love is something stronger than yourself. But then you want to hurt it.

– Why?

– So that it won't destroy you. But you also don't want to hurt it, because you love it; so you want it to hurt you, because this will serve you right, and so will still be loving. So you build it up, become subservient, so that it becomes overblown and topples. And thus after all you will have defeated it. Or you can be like a worm, and undermine it.

– And you think that's what you're doing to me?

– That's what I'm in danger of doing. But because I can see it, it becomes impossible. But there's also a terrible beauty! It's a test to destruction – but also to the heart of things.

– Don't you think you're in danger of overblowing yourself?

– Oh yes of course I am! Exactly.

I enjoyed the power of my sexuality over him. There is so much that I have learned since then about this. Why does sexuality go wrong? It is a runaway system out of control, with no governor.

He would say – But you thus learn things about yourself that you never knew before.

– Animal things.

– Yes.

– Sniffing. Shit.

– If you like.

– And you like playing games –

– But I want to stop.

– Do you want us to be gods and goddesses?

When he left for Beirut he set off without saying goodbye. I knew he wanted to be free of me; but I had not thought he would go. I thought – Well now I have the power to choose whether to be free of you, or go after you.

– Or will I hurt you more by staying away?

The next day I took a plane to Beirut: I found him waiting at the airport. I said – Did you know I would come? He said – No, I wondered. I myself wondered – How many days would he have come to the airport on the chance of my turning up?

In Beirut we stayed in an apartment found for us by Richard Kahn. I don't think Richard liked me: perhaps he thought I was destroying Maurice: perhaps he wanted Maurice for himself. Or perhaps he wanted someone like me.

Richard was at the time making a psychological study of Sunni Muslims and Maronite Christians — the main opponents in the civil war. The Sunnis were openly concerned with gaining political power, the Maronites with maintaining their hold on it. Religion seemed no more than a badge or uniform that dressed up instincts that were the same as those of sexual games. Maurice said to Richard — But nothing I say to your students will mean anything to them in time of war.

— Then tell them that.

— War's a disease that has to run its course?

— But as you say, that won't mean anything to them. So don't worry.

I thought at first that Richard Kahn was a joker, a trickster: he fluttered round Maurice like a moth. But then was it not Maurice who wanted to burn out like a candle?

Maurice took to going for walks round the war-torn city to get away from the strained atmosphere of the university campus. The university was almost never shelled or bombed: Maurice asked — Are people aware of the reasons for that? Richard said — Oh these people don't have to have spelt out to them the hierarchy of commercial considerations.

Maurice said — Whereabouts in their hierarchy is the torture of prisoners?

Richard said — It was you who pointed out to me the brutality of evolution.

In his walks round the city Maurice came across refugees from eastern Turkey who were making a living in Beirut. They were seen as Muslims — everyone had to have a label in Beirut — but they subscribed to few of the beliefs or practices of Islam: they went to no mosques, they did not pray five times a day, they did not observe Ramadan, they felt no obligation to make the journey to Mecca. It was said that they believed in the prevalence of unseen forces such as angels; and although they would not themselves talk much about this, they professed openly that religion was a matter not so much of ritual and dogma as of nurturing awareness in the heart and mind. Their rejection of tradition laid them open to sometimes violent attack by both orthodox Muslims and Christians; and in view of this – and it was this that intrigued Maurice – they felt themselves justified in practising a certain secrecy and dissimulation. Thus little notice was taken of them except when persecution seemed politically required. Richard said they were well established in villages in the mountains of eastern Turkey. They were known as Alevis.

One of the last conversations I remember between Maurice and Richard was on the subject of Alevis. We were in Richard's room where he used to sit rather affectedly on a prayer mat on the floor. Maurice was on the sofa leaning forwards with his hands on his knees.

Richard said 'Yes, those people do seem to be on about the same things as you, not least because you can't pin them down.'

'Are they persecuted now?'

'They mostly get away with it, now that those who dislike them are so busy persecuting each other.'

'But in their villages, do they live in peace?'

'I suppose there's always the threat of persecution, which helps.'

'I'd like to go there.'

'I thought you might know places like that. But you used to say that an orderly society was impossible: any resolution had to be in the mind.'

'Yes I do believe that.'

'So what do you think you would find?'

'I'd like to see what sort of dissimulation works. What is skill, what is art, what is luck.'

One of the questions that Maurice and Richard argued about was what Maurice had been promulgating when Richard had been a student in London. This was the idea that humans could have no experience of autonomy or value, let alone of an orderly society, without a recognition of a force beyond them which it was necessary to respect. Traditionally the word for this force had been God; but the conventional idea of God had become so debased that what mattered was the recognition of the need rather than the word as it stood now. Once this idea was accepted, then how the need could be implemented could be experimented with.

Richard had seen the force of this, but had taken it to be suggesting that 'God' could be reinvented purely as an artifice – as a means to make possible a satisfactory way of life both for an individual and for society – and he doubted whether in a sophisticated world such a fabrication could be effective. Maurice admitted he might once have seen the matter like this; but in the years he had been apart from Richard he had come to suppose, and then to believe, that there was a further consequence to the practice of 'inventing God': that if one recognised the need, and tried to imagine or invent a response to it truly – putting it to the test, that is, in one's daily life, in one's relations with other people – then it did begin to seem that such an invention was true; that what had been conjectured appeared, when tested, to fit the facts of one's experience; to work. Or if it did not, it could be amended – and what could be more scientific than that! Well, Richard would say, almost anything; because in that sense you yourself are the only tester, and the reasons for your conclusions are not open to public inspection. Well, in a way they are, Maurice said, because whatever happens as a result of your conclusions is open to inspection by others; although as with everything people will interpret this in different ways.

I would sit in a corner of Richard's huge sofa and think – And that's all that you two are going to do – go on interpreting things in your different ways for ever.

Richard said 'But if you wanted to test whether the existence of God was what you call true, rather than an artifice, then you'd have to risk more than chatting up students.'

'Such as what.'

'Well, sticking your neck out. Martyrdom. Crucifixion.

That's what people used to risk who wanted to show that God was true.'

'And has that tradition always been effective?'

'I'm not saying it's effective. There's enough appalling evidence for that from what's going on in this town.'

'But you're saying there has to be some risk?'

'Well how else are you testing what is or is not true?'

I said to Richard 'Oh fuck off! You'd quite like him to be crucified, wouldn't you.'

Richard said 'I should have thought that was more in your sort of line.'

I said 'No, that's what men really like. In this town, or anywhere. Lie on your back and open your mouth and let what you call God piss on you.'

I suppose I was a bit stoned at the time. It was easy in Beirut to get dope.

Richard said to Maurice 'Is that what you like?'

Maurice said 'It does seem to be what a lot of people like.'

Richard said 'Ah well, and will you achieve something by honesty?'

Maurice said 'I suppose I can say what I think of what is going on in this town.'

# XXX

When Maisie crossed the road from the café in Beirut where she had been talking with the young man who had turned up so unexpectedly but as if in answer to a prayer, she felt she understood the phrase 'walking on air': she and the young man might both be angels come down to earth to show humans how to behave. She had left her haversack with the young man as a sort of surety, so that he would remain connected to her: she was crossing the road to the apartment building in which was Richard Kahn's flat. The woman who had approached the door and was now talking to the man like a policeman was very beautiful; but she was Richard Kahn's girlfriend, she was not the girlfriend of the beautiful young man in the café. He had said that she was also the girlfriend of a policeman; but this was not the one she was talking to because he had not got a scar on his chin. She was called Leila, and she had a key; but how could she be persuaded to let her, Maisie, into the flat; where she might be joined, later, by the young man from the café? Leila might want to show the flat to the man like a policeman to demonstrate that Richard was not there; and then Maisie could tag along; and then Leila and the policeman would go, leaving Maisie in the flat, who could signal from a window to the man across the road. Leila was dark-haired and olive-skinned and she might have been the sister of the man in the café: surely she, like he, would understand as soon as Maisie spoke to her what was happening, and what was required. All this was already fairly magical.

Neither the woman nor the policeman paid attention to Maisie when she came up. Leila was saying 'But if he's not here, how can I let you in? I was just coming to pick up some of my things.' The policeman was saying 'Then you have got a key.' Leila said 'Surely you know I have.' Then they noticed Maisie standing by them. Maisie said 'Oh hello.' Leila said 'Hello.' Maisie said 'Isn't Richard here?' The policeman said 'Who are you?' Maisie said 'I'm one of his pupils.' Leila said 'Oh are you?' Maisie said 'Is there any trouble?'

Leila was watching her as if she were trying to see what might be behind a bead-curtain of words. Maisie was thinking – I may fall in love with her as I have fallen in love with the man in the café; but I am falling in love with just what is happening; this is a world in which anything seems possible. Leila said 'Richard isn't here.' Maisie said 'Do you know where he is?' Leila said 'Do you have an appointment?' Maisie said 'I hoped he was expecting me.' She was thinking – In this world what should be happening seems to happen if you watch, listen. Leila was saying to the policeman 'Well I suppose I could let you in if she could come with me.' The policeman said 'We're not going to take anything!' Leila said 'Oh aren't you?' And then to Maisie 'Would you trust him?' She laughed. Maisie laughed. She thought – This is amazing. The second policeman had got out of the car up the road and was coming towards them. Leila was feeling in her handbag as if for a key. She said 'Did Captain Leon send you?' The first policeman said 'Oh yes you know Captain Leon, don't you?' Leila said 'No I've never heard of Captain Leon.' She produced a key and opened the door of the building. The second policeman had joined them and they all went in and up some stairs. Maisie imagined she could feel the eyes of the man in the café watching the back of her: she wanted to send a message to him by flicking her fingers behind her. The message would say – It's all right, I think I understand; but is it all right if I give your message for Richard to Leila? She probably knows where Richard is, and will pass it on to him.

They went up the staircase in single file with Leila leading. She said without turning her head 'Do you usually discuss Captain Leon with strangers?' After a few steps the second policeman said 'Who said anything about Captain Leon?' On the top landing there was a door to an apartment and Leila knocked and rang; then she used a key to get in. The others followed. Leila went through to a bedroom and sat on the bed; the second man followed her. Maisie stayed in the sitting room where the first man was looking at objects and papers on a desk. Maisie thought – He has to be doing something that looks professional. Maisie went and leaned against the doorway into the bedroom: she thought – It will seem natural if I am trying to hear what the others are saying.

'Are you saying that you don't know where he is?'

'Yes that's what I'm saying.'

'Do you know a man called Hafiz Ahmed?'

'Oh is Hafiz called Ahmed? I didn't know.'

'He's a colleague of Kahn's.'

'He's at the university, isn't he?'

'He comes here quite often?'

'Sometimes.'

'What is the relationship between you and Hafiz Ahmed and Professor Kahn?'

Maisie was registering – Hafiz? The man in the café is called Hafiz?

Then – There is so much happening beyond the tinkling curtain of words!

Leila was saying 'One or two people come here quite often, as I'm sure you know. We have a bundle of laughs!' She said the last phrase as if it were a quotation he might recognise.

The first policeman came to the door of the bedroom and said 'We meant no disrespect to Captain Leon.'

Leila said 'All right, I'm sure you didn't.'

'We know of his friendship with Doctor Kahn.'

The second man said 'I think we've said enough of this.'

The first man said 'Is there any other way out of this building?'

'There's a fire escape.'

'Where's that?'

'It's through the kitchen.'

'We will just check that.'

The two men came into the living room and then went out of sight through the kitchen. Leila murmured 'What are they doing?' Maisie said 'I think they're just doing what policemen are supposed to do, going through the motions.' Leila said 'That's right.' Maisie said 'Will you be seeing Richard?'

Leila said 'I don't know. I think so.'

'Can you get a message to him? I think it's from Hafiz.'

'You know Hafiz?'

'I think I bumped into him in the café across the road. He asked me to give a message to Richard if I saw him.'

'Hafiz is back? He's all right? He's in the café?'

'Yes.'

'But Richard isn't here.'

'No.'

'I think he's in Jerusalem.'

'I see.'

Leila was watching Maisie as if trying to be sure again of what was behind a curtain. Maisie was thinking – I do hope she thinks I am as beautiful as I think she is.

Leila said 'What was the message?'

'That he thinks it's all a bluff, but they may be making out that it's not, and so anyone may believe what they like, and so it may matter what we tell them.'

'It may matter what we tell them.'

'Yes.'

'And what does Hafiz think we should tell them?'

'He didn't say.'

'Do you know what we're talking about?'

'No. But I mean I think I understand the sort of thing he's saying.'

After a moment Leila said 'All right, I'll tell Richard when or if I see him.'

'Thank you.'

'And thank you. Whoever you are.'

'Hafiz didn't want anyone to see him.'

'No of course.'

'Do you think perhaps he could stay here till Richard gets back? I mean after these people have gone. They won't come looking for him here again, will they?'

'I don't suppose so.'

'And perhaps I could just stay with him and see that he's all right.'

Maisie had to say this last sentence almost inaudibly, because the men were coming back from the kitchen. She did not know if Leila had heard. Leila went on staring at her. One of the men said to Maisie 'Can we see your means of identification?'

Maisie said 'You've got my passport. You kept it at the airport when I landed this morning.'

'You landed this morning? I thought you said you were one of Professor Kahn's students.'

'I am. I come from England. Your people said you'd fix my visa.'

'What flight were you on?'

'I came by helicopter.'

'You came by helicopter?'

Leila said 'Helicopter!'

The man said 'Where are you staying?'

Maisie said 'I don't know. I thought I might stay here.' Then – 'I said I'd let your people know.'

She thought – I suppose we will come down to earth one day, but please with not too much of a bang.

204

Leila said 'That should be possible.'

One of the men said to Leila 'Our job is to help protect Professor Kahn.'

Leila said 'Oh yes, well when he returns, we will let you know.'

'In the meantime will you come along and talk to Captain Leon? Explain things to him.'

'If you like.'

'That would help us.'

As they were going down the staircase Maisie tried to work out what each of them was supposed to believe was happening. She could not quite manage this. Did it have to fit together? She thought – It will have to sort itself out. When they reached the street level she said to Leila 'Oh yes, can I have the keys?' Leila said 'I've left the upstairs door unlocked.' Maisie said 'All right.' When Leila went into the road with the two men she was careful to leave the downstairs door ajar. Maisie went back up the stairs. She thought – But I had to come downstairs, I suppose, just to make sure about the doors.

When she was back in the flat and enough time seemed to have passed for Leila and the two men to have got to the car, Maisie tried to open the window in the sitting room that looked out over the street from where she should be able to signal to the young man. But the window was jammed. Maisie thought – Well I'd better wait a bit longer before I go out to find him. She sat on the bed. She thought – Or shall I just trust that Hafiz will have been watching the building and seeing the people going in and coming out; and he will have worked out just what has been happening; and will trust when to come in. The doors are unlocked. But I do hope he remembers to bring my haversack. Or is this hoping for too many miracles? Then she fell asleep.

# XXXI

Dario was reading –

There was an evening when Maurice and I were invited to have drinks at the Commodore Hotel. This was where journalists stayed in Beirut; where they picked up stories and sorted out what should be told and what should not. Maurice was not at ease with journalists, though he admired those who were brave in doing their job in the war. But in Beirut events were so chaotic and indecipherable that to journalists it often hardly seemed worth leaving the hotel; they depended for the most part anyway on stories brought to them by spokesmen from one faction or another. This might have seemed reasonable to Maurice with his idea that information inevitably consisted of stories largely shaped or invented for a purpose: but what dismayed him was that there was no acknowledgment of this; people who listened to the stories and wrote them up had to make out – and even to believe, such was the convention – that they were true even in detail. To Maurice it seemed more and more that what could be called 'true' lay in realising how much news was manipulated.

Before we went that evening to the Commodore Hotel Maurice had been drinking. He usually drank little and only sensibly – in the evenings to switch off, he said, the buzz of his thoughts. But now in Beirut he seemed to drink almost in order to make himself irresponsible. I do not know how much this was a response to what Richard Kahn had said about the need to stick one's neck out.

Journalists were no more at ease with Maurice than he was with them. He had the reputation of being an unashamedly pretentious would-be guru, and thus was a natural target for journalists who might feel that he felt superior to them – which at this time, such was his self-questioning, he probably did not. But he always found it difficult to convey his more complex ideas in words: he believed they would be accepted only by people naturally sympathetic to them, and this attitude was taken as one of disdain, which increased people's disdain of him.

Maurice and I had been asked to the Commodore Hotel by a group of journalists who said they wanted to hear what he had to say about the war; but it was more likely that they wanted to get a story about him and me – to have some indoor amusement when it was difficult and often dangerous to go out at night. I said to Maurice 'But why do you want to go? You know that afterwards you'll be miserable.'

'One learns from one's mistakes.'

'God, how pompous can you get!'

'Well it's true.'

'Can't we ever switch off? I suppose you'll be thinking it was a mistake you got me to come out here.'

'I got you to come out here?'

'Well, you could have stopped me.'

'How?'

'By being nice.'

'Laura, stop this.'

I knew that I was behaving like one of the people who were maddened by his air of superiority; who thought they were justified in wanting to puncture him and bring him down to earth.

I said 'If you think that's how you learn, do you want to be punished for your mistakes? Do you want to go into your humble penitent mode? Do you want to play one of your masochistic games?'

I half realised that I was involved in some psychological game of my own that was getting out of control. There was something happening to Maurice and me at this time that was beyond his supposed air of superiority and my reaction to this: something was taking over our sexuality. I do not want to talk much about this: sexuality is an area which talk never seems able to deal with truly: it contains too many paradoxes, too much rawness and anarchy; there is such a conjunction of intensity and delight with what, in other contexts, would be seen as squalid or sick. And this I suppose is a subsidiary but vital purpose of sex – that as well as activating godlike forces of procreation it should expose humans to forces beyond their control; so that evolution should not be manipulated, but should be properly random and humbling. Maurice was in many respects so arrogant that perhaps this was a way, through his regard for me, by which nature could compensate in him. And I could be an instrument for this – with my desire to show him how ungodlike he was, to bring him down to earth. Though I, like he, was afterwards likely to feel ashamed and in revolt against this – the need to act sexual charades, to play compensating games.

I said 'I'm sorry, I shouldn't have said that. But you know how you'll hate this evening. And then you'll take it out on me.'

'So it would be better, you're saying, if I admitted that I'd like it if you'd take it out on me.'

'Well wouldn't you?'

'Laura, I don't know. Perhaps it's all too complicated to know. I suppose that's its point. You're very good to me, you want to do what I want, what a part of me that was drawn to you wants, but we don't know where this is going. I suppose with you I am a masochist. I'm having to realise things about myself with you that I only thought I knew previously in theory. With you, there's a conjunction: opposites become real.'

'What does?'

'Love and suffering. Savagery and liberation.'

'And what's wrong with that?'

'Nothing. It's a blessing. But then when you've known it, perhaps you move on.'

'Why? Where to?'

'I suppose, simplicity. Where the whole might seem simple. But I don't know.'

'And you think you might get that by going to the Commodore Hotel?'

'Well that could be a reality and not a game.'

'Just because Richard said you should stick your neck out —'

'Well that might be a way of getting it over with.'

'What?'

'Games.'

'God, you are pathetic. You really do think you're like Christ!'

Perhaps I, Laura, may one day find a better way of talking about these things.

The Commodore Hotel had suffered little damage during the war: it was one of the places like the American University about which it seemed to have been instinctively decided that it would be to everyone's advantage if it remained relatively unharmed; then journalists would have somewhere to go in the evenings where they could meet spokesmen, who would push their own stories about the war.

Before we got there I said to Maurice again 'I'm so sorry. You and I were all right once weren't we?'

'Yes, Laura, we were lovely. We still are.'

'You're not just saying that.'

'It doesn't matter what I'm saying. You should know it.'

One of the reasons I didn't like going to the Commodore Hotel was that the people would be thinking – What is an old

209

man like Maurice doing with a girl like her? She's an intellectual groupie going along for the ride? In which case, might she become available for me?

There were some good-looking Italians, an Australian, and two or three women expecting us in the hotel. They had all been drinking. Maurice entered like an old bear on a chain. I thought – I am the organ-grinder at the other end of the chain.

After a time Maurice was saying – 'But what you people don't understand about this war is that no one wants to win it. That's not so unusual. What's in it for anyone to win a war? They have to take responsibility for their enemies. No one to blame except themselves.'

One of the women said 'You think Hezbollah don't want to win this war?'

'They're not fools. So long as the war's going they've got a purpose, power. If there's peace, they're petty criminals who should be in jail.'

The Australian said 'Keep it up, Maurice. The men from the funny farm will soon be here with their kindness to strangers.'

Maurice said 'Just enough killing but not too much. Pictures of the dead and dying but spilled guts tastefully airbrushed. For mutilated children a bonus, and a holiday for two in the Caribbean.'

'Get the man another drink.'

One of the Italians was making a play for me. I thought that Maurice would pretend not to notice this: that it might be a game for him.

He was saying – 'There are the Christians who are told they win by losing. They don't believe it of course. But they have an excuse to tie themselves up in knots. Which their instincts tell them is an enjoyable thing to do.'

'Tinkle tinkle. Please leave the bathroom as you'd like to find it.'

'But the Muslims now, they're logical. They think they

just like winning. So they cut the hands off anyone who disagrees with them, so they won't have hands with which to masturbate.'

One of the women said 'Bang! You're dead!'

'The Israelis, as usual, are the only ones who make sense. They've taken no responsibility for what has happened to themselves in the past, so why should they take responsibility for what happens to others in the future? God's authenticated game is tit for twat.'

The Australian said 'Fill him up. He's earning it. Last breakfast and all that.'

The Italian who was making a play for me said 'And you, my dear, please will you leave a dummy in your bed tonight, I do not think he will notice the difference.'

Stories that circulated later amongst the gossip-toting crowd about this evening seemed to suggest that Maurice had deliberately insulted all religions in a way in which he must have known might bring retribution on his head; and so was he not suicidal? But this was not the point. I think Maurice was continuing the conversation he had been having with me earlier; he was paving the way to disappear.

At some later stage in the evening he was declaiming theatrically –

'Perhaps the whole Middle East should be run as a gigantic theme park where visitors can enjoy the natural history of humans. Here you will see displays of saintliness achieved through laceration, devotion expressed through betrayal. Here you will see how efforts at peace promote war; how entry to heaven is purchased by armaments. If any mutant sees what is in front of its nose, it is exhibited as a freak.'

The Italian said to me 'Come away, come away, death –'

Maurice said 'Piss off, organ-grinder.'

The Italian said 'Please?'

Maurice said 'Granted.'

I said 'Maurice, come away.'

The Italian said to me 'Are you his keeper?'

I said 'I would like to be, but he won't let me.'

When I had got Maurice out into the street I began to cry. I suppose I was knowing that this might be one of the last times I would be with him. I did not understand this: I did not know if it was my fault: I began to pummel him: we seemed to be on the edge of a precipice. Or might there be a kindly sniper on a street corner who would do the job for us? I said 'Oh God I do hate you! All right, do your imitation-of-Christ stuff, go away, leave me with nothing; but how will I learn if you don't help me?' He said 'How will you learn if I stay with you?' I said 'What?' He was holding me with his arms tightly round me. He said 'I have adored you.' I said 'And I haven't been bad for you?' He said 'No you haven't been bad for me.' Then he began to move away. And I never saw him again.

# XXXII

By the time Ben and Julie with their baby reached the holiday town on the coast where they were due to join up with Ben's mother and father, the baby was a month old and Gaby was still with them. Gaby now sometimes spoke when the occasion required; but not about herself nor her past, except on the evening of the baby's birth when she had talked to Ben. He had gathered that she came from Israel and had for some reason got out: her family would not have known how or why nor where she had gone; and she did not want to go back. When Ben was telling this to Julie he said 'I don't think it was a whim or the result of a family row; I think it was something much deeper, like a conversion.' Julie said 'You did tell her again she can stay with us?' Ben said 'Yes.' Then – 'She says she feels it's like some story that might have been in their scriptures but wasn't.'

On the coast Julie looked for an occasion to talk to Gaby when the baby was asleep in its carrycot beneath palm trees. Julie wanted to tell Gaby something of herself and Ben so that Gaby might feel more confident with them, but she did not want to press Gaby to talk about herself if she did not want to. When they were all on the beach Gaby did not swim; she seldom moved very far from the baby. She seemed to feel it was her role to watch over the baby; not to pick it up nor to fuss over it unduly, but just not to be far away.

Julie said to Ben – 'It's as if she's broken away from her past, and feels that the baby is her task in a strange world.'

Ben said 'We all feel strangers.'

Julie said 'I feel everyone else is a stranger.'

On the beach Julie settled herself on her back with her eyes shaded from the sun. Gaby was only a few feet away. Julie said – 'Gaby, we're all in a sense now refugees – me and Ben and you and the baby. We're trying to find a way not to be trapped by our past, but we can't wholly escape it, we have to learn in some way to carry it.'

Gaby listened with her head turned away and a hand making a pattern in the sand as if it might be a configuration on a landscape seen from a high altitude.

Julie said 'I come from Ireland, where both my father and mother were murdered, and my brother and I were expected to want to kill the people who had murdered them. And if we did not, we were hardly acceptable as fellow human beings. It might even be that our own people wanted to kill us – and they did shoot my brother, in the leg, when he would not shoot at someone as they had told him to do. We had to make out we were a bit unhinged, do you know that word? like a door flapping in the wind, which I suppose was what we were. I don't know where my brother is now, he had to get away. He sometimes talked of coming to this part of the world, he had read of it, of the people in the hills and their religion and their ways of seeing things. I wondered if Ben and I would bump into him; but instead we bumped into you, Gaby; and it is wonderful that this is the way things work.'

When Gaby looked up Julie saw that her face was wet with tears.

'So will you stay with us, Gaby, and we can look after the baby, you and me and Ben, and we can watch her grow. And she will not feel trapped; and she will be able to find things out for herself; and we none of us need talk very much. I think there is too much talk; if we watch, and listen, each day can seem like a miracle. Ben was close to his parents, and they were good to him, but he had to get away: perhaps in some sense just so that he could bump into me. And now there is the baby. So it seems we can be together now – Ben and his mother and father and me and the baby. And you, Gaby: you bring something from a different world.'

After a time Gaby said 'You have guessed about my family.'

'Do they know you're alive? Might they be looking for you?'

'They may think I'm dead. They will mourn. I should some time let them know.'

Julie looked at her baby. The tears in her eyes made it seem that the baby in its cot was floating on a sea.

She said 'We may have to try to become more ordinary, Gaby: the baby will need roots by which to grow. But these will also be not ordinary, because otherwise what will we have learned? It would have been ordinary, I suppose, for my brother and me to have been killed; so many of our people have been killed; as so many of your people have been, Gaby. And you and I and my brother might have been like holy martyrs with our pictures on a wall. And then people would have mourned for us looking at a wall.'

Gaby said 'There is too much mourning.'

'For oneself one need not mourn.'

When Ben's mother and father arrived at the holiday town on the coast – coming from different directions; Ben's mother from England, and Ben's father from where he had been working on a film by the Red Sea – what struck Gaby was how they asked so few questions; about the birth of the baby, about how Ben and Julie had come to be where they were, about why they, Ben's mother and father, had been informed so little about what was happening. And yet although Ben's mother had evidently been sad, they were both now evidently so hugely pleased about the baby, and to be with Ben and Julie, that this was of far greater importance to them than the odd circumstances that had led to it. It appeared that not only had they not met Julie before but they had been apart from each other for some time; so now it was as if the good fortune of the baby had brought them back together. They welcomed Gaby into the family, and seemed a bit in awe of the part they learned she had played at the birth. They made a lot of jokes, and this occasionally reminded Gaby of her own family; but their jokes were like benign admissions of foolishness, whereas her own family's jokes had seemed like protective cladding.

Sometimes when they were having a meal in the rather grand hotel to which Ben's father and mother had taken them, Gaby became conscious of Ben's father watching her almost as if he might be imagining himself as her lover. Strangely, she did not find this disturbing. She thought – I may find I can talk when he is there.

Then one day when Ben and Julie had gone to the beach and Gaby was with the baby in the hotel garden, and Ben's father was lying on a sunbed with his hands folded across his chest like the effigy of some old crusader –

And Gaby was thinking – He is thinking of how we might talk, but he is knowing how anything we say might be misinterpreted –

Ben's mother came out from the hotel and looked at the scene in the garden – Ben's father on his back, and Gaby in the strange costume that she still wore from her time in the hills – and Ben's mother looked from one to the other like a bird considering what morsel it might carry to its brood in the hills: and Gaby thought – When Ben's mother and father are together they seem slightly other than human, so is this why I may be able to talk?

Ben's mother came and sat on the ground by Gaby and said 'Gaby, if you want to talk, this can be like listening to yourself, and your words going winging over the hills.'

Gaby said 'Thank you.' She thought – Perhaps my words will be heard by the man who rescued me in his truck.

Neither Ben's mother nor father watched her.

Gaby said 'I'm called Jewish, as you know, and I found I did not want to go on being called Jewish, I didn't think anyone should be called anything except themselves. To be labelled is to be like a brand product on a shelf: this may be useful for other people, useful for oneself; but I did not think people were to be used like this. I thought people should get off their shelves; but I did not know how to do this for myself.

'This is a difficult story because I do not know what happened.

'I went exploring in a tunnel underneath where the old Temple used to be, where there is now the mosque which some people think should be blown up. This was in an archaeological site where I sometimes went to be still. But there was a fall of rock, and I could not move, I could not get out. I had been thinking that what I wanted was to be born again, and now it was as if I were in some tomb. And what provision is there to get out – to be born again?'

Gaby thought – The two of them, Ben's mother and father, are like people who already know what I am saying, and so can consider it while they listen.

'But I did get out, I don't know how; does one know about one's birth? Or what has been going on before it? It is as if chances have come together from the ends of the earth – to make a construction equal to the great Temple of Solomon, the Dome of the Rock – I know so few wonders! – but how wonderful is a human embryo! A tower that can reach up to heaven. And so beautiful! And the workers knowing where each piece has to go – a bit for an eye here, for a gut or a brain cell there – and the bricks being baked from the clay on which the tower stands; the stone cut from the hills which protect it. And there is a song that the workers sing as they are building; and it is by the song that they know where each piece has to go. But then there was a fall of rock. The tower was collapsing. Had I been trying to sing the builders' song?

'I do not know how to talk of this. I do not suppose I will talk of it again.

'I was being rescued, and this was like a second birth, but I felt I knew that this was for an experiment in which I would die. Is one not born in order to die? and to know this is to be human? This was the second birth – from being animal to being human. How fortunate I was to have learned this! But was there no more to being human?

'I had once imagined that if I was rescued I would be taken back to my family: but I had wanted to get away; so how after all should I be so grateful! The people who had rescued me were for the most part faceless: they were forces that could be called natural. Thank you.

'I dreamed of huge stones being dragged across a desert: lines of slaves were being driven by whips. So this was the tower being built to heaven! But you can ask – What is beauty; what is savagery? Thank you.

'I do not know how to talk about this. The only certainty in this life is death, so you honour it. You dream of a second birth – or is it now a third – but what is this?

'Is it to be born into uncertainty?

'There has to be something coming in from outside, that cannot be known, to interrupt the builders' song with silence. That is, if there is to be rearrangement of the embryo; of what it can know.

'It was evident I had not been taken back to my family.

'The person who rescued me a second time – and this was for a third birth, yes – was there just after I had tried to rescue myself: after I had felt I knew I had been born to die. He risked his life for me: he seemed a bit other than human. Perhaps he felt he might die, and did not mind. He was an Arab: I think he had once been on an assignment to kill Jews. I do not know the truth of this: I do not know if it matters. He took me to a place from which I could go on, and meet Julie and Ben. This happened. And then there was the baby.

'I do not know how to say this. I do not suppose I will ever say it again.

'I saw myself in the baby. I saw the baby in myself. I think this was a third birth, yes.

'Thank you. Now I have been able to say this, perhaps it will be all right.'

Ben's mother was sitting with her head bowed. Ben's father was lying with his hands across his chest. Gaby was thinking – But I have not been talking to myself; my words have gone winging over mountains.

# XXXIII

Hafiz had been lurking at the back of the café, watching the door of the apartment building across the road, trying to see or to imagine what was going on there: he was staying close to the door into the café toilets in case he had to make a dash to escape if the men like policemen came after him. But what did he think he could do? Was there ever a toilet window that one could climb through? He had watched the girl whose name he did not know cross the road, he had seen her talking to Leila and the man like a policeman in front of the building; then the other man from the car had come up, and Leila had produced her key and they had all gone into the building. After a time they had all come out again and Leila had gone with the two men to the car and the girl had gone back into the building. There were so many possibilities about what might be happening, it was impossible to know which one might be correct. Hafiz waited; the car with the two men and Leila in it drove away, but the girl did not reappear. He was very tired, he had been travelling for so long and had had so little sleep in his truck that it had begun to be difficult to distinguish reality from dream.

There had been the girl who had climbed into his truck whose name also he did not know – but he had felt he had known her! – she had seemed not to be of flesh and blood, but some emanation like one of the angels of the people he had sent her on her way to. He had driven her to a village from which she could catch a bus; this would take her to a village that Richard Kahn had talked about, where she might be safe and be looked after. But why had he risked this? Things had seemed to be happening under their own momentum; under the guidance of some unknown imperative.

And now there was this other girl who seemed to have been waiting for him in the café – she was flesh and blood! He seemed to have fallen headlong in love. But was not this likely to be a dream?

After he had seen the first girl off in her bus (he had given her money) he had camped for a time at the base of a holy mountain. He had thought of climbing it and disappearing off the top into the mist; but it had seemed that through his encounter with the girl he had already achieved something of this sort. Before, he had felt it impossible to return home: but now why should he not, if the way that he saw life was changed? Had he not already risked danger? He should report to Richard Kahn about what had been happening. This might be of great import or none. He should still try not to be seen, because he might put Richard in danger.

And so now – having been blessed as it were with his meeting with the girl in his truck – why should the girl in the café be a dream? He must not lose her; he must regain her quickly; he should go and ring the doorbell of Richard Kahn's flat. He was too tired to go on hiding or running, he needed somewhere to lie down and sleep. Had not the girl said that she would get into the building and then would let him in and he could sleep? Or was this a notion characteristic of being in love!

He was beginning to make a move when he stumbled over a large haversack on the floor by his table. This was her haversack? She had left it for him to look after? He could not quite remember. But of course he should take it up to her! She would be waiting for it in Richard's flat.

He crossed the road carrying the haversack and rang the doorbell at the entrance to the building, but the door was not closed. He pushed, and went in and up the stairs. On the top floor he found that the door into Richard Kahn's flat was slightly open too. He thought – This girl with whom I am in love is really extraordinarily efficient! This is a good sign for the future. He went through to the bedroom and saw the girl asleep on the bed.

He thought – Does luck come as the result of some good deed? Such things are spotted in heaven?

Then – But I must first get some sleep.

When Maisie woke in the middle of the night she found Hafiz on the bed beside her and she thought – This does not appear to be a dream, but I am still very sleepy. She needed to go to the bathroom. On her way through the sitting room she saw her haversack on the floor. She thought – This person I am in love with is very efficient: this promises well for the future.

When Hafiz woke in the middle of the night he found Maisie asleep on the bed beside him; but he needed to go to the bathroom. When he went through the sitting room he saw that on the floor beside the haversack where he had left it there was a plastic bag which looked as though it contained provisions. He thought – This is beyond being efficient: this is a miracle. But he was still very sleepy, and hurried back to bed.

When Maisie woke in the morning she did not at first know where she was; it was as if she was coming out from under anaesthetic after an operation and was finding she was alive after all. She looked down at Hafiz who was still asleep beside her; he was unshaven and his face was smudged with dirt, but he was beautiful. She thought – This is a dream I would have always liked but have never had: I will make breakfast for him before he wakes up, I will look after him, this will be the start of domesticity. Then – But will there be any provisions? Then she went into the siting room to go through to the kitchen and there was a large plastic bag beside her haversack which she was sure had not been there when she had come through in the night. She thought – Well it is possible there is some rational explanation.

Within the bag there were eggs and butter and bread and coffee beans and a large sausage-like thing that she thought must be salami. There was no milk. She thought – They probably don't have milk in this strange country: they depend on manna from heaven. In the kitchen there was a machine for grinding coffee. She thought – But I will not use it yet, because I know from my aunt Laura's machine that it will make a terrible noise, and I do not want to wake him until everything is ready.

Hafiz was woken by the noise of the coffee machine that was like a call to rouse the dead. He wrapped a blanket round him – he was still fully dressed – but he thought – This is what people do in domestic life, isn't it? He went through to the kitchen. He said 'Hello.' Maisie said 'Hello.' Then – 'You are brilliant to have brought this fodder!'

He said 'Is that what you call it – fodder?'

'That's what my aunt Laura calls it when she wants to be funny.'

'Your aunt Laura brought it?'

'No, she's in England. I thought you brought it.'

Maisie was having a struggle to get eggs out of boiling water. She thought – I didn't know domesticity could be so perilous. Then – I expect he's making out he didn't bring the bag because he doesn't want to boast about being such an angel.

Hafiz said 'No, I didn't bring it.'

'No? Then who did?'

'I don't know.' He sat at the small kitchen table and watched her at the stove. He said 'You've got an aunt in England called Laura? Laura Simmons?'

'Yes, do you know her?'

'No, Richard talked of her.' Then – 'I see!'

'See what?'

'Did Joshua send you?'

'What?'

Maisie was pouring coffee into mugs. She sat at the small table opposite Hafiz. She thought – Well now it really is as if we were married and in a balloon above where there are shapes and patterns.

She said 'Do you want some toast?' He said 'Yes please.' She was thinking – I did not think I could ever be as happy as this.

He said 'Perhaps Leila brought it.'

'Brought the bag? Oh yes, she kept her keys. I asked her for them, but she told me to leave the doors open so you could get in, and I suppose so that then she could get in too.'

'That was very sensible.'

'Yes.'

'So that explains it.'

'Yes.'

Hafiz thought – Though how any of this can in fact be explained, I can't imagine.

Maisie watched him eating his egg. She thought she might ask – Is your egg all right? This was not the sort of thing that her aunt Laura would ask, but she did not think her aunt Laura was good at domesticity.

She said 'Leila is very beautiful.'

'Yes.'

'I gave her your message.'

'You did?'

'She said she'll pass it on to Richard Kahn.'

'Is she going to see him?'

'I'm not sure. But when she does.'

Hafiz was thinking – As soon as I have finished this egg surely we can go back to bed. With any luck we can stay in bed the whole day. I am someone who has come to an oasis out of the desert and I want to plunge into the water head first.

224

He said 'Were those men with Leila policemen?'

'Oh yes I think they were. But neither of them had a scar on his chin. Is the one with the scar called Captain Leon?'

'Yes. Will Leila get in touch with him?'

'Yes. I think she was using him to frighten the others. They asked her to come back with them so that she could make things all right.'

'She is a genius.'

'Yes. But she is the friend of both Captain Leon and Richard Kahn, isn't she?'

'Yes, why do you ask?'

'Because I think that in that case we might be able to stay here until Richard gets back.'

'Oh I see.'

Maisie was thinking – I do wish he would hurry and finish that egg.

Hafiz stood and carried the mugs and plates to the sink. Maisie watched him. She said 'I didn't think Arab men did that.'

'Did what.'

'The washing-up.'

'They don't.'

'Then I'll do it. But later. Now we should go back to bed. I want to do everything properly.'

'All right.' He left the plates in the sink. He followed her into the bedroom and stood in front of where she sat on the bed. He said 'What's properly?'

She said 'I'm not sure. I haven't done it much. You can show me.'

# XXXIV

Dario was reading –

I, Laura Simmons, did not report Maurice missing for three days. What was the point? The police would look at me like they look at people in films; they would be thinking – Do you fuck? Have you had a lovers' quarrel? And I would say – Yes we do, and yes we have. And there would be the ghastly schadenfreude of people who hear of lovers' quarrels; also the thought that I might now be available. I only eventually went to the police because people in the neighbouring apartment were getting suspicious; they had heard us quarrelling the evening we had gone to have drinks at the Commodore Hotel, and perhaps they thought I had murdered Maurice. I had said to him 'If you go to Jerusalem I'll follow you.' He had said 'I'm not going to Jerusalem.' I had said 'Oh aren't you going to go up like Mohammed on a fucking horse, or was it a cloud?'

When I did go to the police I told them a version of the story and they wrote nothing down but kept my passport and told me to come back in two days. I did this; and by that time they seemed to have received some information which had made them more interested.

'What was your relationship with Maurice Rotblatt?'

'The usual.'

'What do you mean by that?'

'We were not accomplices in one of the ludicrous games that you like to call intelligence, if that's what you think.'

'Why should we think that?'

'It sells better nowadays than sex.'

I thought – Do I really want to put their backs up so that I get myself 'disappeared' like Maurice; because what other dignity is possible?

'Your relationship was physical?'

'Hot diggety dog.'

'Had you quarrelled?'

'Violently.'

'When.'

'The evening he disappeared.'

'What about?'

'About whether he was trying to be more like Christ or Mohammed.'

'Miss Simmons, why have you come to us?'

'To provide cover for myself. So you won't be able to ask me why I haven't.'

'We will be in touch with you.'

'He might have gone to Jerusalem. He had an ex-wife in Jerusalem.'

'Why didn't you tell us this before?'

'I don't like to think of it.'

'We will be in touch.'

There was a younger policeman listening in on this conversation. I wondered if he was from some higher intelligence organisation. He was handsome, and had a large scar on his chin. He was also the sort of person who would be wondering whether he had any chance with me.

When I left the room, the young policeman followed me. I thought – Well why not? This would seem some revenge on Maurice.

He said 'What was your friend doing in Beirut?'

'He was giving lectures.'

'Why Beirut?'
'He was invited.'
'Who by?'
'The American University.'
We were going down a corridor towards an outside door. He had been speaking to my back. Then he moved past me and opened a door into a side room. He gestured me to go in. He said 'Please.' I thought – At least I will not be self-pitying.

The room was just another interrogation room, with a table and two chairs on either side of it. The young policeman gestured me to a chair and he sat opposite me. He was in fact very handsome.

He said 'What were the lectures about?'
'People's need for violence. About why people like self-destruction.'
'And why do they?'
'Shouldn't I be asking you that, in this god-awful town?'
'But what does your friend say?'
'It's humans' contribution to evolution. Eliminating waste.'
'Interesting.'
'Yes.'
'And what did he think one should do about it?'
'I don't know.'
I suddenly felt my belligerence, my prickliness, draining away. I thought I might even cry. We were all in the same fragile boat as the people in this awful town.

He said 'There are a lot of young people now who think that everything not of immediate profit can be destroyed, without asking what might come after. Does your friend agree with that?'
'He wasn't young, he was as old as the hills.'
'Then do you agree?'
'How can you tell what will come after? The future goes its own way. People will soon find it is a delusion that they might manipulate it.'

228

'How?'

'My friend thinks a technological revolution is coming, through which endless information will be available, endless choices will be available, but there will be no information about what to choose.'

'And the old guidelines will have gone.'

'Yes.'

He had gentle eyes. They were like those of someone trying to find their way in a darkened room. I thought – Oh bugger, I can't get away from the terrible curse, or is it a guiding star, of attraction.

He said 'It seems to me there is soon going to be a great conflagration, not the stupid squabbles that are consuming this town, but between the people who think that evolution depends on stability and progress, and those who think that for the sake of evolution one has to pull all forms of stability down. But there will also be those who see that this may be happening, but think there may then be freedom for small numbers to affect things for evil or for good.'

'How?'

'While the rest are occupied, to sow the seeds of what will come after.'

'That's what Maurice thought.'

'And what do you think? Oh no, I have asked you that.'

'Yes I think that. But who are these people? And how would one know them?'

'Well, there may be something called intelligence, even if it is not of the sort that you understandably mocked.' He stood up. 'The intelligence of people who learn to go their own way, but also that by this they are not on their own. Please feel free to get in touch with me if you would like.'

'Thank you.'

When I was back at the hotel I lay on the bed and thought – In this mad town do people really think there is some alchemical substance being forged like the philosopher's stone at the heart of a furnace?

I thought I should stay a few more days in Beirut to see if Maurice turned up. I did not get in touch with the handsome man with the scar on his chin because I thought he had made his point, which we had understood, and whatever this was might become apparent in its own time.

The British consul came to see me. He said 'Well he doesn't seem to be in Jerusalem. They've got no information there.'

'Well they'd have to say that, wouldn't they.'

'You think he was some sort of agent?'

'I don't know. But I think his friend Andros is.'

'Professor Andros?'

'Is he a professor?'

'Well they're supposed to be intelligent, these professors!' The consul laughed. He was a quiet, sandy-haired man. I thought – Well for God's sake, at least he's not after me.

I said 'They like making up stories. They think they can influence things by making up stories.'

'You think Professor Rotblatt is making up this story?'

'He's not a professor. But it would be a good story.'

'You think he's faked his disappearance?'

'Oh no, I mean the story that there's going to be a great conflagration between the people who think everything has to be pulled down and those who do not; and then there will be those who do not think this is the point at all.'

The consul laughed. 'And so what is the point?'

'That's what you can't tell with evolution.'

I thought – We are like people dropping sticks into a river.

It was only after a week that I got in touch with Richard Kahn. I did not do this before because I had been hostile to him when I had last seen him: he had seemed to be challenging Maurice to make some move other than talk. I had thought he was jealous of Maurice and had wanted to be rid of him. But now I didn't know. It was possible that Maurice had known what he was doing and had been using

230

Richard? Had we not all colluded in Maurice's disappear-ance? I rang Richard and we arranged to meet, not in his apartment but at a café on the sea-front.

On the beach the waves were coming in and crawling back like unborn creatures that could not make up their minds to come on to the land. I said 'I thought you might blame me for what's happened to Maurice.'

He said 'What has happened, do you know?'

'No.'

'I thought you might blame me.'

'I think he just wanted to get away.'

Richard seemed neither sad nor angry. It was as if he might be looking for somewhere to fall asleep.

I said 'Might he have gone to have a look at those people that you and he were talking about?'

'What people?'

'Those people in the hills. He wanted purity.'

'Which he won't get.'

'Oh he knows it has to be in the mind!'

'Which perhaps he has also learned it isn't.'

I thought – Richard must have once been a bit in love with Maurice.

I said 'I thought you might think I was bad for him.'

'There's no sense in thinking what's bad and good for Maurice. He can use both or either.'

'So I needn't feel guilty.'

'None of us should feel guilty.'

'Do you think there's a great battle coming up between the people who think there's no such thing as good and bad but have to insist there is; and people who know that there is but think they can use it?'

'Good heavens, did you get that from Maurice?'

'No, from a man at the police station.'

'The things you do!'

'Well, what shall I do?'

He laughed. He said 'Go home.' I thought – And please

231

don't say: And work for your salvation. He said 'And work,
like all the rest of us, for your salvation.'

I said 'Do you understand what Maurice meant about
God?'

'I think so.'

'What —'

'It sometimes seemed that he was saying one could make
of God what one likes; but he wasn't, he was saying that that's
what people usually do. He was saying that one had to look
for God, and then it is often God who makes what he likes of
you.'

'And do you think that happens?'

'It can do.'

'But do you just wait?'

'I suppose you enjoy things while you can.'

# XXXV

It was Ben's mother, Melissa, who knew the Maurice Rotblatt story; not only from what had been in the newspapers but because she was a friend of Laura Simmons and they had talked about it over the years. Melissa, who was a psychotherapist, had said – I don't think one can plan to turn oneself into an archetype or part of an archetypal story: surely that either happens or it doesn't. Laura had said – I suppose one can give it a whirl, as we used to say.

Laura had gone to talk to Melissa when she had got back from Beirut after Maurice had disappeared. Melissa had not seen her professionally because this was precluded by their friendship according to the conventions of psychotherapy. Laura had said 'I don't understand why it's thought that friendship screws things up.' Melissa had said 'Don't you?' Laura had said 'You think it's ever possible to be objective?'

Melissa had said 'You think Maurice was conscious of being taken as a Christ-like figure?'

'He might have thought he could be in that sort of way effective.'

'And was he?'

'Well that's the question.'

Melissa was remembering this conversation when, years later, she, Ben and Julie and Ben's father, Harry, were sitting under umbrellas by a bright blue swimming pool in a hotel to which they had moved by the Red Sea. This was where Ben's father had been doing reconnaissance for a film. Melissa remembered saying to Laura, 'The wonder is how someone like you ever got involved with Maurice.' Laura had said 'I thought he had all the answers.' 'And that was all?' 'No of course not.'

Now, under the bright blue sky, with the baby in its cot under its own umbrella, the girl whom they knew as Gaby was swimming far out to sea.

Melissa was talking with Ben and Julie while her husband Harry lay with a hat over his eyes, appearing not to be listening. Melissa was saying 'But Maurice didn't say that you could make one thing happen rather than another, what he was talking about was a state of mind, an attitude, a style.'

Ben said 'But one thing will be more likely to happen rather than another if you have a lively attitude, style, rather than another.'

'Just you on your own?'

'That's scientific, isn't it Dad?'

Ben's father Harry after a time said 'What?' Then he sat up and tilted his hat back and looked out to sea. He said 'Scientists make up stories to describe what they see. Or what they think they see. But what happens happens.' He seemed to be checking that Gaby was still in sight. Ben said 'But no one knows what happened to Maurice Rotblatt.'

Melissa said to Ben – 'Your father was rather keen on Laura.'

Harry said 'Oh yes I was, wasn't I?' He lay back and put his hat over his eyes.

Julie sat up to see that her baby was all right. She said 'I still think he was that old man at the dig.'

Ben said 'Oh of course he wasn't that old man at the dig! He was an Armenian.'

'Couldn't Mr Rotblatt have been an Armenian?'

Harry said without removing the hat from over his eyes –

'Surely he could be anything, that's the point – a bird, a tree, an Armenian, an Englishman.'

Melissa said 'I do wish you'd be serious.'

'I am being serious.'

'But I knew him!'

'I thought we were talking about a style, an attitude of mind.'

The others were now looking out to sea, to where Gaby was swimming parallel to the shore, her head bobbing up and down like a mooring, not getting closer nor farther away.

Julie said 'The point of this old man at the dig was he seemed to know what we wanted. He took us in his car to the village thirty miles away.'

Melissa said 'But you're saying this was what you wanted.'

Ben said 'Yes but we none of us knew this.'

Harry said 'So that might be called "Doing a Maurice Rotblatt".' It was as if no one had heard this.

Julie said 'He said he'd spent some time as a young man up a holy mountain.'

Melissa said 'I thought you said you didn't know the language.'

Ben said 'I was learning it.'

Julie said 'He said that almost from the beginning Islam had gone wrong. The rightful heir to Mohammed was his son-in-law Ali, this was who Mohammed had chosen to be his heir; but Ali was peaceable and spiritual and insisted that Allah was the lord of everyone and so did not have enemies. So Ali was murdered, because everyone wanted enemies.'

They saw that Gaby suddenly appeared to have reached a small outcrop of rocks that stretched from the land into the sea. She was climbing out of the water with her bare feet treading delicately on the sharp rocks.

Melissa said 'But you still haven't answered my question. Was he just saying that if you're attentive you notice more of what's there anyway, or that you bring into existence what was not there before?'

Ben said 'You make connections which were not there before. You bring into actuality what were only possibilities before.'

'Well, which?'

'But the possibilities exist.'

'Presumably.'

'And you choose.'

Harry said 'Or are chosen.'

Melissa said 'Can't you either be part of the conversation or not?'

'No.'

Ben said 'You mean it's not arbitrary.'

Harry said 'It's the way the cookie crumbles.'

He sat up and propped himself on an elbow. He watched Gaby as she was coming towards them along the beach. They had all stopped talking to watch her. She was wearing a brief two-piece bathing dress. Harry was thinking – She is Aphrodite's child: the hidden pearl in the oyster shell, coming skimming in to the land from the sea.

Melissa called 'Did you have a good swim?'

'Yes thank you.'

'When did you learn to swim?'

'I think I've always known.'

Harry said 'If you drop babies in the deep end they know how to swim.'

Gaby went to where the baby was lying in its cot and stood looking down at it. She draped a towel round her shoulders. Ben's father thought – There is a painting of the Nativity like this, in which the people standing or sitting around are looking at what appears to be a nest from which the birds have flown, while the baby is on its own and gazes contentedly out of the picture.

Gaby said 'I think I know this person you sometimes talk about. I think he came to visit my uncle once in Jerusalem.'

After a time Melissa said 'Maurice? You knew Maurice Rotblatt? When was that?'

236

'I must have been ten, eleven.'

'But was this before or after he was supposed to have disappeared?'

'I understood he had come from Beirut. They were discussing where he should go.'

'Who is your uncle?'

'He is a teacher of theology at the university. Or he was. He was expelled for saying that he wasn't certain of anything any more.' Gaby was looking down at the cot, as if she were telling this to the baby.

'And where did they think Maurice should go?'

'I don't know. I don't think they knew.'

'What else do you remember?'

'My uncle said that this man Maurice was one of the few people he knew who believed in God. Who behaved as if he did.'

'How did he behave?'

'I suppose he trusted.'

'Trusted what?'

'I'm sorry, I should have talked about this before, but I did not want to think about the past, and I did not trust talking.'

Harry said 'That's all right, Gaby.'

Melissa said 'But you think it wasn't more than six or seven years ago?'

'I think my uncle said that this man just assumed that everything was all right.'

Harry said 'And everything is, Gaby.'

'Do you think I should go back?'

Melissa said 'Where to, Jerusalem?'

'To tell them.'

'Tell them what.'

'That everything is all right. That people should no longer keep to themselves as Jews, or Muslims, or Christians, because to see oneself like that is not properly to have been born.'

Harry said 'Then how should one see oneself, Gaby?'

'In relation to God. Who is all right.'

The baby had begun to make a slight singing sound. Gaby picked it up and handed it to Julie, who took out her breast and began to feed it.

Melissa said 'Well we've all got to go home. And pick up the pieces.'

Julie said 'I still think you should come with us, Gaby.'

Harry said 'And what would your uncle tell them? The people in Jerusalem?'

Gaby said 'He used to say it all had something to do with the book of Jonah.'

Melissa said 'What does the book of Jonah say?'

Ben said 'Jonah sheltered underneath a gourd, which withered.'

Julie said 'I thought he was swallowed by a whale.'

Gaby said 'It seemed to me in that tunnel that I'd been swallowed by a whale.'

Harry said 'The story of Jonah is that God told him to go and preach to the gentiles of Nineveh, and he refused, and tried to escape on a ship. But he was chucked over the side of the ship because the sailors thought he was bringing them bad luck. He was eaten by a whale who deposited him on the shore of the people of Nineveh, and God told him again to preach to them. But he still sulked, and told God he thought he should just destroy them, because they were wicked gentiles. But God said he didn't want to destroy people any more, so instead he destroyed the plant that Jonah was sheltering under, to teach Jonah a lesson.'

After a time Melissa said 'And what happened then?'

'We don't know. That's the end of the story.'

'But that's most unsatisfactory.'

Gaby said 'But the people of Nineveh did repent.'

Harry said 'Oh yes, they did.'

Julie said 'Do you think Jonah repented?'

'We don't know. It's as if that end of the story has been cut off.'

Melissa said 'So what do we do?'
Ben said 'Let's all go to Nineveh!'
Harry said 'You mean Jerusalem.'
'Oh, Jerusalem. Nineveh. What's the difference!'

# XXXVI

When Richard Kahn reached Jerusalem after the plaster had been removed from his leg – having travelled the circuitous route by bus and hired car through Syria and Jordan because the frontier between Lebanon and Israel was closed – he went to see Professor Nathan, Lisa's uncle. Nathan was in his room at the top of the high-rise block that looked out over the old city. He sat in a wheelchair with a rug over his knees. He said 'I didn't think they'd let you in. Does this mean they don't know about you or they do?'

Richard said 'They'll know what they want to know. I suppose they keep an eye out.'

'What'll they make of your coming here?'

'I don't think it matters.'

Richard had been walking with a stick. He sat down heavily. The professor, watching him, said 'I thought your fall was a story.'

'And I thought that's what people would think. So I broke my leg.'

'A natural hazard?'

'Yes.'

Richard was thinking – I am exhausted. Perhaps I have come all this way because this is a place where one might be put to rest by a suicide bomber.

He said 'So what's happening.'

Nathan said 'We're getting a government that believes in an eye for an eye and a tooth for a tooth and calling it plastic surgery.'

'That's the latest joke?'

'It keeps things going.'

'They think people will get tired –'

'No, no, they see people need to be tired.'

'So they won't think of disaster happening?'

'Quite.'

The professor wheeled himself to a sideboard where there was a bowl of nuts. He held this out to Richard.

Richard said 'I wanted to ask you about this story that an old scroll, an old document, has been discovered under Temple Mount.'

'Whatever it is, they're sitting on it.'

'But what does it say? What's it supposed to say?'

'There was a team years ago doing excavations under Temple Mount. They found some document. But it wasn't an old one; it is the confession of someone who said some old document had been destroyed.'

'Why?'

'I don't know. Presumably because it might upset the status quo.'

'The status quo being instability?'

'Yes.'

'But why confess?'

'Presumably so that everyone could make of the situation what they liked.'

'It wasn't a forgery?'

'Oh indeed, who knows?'

'Did it say what the document was that was supposed to have been destroyed?'

'It was hinted. The usual Christian stuff, but pre-Christian. About being responsible for the gentiles.'

241

'But it's now this document that's supposed to have turned up?'

'That's what they won't say. There was some sort of explosion: a fall of rock. Whatever was discovered, they're keeping it quiet.'

'To stop the threat of stability?'

'Well it wouldn't be stability, it would be an obstacle course.'

'That's what our old friend Maurice Rotblatt thought.' He pushed the bowl from him as if he were making a show of dismissing temptation.

'What?'

'Not just doing what you like. A journey of discovery. An adventure.' Then – 'Did he come to see you?'

'Who, Maurice?'

'After he disappeared. Was supposed to have disappeared.'

'Yes he came to see me.'

'You never told me!'

'Would you have wanted me to? All right, yes, an obstacle course!'

'He converted you!'

'What to?'

'His own particular brand of comprehending how the universe is incomprehensible.'

'Oh yes, he was good at that.'

'So one knows that one doesn't know, and so on. And so one knows where one is.'

'You know where Maurice is?'

'Oh no, I don't know that.'

Richard went to the window that looked out over the Old City. He thought – But I know why I have come here: to talk with someone who knows what we're not quite talking about.

Nathan said 'Do you know anything about my great-niece Lisa?'

'No, should I?'

'You've got the entrée to such things. She's disappeared. Like Maurice.'

'Did she know him?'

'I remember she met him the time he came here.'

'Perhaps she's gone to join him. I like the image of the happy hunting ground.'

'You think he's alive?'

'Do you know where he is?'

'Oh no, I mean in the mind. Join him in the mind.'

Richard thought – But it is impossible to hold what we're not quite talking about in the mind: sometimes it is there, and sometimes it is not. But we always have to be looking for it?

Nathan said 'What happened to that student of yours, the one who was involved with that absurd biological weapon?'

'He went off to try to find out what was happening.'

'And he hasn't got back?'

'No. And you haven't heard anything?'

'And you risked coming here? That was good of you.'

'But there is the danger, yes, of madmen working on their own.'

'They're not the first madmen who've had power.'

'No indeed. Have the sane ever had power?'

Nathan was trying to remember what he and his niece Lisa had talked about the last time he had seen her. She had been being taught about the Holocaust. She was training to be a nurse: it was as if she felt she had some task to do. They had talked about how in the old stories people had felt they had tasks to do.

He said 'My great-niece Lisa wanted to stop being a Jew.'

'And what did you tell her?'

'That this was not possible. Not until everyone stopped branding people or being branded in this way. She would simply be branded as someone who wanted to stop being a Jew.'

'That didn't put her off?'

'I don't suppose so.'

'So what happened?'

'That's what we don't know.'

Nathan appeared to be going to sleep. Richard thought –
We might just stay sane. We don't know if we have any
further power.

Richard began to wonder how soon he could set off on his
journey back to Beirut. He would have to retrace the long
journey through Jordan and Syria: but perhaps one of the
functions of war was that it gave one chances to think.
Perhaps he might find something pleasant to do in his hired
car by the Sea of Galilee. It had been right to want to get
away from Beirut, because if anything had happened to Hafiz
they would have wanted to question him. He hoped that
Leila was looking after the apartment.

Nathan suddenly lifted his head and said 'There's something we're not getting.'

Richard said 'What?'

'If the universe is comprehensible but not in words –'

'Or symbols –'

'Quite. But the young are getting it.'

'Well they would, wouldn't they. In the evolutionary
course of things.'

'My niece is only seventeen. She's remarkable.'

'Then it'll depend on where she lands up.'

'God be merciful. But if she'd been hurt, she'd have been
identified. And I'd know.'

'And you don't.'

'No.'

Nathan suddenly wanted to be on his own. He wanted to
use his imagination. He said to Richard 'How old is this
student of yours? The one who's been involved with the
experiment –'

'I think twenty-four.'

'They know that the danger is of the madman with the
bomb.'

'So what do we tell them? Or what do they tell us.'

'If evil isn't organised, one's responsibility is to hop out of the way.'

'They know it would be an obstacle course.'

'As a matter of fact it does seem likely that there's some danger like that in the pipeline.'

'Yes, so I've heard.'

'Well thank you for coming all this way. It's extremely good of you.'

'Oh that's all right.'

# XXXVII

Dario was sitting in a deckchair holding a typescript. Laura was lying on the lawn beside him, wrapped in a rug like a mummy. There was a wind that sometimes disturbed Dario's pages. Dario was reading aloud –

'During the second half of the twentieth century it had become accepted by rich nations that nationalist wars were not worthwhile; that victory as much as defeat cost enormous sums of money because then there was the burden of responsibility for the enemy. Peacetime was more profitable, which could be manipulated so that the rich simply became richer and the poor stayed poor.'

He broke off. He said 'But we've had this.'

Laura said 'People like reading the same things over and over. It reassures them.'

'Even things telling them how ghastly they are?'

'Especially. Then they feel important.'

Dario read –

'At the same time it was glimpsed by a few that with the rich and powerful being made hollow by deception and overwork, but like efficient robots still keeping the whole thing going, there was a chance for them, the few, to go their own way – either for evil or for good. There would have to be some dissimulation; but this would be recognised for what

246

it was by others of the same kind, and so in this context could be taken as authentic.'

Dario broke off. He said 'But to most people this is meaningless.'

Laura said 'Exactly. Just as terrorism has a chance to flourish secretly, so might the force of good.'

'People wouldn't recognise it so they wouldn't want to crush it?'

'With luck.'

Dario read –

'Maurice Rotblatt wrote his articles, lectured, gained a small but devoted following. But he was known as a maverick, a mystery man, who seemed to have something interesting to say but not a generally intelligible way of saying it. He implied – You make your own story; but this is not arbitrary; it has to be authenticated by observation and experience.'

He broke off. He said 'But if this has been done –'

'It hasn't. It's handed on. It's happening. Everyone has to do it, to say it, in their own way.'

'All right I'll try. But it'll take some time.'

'You can stay here.'

'But you and I are not to be allowed to have what's called a relationship?'

'I thought you were queer.'

'Can Joshua come?'

'I thought he was with Andros.'

'That was an arrangement. They could both be a help. In this climate where the few perhaps need to know they exist.'

'And what would I be doing?'

'I see you as the madame of a glorious spiritual brothel.'

'I wouldn't mind that.'

'And then of course we might all stagger off to war. But having first been comforted.'

Laura said 'Go on.'

Dario read –

'Words are either written, in which case they can be held

up for inspection, or they are spoken, in which case they are gone with the wind.' He broke off. He said 'You can't say "gone with the wind".'

'Why not.'

'It's a cliché.'

'Everything is either a cliché, or likely to be misunderstood.'

'But you can at least hold it up for inspection.'

'This isn't getting anywhere. This is playing games.'

'What about this – "It's second thoughts that matter, when you yourself are trying to work out what you are trying to say."'

'Well what are you trying to say?'

'Did you go on seeing that policeman? The one you liked. The one with the scar on his chin.'

'What has that got to do with it?'

'It might have a lot to do with this story. How do you know? How do you ever know all the ramifications? Isn't that the point? You and the policeman were attracted. Attraction isn't just for procreation, it's for connection. You might have changed his life. He might have changed other people's lives. You might have made him interested in Maurice. He might have gone cannoning off on a course he wouldn't otherwise have gone on, rescuing countless people and preventing a third world war.'

'Well, we did have a fling.'

'You see? And that's a story. Do you know what's happened to him?'

'Well I think he did go on making enquiries about Maurice.'

'You see?'

'But where would this end? If everything has an incalculable effect on everything else, which you can't tell –' She broke off. 'You mean, it's all part of the same story? If you hadn't been trying to seduce Maisie in the basement of my house –'

248

'Me trying to seduce Maisie in the basement of your house?'

'– then Maise might never have bumped into Andros, and not been given the idea of going off on a journey.'

'You think Andros gave Maisie the idea of going off on a journey?'

'Didn't you say he did?'

'I can't remember; did I?'

'But that would be endless.'

'Yes. But that's what Maurice said would be right.'

'What?'

'Not knowing. Wondering. Wonder. That would be the point.'

'The point of what –'

'God.' Dario went on reading quickly – 'I should like to go to one of the trouble spots of the world where anarchy is settling in and just be there, with no intention, not knowing if this was making any difference –'

'Who wrote that?'

'Wouldn't it be Maurice? Does it matter? Or this – "Anyone who reads this may know what had happened to me, but if they do not, I would like them to understand what is the point of this experiment. Since there is no proof of anything beyond the bounds of determinism – and that cannot be proved – then what is left except a journey of speculation in which one catches an occasional glimpse of a Flying Dutchman or a Wandering Jew –"' He broke off. He said 'Those are ridiculous images.'

'Why?'

'It sounds more like Andros.'

'No it's not like Andros.'

'Did you live with Andros?'

'Oh, for a time, yes.'

'That's not clear.'

'I hope not. What have you got against Andros?'

'Nothing.'

249

'That he didn't make a pass at you? That you wanted him to make a pass at you, so you could turn him down?'

Dario said 'Or what about this?' He picked another sheet of paper from a pile beside him. He said ' "You know that young couple you told me about who didn't want their baby born in England or Ireland and so went on a journey –" '

'But how did that get in! That was years after Maurice disappeared!'

'Yes.'

'What is it? A letter? A fax? It's got nothing to do with Maurice. It was just the other day.'

'I wanted to prove my point.'

'What point? How things are connected?'

'Yes. You don't know. It might have something to do with Maurice.'

'It's a fax from me to Melissa. No it couldn't have been. Or was it. Did you put it in?'

'Why have you never tried to find out about Maurice? Whether or not he's still alive?'

'He wouldn't have wanted me to. Then it can go on seeming that he might be.'

'Exactly.'

'It must have been a fax from someone I was asking for information. Melissa had asked me to find out about some places Maurice had talked about –'

'You see?'

'Oh you are impossible!'

'It's the ramifications. It's the effect he has on others.'

'You mean I'm getting rattled?'

'Well aren't you? We're having quite a relationship. But we can't just leave him up in the air.'

'All right, bring him down.'

'You think he might have been going to Jerusalem?'

'He had a wife who had some sort of adopted child there.'

'Oh yes, wasn't I saying I might be his child?'

'Well you're not. Are you?'

'Why shouldn't I be? But where on earth were these people going to have their baby?'

Dario rummaged about among other papers on the ground beside him. Laura watched him. He said 'I don't think we're making enough of the baby. What is it about babies? With them we do have a power, one way or another, to alter the world?'

Laura said 'All right, I can't stand it. Do ask Joshua down if you want to.'

'Thank you.'

'But not Andros.'

'Why not Andros? He might be able to tell us about Maisie.'

'Why should he be able to tell us about Maisie?'

'He was going to see her.'

'He was? Why didn't you tell me!'

'Didn't I?'

'All right, and Andros.'

'But no mucking about? Stick to Flying Dutchmen or Wandering Jews?'

'They're not what's on offer in a spiritual brothel.'

'So what is?'

'You tell me.'

'Perdita? Marina? What is lost is found?'

# XXXVIII

During the three days that Maisie and Hafiz had been in Richard Kahn's flat they were careful not to go near a window nor turn on a light in the sitting room: the men who had been waiting for Hafiz or Richard might be waiting again outside. It also suited Maisie and Hafiz to feel they were besieged. Maisie said 'If we have to stay here till the food or air runs out it will be more economical to stay in bed.' Hafiz said 'There's a French film like this.' Maisie said 'There's an opera like this where people are entombed.' Hafiz said 'I wouldn't mind.' Maisie said 'I would.'

The food in the refrigerator lasted, and three bottles of red wine. The telephone had rung several times and they had not answered it. They talked in murmurs in case they might be heard through the walls: they watched television with the sound turned low. It seemed to each of them – This is perfect conjugality: we can't go out, no one is likely to come in, we are in thrall to a force which is greater than ourselves –

– This would not be possible for the whole of our lives?

On the morning of the fourth day Maisie studied the refrigerator which was now bare. Hafiz, watching from the bed, said 'Shall we expire quietly, or make a dash for it like Butch Cassidy and the Sundance Kid?'

Maisie said 'Fancy your knowing all these films!'

'You thought I'd be primitive?'

'I thought you were spiritual.'

'I am. I don't like unhappy endings.' He pulled the bed-clothes back for Maisie to climb in. He said 'Richard gave a seminar once on why people like unhappy ends.'

'Well why do they?'

'They feel cheered up.'

'Well I couldn't feel more cheerful.'

'So there is no need to think about ends.'

She came back to the bed and lay on top of him. She thought – But why do we think that this can't go on for ever? Just because the food's run out? She said 'So what do we do when we get out of here?'

'Do we need some great cause to fight for?'

'I think we need something quite ordinary for sixteen hours a day for sixty years.'

'This'll do.'

'I could cook. I could sew.'

'I could go back to my job.'

'I thought you said you couldn't.'

'I'd have to think of a story.'

'We could go to England.'

'I thought you said you didn't want to.'

'I'm not particular.'

'We may just have to see what happens.'

'But nothing will split us up?'

'Well, even if it does –'

'What –'

'We might be twice as effective.'

'Oh I see. Yes. That's terrible.'

Masie got off the bed and paced up and down, naked. She seemed not to want to hide how thin she was. She became slower and slower. She stood still and seemed to listen.

Hafiz said 'When I was on my journey, trying to find out what was happening, I arrived at a village which seemed to be the one where they were doing the experiment I've told you

253

about. But I haven't told you this part of it. There was something unexpected.'

Maisie said 'Which of course I will understand.'

'There were two trucks parked outside the village so that something seemed to be going on inside. I never had time to see exactly what. I'd got out to have a look, and had got just inside the village, and there was some sort of technician, doing something up a pole. I thought I should get away quick, and I feared that afterwards I might be rather ashamed. I mean this was a village where they might have been trying out the effects of some poison. But then when I was going back to my truck I saw someone, a girl, crawling out of one of the parked trucks and trying to climb into the back of my own. It was as if she was wounded, or sick. And so I helped her into my truck. But how did she know how to do that?'

After a time Maisie said 'You're trying this out on me?'

Hafiz said 'Yes.'

'You mean, how did she know to get into your truck, or that you would help her?'

'Yes. How did she know I wasn't one of the people who had brought her to the village?'

'I suppose, what else could she do?'

'Yes I see.'

'So you rescued her?'

'I drove her to the frontier. Just over. There was a bus to a village that Richard had said he knew about.'

'And how long did that take you?'

'Two days.'

'Yes I see.'

'I wanted to tell you.'

'She was in the back of your truck for two days?'

'She came to the front when we were driving.'

'And this is what I might have been difficult about?'

'Yes.'

'Well I'm not.'

'Good.'

'How old was she?'

'I should say, seventeen.'

'Well you were lucky, weren't you. I mean she was lucky.' Maisie began picking up her clothes that were scattered on the floor.

Hafiz said 'She was an Israeli. She didn't want to go back. She thought her people were always seeing themselves as the victims in some experiment.'

Maisie was putting on her clothes. She came and sat on the edge of the bed with her back to Hafiz. She said 'Nothing quite like that happened to me.'

Hafiz said 'What did happen to you?'

'I did have a chance to help someone. There was a soldier in the train who wore an enormous army overcoat. It was very hot. I helped him to masturbate.'

'You helped him to masturbate?'

'Yes, but only by talking. I think he was desperate. I thought he might have jumped on me.'

'What did you talk about?'

'Pollution. The sicknesses in people, in the landscape. Shouldn't it be possible to do something about them. I just kept talking while he watched me. He watched my mouth. There's a film like that. He beavered away inside his overcoat.'

'You have such good words – beavered!'

'He was a sweet man really. It was as if he were being eaten inside. He gave me some chocolate. Which I ate. I was so hungry.'

Hafiz pulled himself up and put a hand on her shoulder. He saw that she was crying. She said 'But it's so awful!'

Hafiz said 'But it's not.'

'He said I was an angel.'

'Well you are.'

'I hadn't been hungry for so long. You don't mind my being thin?'

'No.'

255

'But we're not going to be able to stay here, are we?'

'Not here.'

'Then mightn't that be awful?'

'What was it those people said in that movie – We'll always have Paris.'

'Oh yes. But it was – "We'll always have Paris, which we didn't have before."'

'That's right.'

'But they split up.'

'But they were in a movie. We're not in a movie. We make jokes about movies.'

'Yes. I see.'

Maisie watched Hafiz as he put on his clothes. She said 'So you mean we might be ordinary.'

'Not ordinary. Ordinary's confused.'

'So what are we going to do?'

Hafiz said 'Shouldn't we just go out and have dinner?'

Maisie sang: '– and nothing else will matter in the world today –'

'What's that?'

'A song.'

'It sounds a happy one.'

When they were both dressed they went to the door on to the landing and listened. Maisie said 'What do you think is happening to the girl you helped?'

'I should like to know one day.'

'Can I come with you?'

'I hope you will be with me.'

'How is it that you speak such good English?'

'I spoke English with my friend Joshua.'

'He's the one who's homosexual?'

'He's the one who's gone to see your aunt Laura in England.'

As they were going down the stairs Maisie stopped and said 'Let's just try it.'

Hafiz said 'Let's just try what?'

'Being ordinary. Say – I love you.'
'I love you.'
'Yes. I love you. It's not too difficult.'
'No. I love you to distraction – ?'
'No, that's confused. It's silly.'

# XXXIX

Three days after he had left Laura in Beirut, Maurice Rotblatt arrived in Jerusalem – having travelled by bus the circuitous route through Syria and Jordan; having half expected to be detained and questioned at each frontier, but also telling himself – I do not have that importance. When in Jerusalem he walked through the streets of the Old City where he had not been for several years: he wondered – Did Jesus come to have a look at these jumbled streets after his death? does he haunt them now, to get schadenfreude at these people's misfortunes? Or would he think they are fulfilling their destiny. Maurice was on his way to see if he could bump into Professor Nathan somewhere on his way between the university where Nathan worked and the Armenian quarter of the Old City where he had chosen to lodge; he used to set off on this journey on his bicycle, then get off to push when he reached the narrow streets, guiding it through the crowds as if it were a donkey. Maurice thought – He is an Old Testament figure, although he is rebelling; or should one say learning? Maurice had heard that Nathan was soon going to have to move out of his lodgings because pressure was being applied to segregate more rigorously the various ethnic groups in the old town: also Nathan had made it known that he objected to this policy. Maurice wanted to come across

258

Nathan unannounced, because he did not want to embarrass him nor to let anyone else know that he, Maurice, was in Jerusalem.

Outside Nathan's lodgings there was a small open square with a café and stalls selling food. Maurice saw Nathan standing talking to some soldiers at the far side of the square; he had his hand on the shoulder of a young dark-haired girl. Maurice thought – He is explaining to the girl as much as to the soldiers how segregation makes no sense: the girl should know she has a right to be here.

While Maurice waited for the soldiers to go he bought a bag of nuts from a stallholder whom he judged was Palestinian. Maurice wondered – Are they now setting about separating the Armenians and Palestinians? He thought that Nathan had spotted him but was pretending not to know him: this would be the sort of caution they would have both got used to. Then the girl was coming over to him as if to let him know that she knew what was happening and she wanted to make sure that he did. The stallholder held out a scoop of nuts to her but she smiled and shook her head. The stallholder murmured something that seemed to mean 'Go on, it's a gift.' The girl took the nuts and she and Maurice stood eating side by side. Maurice wondered – In some sense she knows me? After a time the soldiers left the square and Nathan came over. He said 'This is my niece Lisa. She makes a point of going where she is told not to go.' The girl, who looked about ten, said 'It is so stupid.' Nathan said 'All right, but now off you go.' Maurice said 'Would you like the rest of my nuts?'

The girl said 'Thank you. Would you mind if I offered some to children on my way home?'

Maurice said 'No.'

Nathan said 'Let's have some coffee.'

He and Maurice crossed the square to the café. The girl followed them eating nuts from the bag. Nathan seemed not to be worrying about her still being with them. He and

Maurice ordered coffee. Nathan said 'I heard you were in Beirut. There were people asking if you would be coming here.'

'What had you heard?'

'That you'd insulted everyone equally, Muslims, Christians and Jews. I supposed you'd done it in order to get away.'

'I've started making mistakes.'

'What?'

'I can't manipulate people. I mean I don't think stopping that is a mistake.'

'Ah.'

'I want to get away, yes. But I wanted to see you first.'

'Thank you.'

'But what does God want: is that a stupid question?'

'Yes. I'm not sure.'

The proprietor emerged from the café and recognised Maurice from the years when he had been in Jerusalem. The proprietor said that he had something he'd like to show him, which was an icon of St Gregory the Illuminator, who was the patron saint of Armenia. Maurice said he'd like to see it. The proprietor went to fetch it.

Nathan said 'But I'm like you. I'm being chucked out.'

'Out of your home?'

'Out of the university.'

'What for?'

'What I think would be called Holocaust impatience.'

The girl who was standing by them eating nuts, said 'What's that?'

Nathan said 'Wanting to get on with things.'

'To get on with what?'

'Whatever will come after.'

'Is that why asking what God wants is a stupid question?'

Maurice said 'That's clever.'

The café proprietor came out with an object wrapped in a cloth. He sat at their table and unwrapped in reverently. It was a painting on wood of a beautiful young man with a whimsical smile and one finger held up pointing to the sky as if he were expecting to hear the answer to a riddle.

The girl said 'Who was Gregory the Illuminator?'

Maurice said 'He spent fifteen years locked up in a pit, and then was let out and converted everyone around him.'

'Wasn't that what God wanted?'

'Well it was what came after.'

'He looks very cheerful.'

The café proprietor said 'He was a true martyr.'

There were some soldiers coming back into the far side of the square. They had guns slung over their shoulders like wings. They began to argue with the Palestinian family with their stall of fruit and nuts.

Nathan said to Maurice 'I'd been teaching the case against Jewish exclusiveness. The book of Jonah.'

'And were you getting anywhere?'

'No.'

The girl said 'You mean you can't ask what God wants because he wants you to want it?'

Maurice said 'Yes.' Then to Nathan 'People would die rather than change.'

Nathan said 'People would kill rather than change.'

Maurice said to the girl 'So what are you making of this?'

The girl said 'Gregory is very beautiful.'

The café proprietor said 'Thank you.' He began to wrap up his icon again. He said 'But there are still people who would want to destroy it.'

The girl said 'So how would you know how to want what God wants?'

Nathan said to the girl 'What do you think he should do with the icon?'

The girl said 'Perhaps he should hide it in a pit. Then when the time comes it can be uncovered and convert everyone around it.'

The café proprietor said 'You should be careful. You will get us all into trouble.'

Maurice said 'I've got a god-daughter like you.'

'What's she called?'

'Maisie.'

At the far side of the square there was an altercation going on. The soldiers had taken hold of the barrow on which were set out the stallholder's spices and nuts and were trying to move it. Some women who seemed to be the family of the stallholder were hanging on. One of them tried to grab a gun from the shoulder of a soldier. The others took down their weapons and stood back and held them pointing at the family.

Maurice said 'I'd better be going.'

'Well thank you for coming.'

'It's good to know that people are alive.'

'Yes. Are you going to see your wife?'

'I hope so.'

'Give her my regards. I'm told she's doing some experiment in the bowels of the earth. Sensory deprivation.'

'Yes I'd heard that.'

'No noise, no radiation. Nothing but your own brain's radiation.'

'The language before Babel.'

'Ah well, that might explain that inexplicable story.'

At the far side of the square there began to be a wailing, a lamentation, as the family's stall became tipped over and the contents were strewn on the ground. The girl was watching. She said 'Why is the story of Babel inexplicable?'

Nathan said 'I told you to go home.'

The girl said 'I know.'

Maurice said 'Because why didn't God want humans to get up to heaven?'

The girl said 'Perhaps he wanted them to get things right down here.' Then – 'I think I'll go and ask them.'

'Ask them what?'

'Why they think it's right doing ethnic cleansing.'

# XL

Andros and Joshua entered a large open-plan room in which numerous computers on desks were separated by shoulder-high screens and interspersed with tables of biological and electrical equipment. Men and women, most wearing white, were seated on swivel chairs in front of the computers. A few swung round to take note of Andros as he came in; but it was evident that he was there to show the place to Joshua. He was saying 'Your friend in Beirut worked in somewhere like this?' Joshua said 'I think so.' 'How much did you gather of what he was doing?' 'I think he was trying to find out something of the genetic make-up of the brain.'

'And what did you gather of that?'

Joshua said, as if he were performing for the sake of the people in the room – 'I think that since the genes of a chimpanzee and those of a human are so nearly identical, what gives humans their special brand of consciousness either exists in very small genetic differences that are hardly discernible, or is not represented so much in the genes as in an organising ability of the billions of cells in the brain.'

Andros had seated himself on a chair that could swivel from facing Joshua to the other people in the room. To a young woman who happened to be close to him he said 'Does that make sense to you?' She seemed at first not to register he was talking to her, then nodded.

Joshua went on 'He thought that it was by discovering more of what these differences might be – either in terms of genetic components or in patterning – that one might understand what might be a next step in human evolution. If one could discover how human consciousness had arisen, that is, then one might discover how it might develop. There might be a lead to some higher form of consciousness: at least by the elimination of some of the more unpleasant traits at the moment prevalent in humans.'

Andros said 'By genetic engineering?'

'Well, if this were feasible or desirable. But more probably by considering other ways of altering how we think.'

There were a few cautious smiles at this among the people in the room; as if a topic had been broached that was slightly indecent.

Andros said 'Thank you.' He swivelled to the half-attentive audience and said –

'What I was saying in my lecture some weeks ago that was so fortuitously interrupted – perhaps I should say fortunately, because in the meantime my thoughts have moved on – what I was saying then was that while the mapping of the human genome is giving us the chance of much power to treat and eliminate abnormality and disease, the prospect of planning to alter or enhance human nature remains something of a fantasy. Scientists cannot tell the results of their experiments until they have been tested; and phenomena in the brain and in the outside world are so intricately interconnected that possible effects and side effects are almost infinite, and cannot be known in advance. So it seems that what might be called enhancement of human nature will continue to remain in the realm of chance and natural selection. However, it can be claimed that what scientists call "chance" might be subject to enquiry outside the realm of science: and in my lecture I had begun to say that this was what my old friend Maurice Rotblatt was doing with his theories about what he called aesthetics.'

To this there was no reaction at all from the people in the room. So after a time Joshua spoke up as if he were the feed-man in a double act – 'You mean, might there be something outside us, as there seems to be in what gives us the idea of beauty, that might in the matter of evolution be telling us what it is right do?'

'Exactly!' Andros beamed. 'Science gives us no informa-tion about ethics or aesthetics.' One or two people in the room rolled their eyes.

Joshua went on – 'And isn't there a case to be made that evolution itself has depended on consciousness as well as creating it? That there is something here that might give us insight into dealing with what is otherwise called chance?'

Andros frowned and shook his head, as if he were in sympathy with the people who found this embarrassing. He said 'Let's stick to science. We know a great deal now about our genes: and it seems that at least a third of them play a role in the development of the brain. But we still know very little about the brain's functions. We know little about the ways in which the brain affects other parts of our body, let alone how it interacts with the outside world, either on its own, or in combination with other brains. Since it seems at the moment impossible to assess the effects of consciousness scientifically, some people are driven to say that conscious-ness as a scientific concept does not exist. As a result it is difficult for scientists to assess in what style in this area they should proceed.'

Andros shook his head again; but this time as if reproving himself for having strayed outside his brief.

He said 'But I have not yet told you how my thoughts have moved on since my lecture. I was saying then that it seemed unlikely that human nature would be enhanced by genetic engineering. But I was thinking as a theorist, and was not considering the cumulative effects of piecemeal engineering. Diseases can and will be eliminated; abilities to thrive can and will be chosen and augmented. And thus more and more opportunities are likely to become available for couples or individuals to choose, or to think they can choose, what sort of people they want themselves and their children to be. But the results of such powers, as I say, are unpredictable. This is what more and more we may learn. And then, as we continue experimenting, we may learn humility, and wonder.'

He was silent for a time, biting his lip and looking down at the ground. Eventually Joshua said 'You mean, we may learn through failure; even disaster?'

Andros said 'Either that, or we will have learned a new style.'

After another silence, in which the embarrassment in the room seemed to be occasioned by the presence of someone perhaps mentally ill, Joshua said 'Such as –'

Andros stood up abruptly. He said 'Well let's call it a dance. In honour of art, of skill, of enlightenment. In honour of wonder.' Then he walked out of the room.

Joshua smiled briefly and as if apologetically to the people in the room. Then he followed Andros.

Out in the street Andros said 'Sorry about that.'

Joshua said 'I thought it went rather well.'

'One does stop being able to bear the sound of one's own voice.'

'You didn't bring in God.'

'No, they've got to work that out for themselves.'

They were walking through streets that were similar to the ones in which Andros had bumped into Maisie some time ago – raucous with lures and advertisements for sex, and with people standing and drinking outside pubs. As Joshua walked, maintaining his usual rather formal distance from Andros, he was thinking – It's all very well to say that one can't plan the future, but Andros and I have been friends for some time now and we still haven't done or said anything about sex. And Andros has his commodious flat, and I am fed up with staying in cheap hotels. I suppose he knows that it's Dario I am in love with, and I suppose he is a bit too: but we have both of

266

us chosen not to live with Dario, and so why should not something evolve from that?

Andros said 'Let's go in here.'

They had come to the outside of a pub that seemed more quiet and old-fashioned than most in the area, with windows of etched glass. But when they were inside they realised that the customers were only men. Andros thought with amusement – But I have taken him to a gay bar! Will he think I have done this on purpose or by chance? He said 'Oh dear.'

Joshua said 'I like this place. Let me buy you a drink.'

He went to the bar leaving Andros at a table. He thought – Perhaps this will be a catalyst: has he come here on purpose, or by chance?

As he was returning to Andros with their drinks there was a man with a small black moustache entering the pub with a group who looked like bodyguards. They settled at a table next to Joshua and Andros. When he saw Joshua he said 'Well well well, here's the poncy film director!'

Joshua knew he had seen the man before but could not at first remember where. Then he recognised him as the man on the Heath who had been trying to blackmail or to beat up Dario.

The man with the moustache said 'He takes films of small boys.'

One of the men who was with him said 'Does he now!'

'And in public, too. Au naturel you know.'

Andros said in a camp voice 'Oh I'd like to see those.' And to Joshua 'Why haven't you shown them to me?'

Joshua wondered – You mean, you may know how to handle this?

The man with the moustache said to the man at his table 'Did you hear that, Mick?'

Joshua said to Andros, 'What, you with your heart condition?'

Andros said 'Oh the old ticker can still take a bit of tock.'

The man with the moustache said to Joshua 'You haven't

267

got your fucking film crew here. I don't believe you ever had a fucking film crew.'

The man called Mick said 'We don't like fucking peedifillies.'

Andros said loudly 'Then why don't you suck your mother's cock.'

The man called Mick jumped up and punched Andros on the side of the head. Andros toppled over backwards in his chair still in a sitting position. The man with the moustache shouted 'That's the wrong bugger!'

Joshua shouted 'He's got Rotblatt's degenerative heart disease! You've probably killed him!'

The man called Mick said 'No one's going to say that about my mother!' He made as if to kick Andros on the ground.

The man with the moustache said 'Hold it, Mick!'

Andros lay back on the ground and closed his eyes. He murmured, 'Kiss me Laurel.'

Joshua shouted 'Murder! Get an ambulance!'

A man came out from behind the bar and said 'Get him out of here!'

Joshua knelt by Andros. He was thinking – If I can get him back to his flat, then I can stay and look after him. And we won't have manipulated it!

The man with the moustache said 'Is this another of your fucking tricks?'

The man who had come from behind the bar said 'And I want you lot out, now, quick.'

Joshua yelled 'Don't let them go!'

The man with the moustache and the man called Mick hurried to the door and out into the street.

Joshua and the man from behind the bar lifted Andros up onto a chair. Andros was saying 'No, I'm all right.'

The man from the bar said 'You're not all right till I've got you out of here too.'

Andros said 'That's probably true.'

Joshua said 'You were wonderful!'

The man from the bar said 'Get a taxi.'

Andros said to Joshua 'Perhaps we could go to my place. You could stay there.'

Joshua said 'That would be very nice.'

Andros said 'But what an experiment!'

# XLI

When Maurice had left Professor Nathan in the café in the
Armenian quarter of Jerusalem's Old City he went to look for
his wife Linda who was the other person he wanted to see
before he made a further move to get to where people he had
known would not find him. He telephoned Linda's office at
the Institute of Cognitive Psychology, and a voice told him
that she was working at an archaeological site at the base of
Temple Mount. Maurice said 'What is it that's there?' The
voice said 'There are tunnels dug at the time of King
Zedekiah to provide supply routes or escape routes in or out
of the city.' Maurice said 'Yes, I see.' The voice continued as
if it were a recording on a machine – 'At the moment the
political situation is such that work on the site has been
postponed because of the security risk.' Maurice thought –
You mean with her cognitive psychology she's studying
escape routes in and out of the brain?

Maurice went on a detour through the new town to reach
the far side of the Old City. He noticed how many people
were holding mobile phones to their ears: it was as if they
were protecting themselves from a plague of locusts. Mobile
phones were still a fairly new phenomenon, but they seemed
to have taken hold with particular vehemence in Israel.
Maurice thought – They were building up a tower to heaven
here and already it is Babel.

At the entrance to the site there were security guards who would not at first let him through. Then a colleague of Linda's appeared and recognised him and said 'What on earth are you doing here?' He said 'What are any of us doing here?' The woman said 'Linda's down one of the tunnels doing God knows what. No one for sure can do anything with her.' Maurice said 'Can you get them to let me through?' The woman said 'These tunnels are unsafe, that's why they've closed them.' Maurice said 'Then tell them I'll be trying to get her out.' He was thinking – Perhaps I might join her?

The woman got him authorisation to go through, and she lent him a torch. Maurice went crouching down the low-roofed tunnel. He thought – Now let me guess: she is studying sensory deprivation, oh yes. Or she wants to find the resting place of the Ark of the Covenant and she doesn't know what she's doing, she wants to find a new covenant. Did they have any idea of what they were doing at the time of King Zedekiah? The roof of the tunnel was crumbling. He thought – Or it seems more likely that we'll end up entombed like those boring lovers in *Aida*. He had never quite stopped feeling married to Linda: they had separated when it had seemed that they had had different tasks to do; then they perhaps each in their different ways had found these tasks impossible. That might have been a reason to have stayed together? But would it not have been giving up, if they had stayed together?

The light from his torch was lurching ahead of him down the tunnel like a ghost. He thought – What does the mind do when it is deprived of sensation? Does it start eating itself? Knowing itself? Having a conversation with itself? People were thought to have been having a conversation between the two halves of the brain when in the old days they were under the impression they were being spoken to by gods. They would now be thought mad. Linda's voice came out of the darkness: 'Is that you?' Maurice thought – We may be mad? Linda's voice said 'I thought it was you!'

His torch flickered over and lit up an alcove that had been hollowed out from the side of the tunnel, perhaps originally as a storeroom or a place where people carrying loads in opposite directions could pass. It seemed to have been fitted up now as a makeshift living space, with a low camp bed on which Linda was sitting, some basic cooking equipment and what seemed to be containers for food and water. There was also a computer and what looked like electronic equipment for recording sound waves or radiation. Linda said 'Oh do turn that thing off! I'll light the lamp.'

He turned the torch off and in the darkness she stood, and they embraced as they used to do by putting their cheeks together briefly first on one side and then on the other. Maurice felt suddenly, with an impression like an electric shock, that he was on the edge of something huge and unearthly. What had been those old people's impressions of gods and goddesses?

He said 'That's the sort of thing you've been doing here?'

'What?'

'Wondering if you'd know if it was me.'

She had pulled away from him, and she was striking a match and lighting a hurricane lamp that hung from the ceiling. Maurice thought – It is as if she is inserting some new material into an embryo. She said 'Well someone did think they had seen you.'

When she turned to him he saw that the soft skin of her face had become etched with innumerable faint lines, but her features in middle age had kept their beauty. She had no make-up; her fair hair was cut short and roughly as if just to keep it out of her eyes and to protect her head.

He said 'Can you get the electronic stuff to work here?'

'I brought batteries, but I don't use them.'

'What was the stuff supposed to do?'

'Guess.'

'With noise, radiation, cut out, measure what might be generated by your own mental activity?'

'Oh you would get it right!'

'I'm cheating. Nathan mentioned something.'

'What does he know!'

'Does it work?'

'None of that sort of thing can be measured. It's there, but it's not scientific. They can't find out much about it with animals or birds, let alone humans.'

'If you measure it it ceases.'

'Yes.' She had sat down again on the camp bed. He was standing above her, looking down. She said 'Your brain has its radiations, and if they're not drowned by noise they might be received by other brains. But I don't think we're adapted to that sort of thing. We communicate best not even by speech, but by making things.'

'Like before Babel.'

'Yes.'

'As if we were on our own.'

'Which we are. But then not if we're making things.'

'Like those people who made drawings in caves.'

Linda was watching him as if she were intent on memorising the contours and shadows of his face so that she could make a drawing of him when he had gone.

He said 'So what have you been making.'

'You and I, we never quite accepted how this works.'

'Oh well we did, except that we wanted to alter things.'

'I've thought of forging a document, supposedly from the time of King Zedekiah, that might alter things.'

'Now that's an idea. What would you say?'

'What would you? That's more your sort of thing.'

Maurice had begun to lower himself gingerly on to the far end of the camp bed on which Linda was sitting. He said 'Pull your fingers out. Grow up. You're supposed to be responsible for everything.'

The bed suddenly tipped; and as he tried to right himself it buckled and heaved. He and Linda were thrown first together, then apart; Maurice landed up on his back on the floor. Linda was laughing. Maurice said 'Fancy a quick one?' Linda said 'This'll do beautifully.'

When they had straightened themselves, and were sitting side by side on the rickety bed keeping close for fear of it collapsing again, Linda said 'Do you still do it with old Piss-in-Boots?'

'Why do you call her Piss-in-Boots?'

'I don't know. It seemed to suit her.'

'No, I've left. So I came to say hello and au revoir.'

'Where are you going?'

'I don't know. I've got to stop talking. Stop teaching.'

'Then you are the same as me.'

'Yes.' He was thinking – But what exactly would one say in such a document? A continuation of the book of Jonah?

She said 'I suppose I'll stay here. I mean, in Jerusalem. I've still got Nathan to talk to. And there's Dario. We don't see his father.'

'How is Dario?'

'He talks of going to England. I think he'd like you to be his father.'

'He's only, what, twelve? thirteen?'

'He's very intelligent.'

'Perhaps we should have had children.'

'It didn't happen. It doesn't matter. What will you do if you don't teach?'

He said 'About that document – what about a last chapter at the end of the book of Jonah? Where he makes up his mind to agree to be responsible for the people of Nineveh?'

'I suppose that wasn't written because people weren't ready for it.'

'Or it was written, and was censored.'

'But are people yet ready for it?'

'But what if it's been lying in the depths of the gene pool like one of those fishes with such monstrous whiskers that it can tell when a loved one is approaching along a dark tunnel at a hundred paces!'

'Dear Maurice, what would we do without you!'

'I'll write it. You fix the dating.'

'Perhaps it'll just happen. It's a beautiful idea.'

'As a matter of fact I was given the idea by a child: a niece of Nathan's.'

'Oh yes, I know her.'

'And they are the most beautiful fishes that have hardly yet been seen, at the bottom of the sea!'

# XLII

Richard Kahn sat in his hired car at the side of a road over one of the hills that overlooked the Sea of Galilee. He had thought he would stay here till the sun went down, and in the meantime he could listen to the news on the radio. He had seen the people he had wanted to see in Jerusalem and Tel Aviv; he was reluctant to hurry back to Beirut because there might still be no news of Hafiz – or, with increasing probability, news that he would not want to hear. And now that he was in Israel – perhaps for the last time, the way things were going – he wanted to take the opportunity to visit some of the places that had meant much to him in the past.

The people in Tel Aviv had told him that the Americans had carried out more air strikes against installations in Iraq, and now reports and rumours were increasing of the likelihood of a massive terrorist strike against America. On the West Bank and in Gaza there was ever-escalating retaliatory violence which it seemed nothing would mitigate except all-out war. In Europe a meeting of world leaders had been attacked by anti-capitalists who had themselves been savaged by police; there was a new computer game with this theme on the market. Richard thought – What will I say to my students when I get back to the university? In a context in which people are supposed to have almost limitless freedom to enjoy what they like, to choose what they like, what they go for is violence and suffering. I have said that God is a guarantor of our freedom; what if God gets fed up?

Would it be any use now to say – Our freedom is only of any value if we have the chance of coming up against what we do not like – or may not know we like – and so we have a chance to learn?

When Richard had left Tel Aviv he had tried to contact Joshua in London but he could only get Joshua's answering service. He thought – Perhaps the structure of Babel is breaking down. He had wanted to ask Joshua if he had any news of Hafiz; but why should Joshua have news of Hafiz? Was he, Richard, falling into the trap of assuming that by pressing buttons and speaking into a machine he was doing anything more than trying to reassure himself?

He was glad to be having this time on the hillside: the evening light was so beautiful! The water on the lake was still and burnished as if it might be a surface on which one could walk – though yes, it would be slippery, and if one made a false step one might fall as if through ice. This hillside was a place of true and quiet sacredness: so different from the cacophony of the towns. Richard had been listening with part of his attention to the news. There was a voice saying that in the not-so-unconscious reasoning of the anti-capitalist rioters they would soon have attracted enough attention to think it worth becoming capitalists themselves: that the real danger to capitalism was from religious fundamentalists with bombs or chemical weapons.

Richard turned the radio off and got out of the car; whatever happens in the world would surely happen without any intervention from him. Or had Maurice been right that one should at least make gestures? that there were resonances from individual effort that went out like radio waves round the world, however difficult it was for anyone to believe this – even for him, Richard, who would wish to. This hillside was a place to which he had once come with Maurice years ago as a tourist – was this why he had come again now? His journey to Jerusalem, his talk with Professor Nathan, had stirred in him again the impression that the story of Maurice was one still waiting to be filled in, filled out. What might have happened to Maurice had become the stuff of legend – which he, Richard, had played some part in promulgating. But then, what was the force of legends?

There was a monastery across a valley on the top of an adjacent hill: it was behind a high wall at the outside of which in the old days there were likely to have been busloads of tourists. For some time now these had been scarce – this was a territory around which there hung a fear of violence as if it might be a contagious disease. Yet this place had once been the focus of such hope and heroism! Surely fear should not be a reason for travellers to shun it. Richard went down towards the valley. Perhaps at some time he might like to enter a monastery. Was this what Maurice had done? At the moment he, Richard, was missing Leila. But now that his leg was mended, would it be right for Leila to stay with him? He did not feel it was his task to become domesticated and settle down.

Richard lay on the grass on the slope of the hill and looked down towards the lake. The sun was setting behind him and was making a path on the water like a red carpet for a king. There was a lone figure by the lake: this was unusual: people did not go out alone in this landscape now. The figure was still; it was looking out over the water as if in meditation or prayer. He must be a monk from the monastery, Richard thought, who had got special dispensation to make a lone obeisance to God in this way. This was what he, Richard, would like to do if he became a monk – let his mind, heart, roam like a scanner to pick up resonances that might otherwise be unheard. Or if there were none, then to offer up some resonance himself – without needing assurance that it would be heard.

The figure by the lake had bowed his head as the sun went

278

down; it was as if the red-gold carpet was being rolled out in front of him. Then he turned and began to move up the valley between the hill on which there was the monastery and the slope on which Richard sat. Maurice might indeed have retreated to a monastery such as this – as protection against imagined or real threats against him, or more realistically as a way of resolving tensions in his life that had seemed to have become unbearable. He would be an old man by now; he had sometimes talked with approval of the Hindu idea that towards the end of his life a man should hand over his worldly goods and aspirations to his dependants and become a beggar: this would be both in preparation for death, and to show respect to life which had to be carried on by others. But it was more likely, Richard had felt, that if Maurice was alive and free he would have gone to one of the villages in the northern hills he had talked about. The old man moving up the valley at an angle to Richard had a long white beard; the cowl of his habit was thrown back; he raised his head to look at the sky; he was like a vision from an earlier time when people naturally saw visions. Richard thought – Now they imagine they see reality?

But he wondered, if Maurice were alive now, what message he would want to give to the world. Jesus had not said much in his last messages: his brief announcement about the coming of the Holy Spirit had not been paid much attention to. The disciples had been left with the impression that Jesus would soon be coming again to the world to dispense order and justice, and when this had not happened there had been confusion and misunderstanding. How would Maurice see things now if he had spent the last seven years in a monastery? – Of course there is no settled order and justice! But is there evidence of a spirit?

Could anyone make up this sort of story?

Richard sometimes regretted the story he had told of the sticks or bones he had found in a cellar; he had not foreseen how the story would be taken up. Of course it was conceivable the sticks might have been bones! and people anyway believed what they wished to believe. But still, as Maurice had so often said, stories were true when they stood up alongside reality. Oh yes, one could blather on about what was reality.

The old monk – for this Richard was now sure was what the figure was – had now reached a place in the valley between the darkening hillside where Richard sat and the path which would take him up the opposite hill to the monastery. He stopped and turned and regarded Richard. Richard at this moment became overwhelmed by the impression – But this is Maurice! I know it! Why should it not be Maurice? He took refuge in this monastery which he had felt friendly towards before, and he is now an old man with a white beard. Naturally I did not recognise him at first, but he recognised me who have not so much changed; but I recognise him now! Richard raised his head and opened his mouth as if to speak, but no sound came out. He thought – I am like a young bird wanting to be fed with a fish.

The old man bowed slightly, then turned with his back to Richard and went on up towards the monastery. Richard thought of calling after him: but he thought – He did acknowledge me, and that is what matters. And then very quickly – Of course this is absurd.

But he need not make up a story? It had happened. He could say –

– I was outside a monastery on a hill by the Sea of Galilee and I thought I saw Maurice Rotblatt. Oh make of it what you will! I know it's almost certainly impossible. The person I imagined was Maurice just paused, seemed to give me a sign of recognition, then went on up the hill. But I did feel a sort of enlightenment. This is what matters. It seemed we were both people who were coming into the possession of the keys of our house.

# XLIII

Laura returned to her home from London where she had been seeing Andros and trying to find news of Maisie and attending lectures on cognitive psychology. She found Dario in the room assigned to him seated in front of a desk-top computer and a printer. He said 'There's quite a lot coming in. Who started this site, do you know?' Laura said 'Wasn't it Richard Kahn in Beirut?' Dario said 'He and Maurice had this plan? They thought they could influence things?' Laura said 'I don't think Maurice thought that the Net would ever be much except noise. But of course he often said that randomness can have a life of its own.'

'But people wouldn't see this unless they wanted to? They'd only hear the noise?'

'And what is randomness!'

Laura leaned with her hands on the back of Dario's chair. On the screen there had come up –

Ancient documents are said to have come to light as the result of an explosion and a fall of rock in one of the tunnels being excavated under Temple Mount. These tunnels are being explored with the intention of their one day being opened up as a tourist attraction. On the other hand it is not known if the explosion might have been the result of terrorist activity.

Laura said 'What ancient documents?'
'It doesn't say.'
'But what do the documents say?'
'They're not saying that either.'
Dario clicked and on the screen there came up –

The identity of the archaeological student who is said to have stumbled on this document is being withheld under security restrictions. Professor Nathan, retired Professor of Comparative Religion at the University of Jerusalem, is reported to have said – Of course such documents are likely to be forgeries. On the other hand it is possible that they are being kept under wraps because they give backing to views at present inimical to the ruling forces in this country and others.

Dario said 'What does it mean – "and others"?'
Laura said 'But Maurice knew Nathan! They used to correspond. Nathan was a maverick. He used to say that religions had been turned into brands. Maurice would have loved this. He'd have seen Nathan if he'd gone to Jerusalem.'
'You still think he might have done?'
'But someone must have a theory about what the documents are supposed to have said.'
'I'll try.'
Dario manipulated the computer. Laura wandered away. She sat in an armchair and took her shoes off. She said 'It sounds like the Dead Sea Scrolls.' Then – 'I think "and others" means that no one wants to upset the apple cart. To get the apples back on the trees.'
'That was a saying of Maurice's?'
'Yes.'
'Could we get in touch with Nathan?'

'He wouldn't have e-mail. But I could try Melissa. She said they might be going to Jerusalem.'

'Is she the one who's having a baby on Mount Ararat?'

'No she's the mother of the one who's had a baby on Mount Ararat.'

'But look at this.' He held out to Laura a piece of paper that seemed to have emerged from the printer. When Laura did not take it, he read aloud –

The idea that every individual would be linked up to such digital machinery that, at the touch of a button, one could view what one liked, order what one liked, and in time indeed get machines to do almost any task that one liked, has been seen as a triumph for freedom of choice. But in fact it is the opposite: because in these conditions how could one discover what one liked? There would be available only what was manufactured and provided by programmers and technicians: so that the mass of people themselves would have become themselves like machines.

Laura said 'But this is just what we've been saying!'

Dario said 'Indeed.'

'You mean this is randomness? Not randomness?'

'Well it's as if something knows what it's doing.' He read –

However, the system would give opportunities for those subtle and wise enough to take advantage of it and not to fall prey to it. For they would be moving freely in a world in which what they come up against would be likely to be mechanical. And so it would be up to them to use such means in relation to it, such blandishment or weapons, as are specifically human.

Laura said 'Well we're not doing too badly.'

Dario said 'Do you know that problem about how to devise a test by which, if a person was isolated in a room but was in contact with just a voice, he or she would be able to tell whether they were conversing with a human, or the most skilfully programmed machine?'

'Well, how would they?'

'I can't remember. I thought you might know.'

'No. Something to do with seeing connections?'

'But humorous connections? A machine couldn't tell what's funny?'

'Perhaps witty. I don't think a machine could be programmed to be witty. Maurice used to say that he thought that God was witty.'

'Wit can be cruel.'

'Indeed.'

'Freud wasn't witty even when he was writing about jokes.'

'You think Freud was a machine?'

'Well he tried to be scientific.'

'Dear Dario, you're so well-read.'

'And we're both so witty.'

Dario tapped some more keys on the computer which led it to play a faint jangling tune. Laura sat up and leaned with her elbows on her knees.

She said 'I saw Andros in London. They're coming down here.'

'Andros and Joshua? When?'

'Any time now. They'd like to come and stay. In London they seem to think they're being pursued by malignant homosexuals.'

'I expect those are the puritan parts of themselves.'

'Dear Dario, that's witty.'

'They'll need to be chaperoned.'

'Well you'll do that, Dario.'

Laura stood up and moved around the room. She said 'It appears that Andros spent a weekend with Maisie in Paris, and then bought her a train ticket to Istanbul.'

'A *train* ticket to Istanbul?'

'Apparently that was what she wanted.'

'Is Andros back in the closet?'

'I don't know what is in or out.'

'I knew someone who could only do it in the closets of trains.'

'Dear Dario, you are disgusting.'

'You couldn't tell by that that he wasn't a machine?'

'I shouldn't think so, no.'

'Oh and look. This came through on your e-mail.' Dario clicked, and manipulated, and then read out – 'Dear Laura, I cannot raise you. Have you got your mobile switched off?'

Laura said 'Who's that? Melissa?'

'She's the one on Mount Ararat?'

'Well, metaphorically on Mount Ararat.'

'And we think Maisie might be on her way there?'

'But not to have a baby!'

'Why not to have a baby? And don't we think Maurice might be on Mount Ararat?'

'Where exactly is it, for God's sake?'

'It's where the Ark came down.'

'That I know.'

Laura had come and stood behind Dario and they were both watching the screen. Laura put a hand on Dario's shoulder. She was thinking – Dear Dario, if we go on like this, I'll have to inveigle you back into, or is it out of, the closet.

There was the sound of a car arriving on the drive outside. Dario said 'Oh God, is it them?' He tipped his chair so far back to look out of the window that he lost his balance. He toppled backwards and flung his arms about wildly. Laura reached out and caught him as he fell to the floor. She was pulled down on top of him, and lay there. Dario said 'At last!' Laura said 'I did say I do love you!' There were the noises of car doors opening and closing; then Andros's voice saying 'Coo-ee!' Laura murmured 'Coo-ee!' Dario said 'But they should have counted up to a hundred!'

# XLIV

When Hafiz and Maisie emerged into the street on the evening of the fourth day of having been holed up in Richard Kahn's flat, they each had the impression that they were coming into a world that they had not properly noticed before. The people in the street – what oddities! – so intent on what they were doing, and yet what on earth did they think this was? Hafiz and Maisie were trying to act normally – but in this context what was normal? – to move as if haphazardly, and yet to follow trajectories imposed by the programming of their minds? Would Maisie and Hafiz have to learn the customs of this strange tribe? They had discussed whether they should go out separately or together: if the apartment was being watched, it would be better to split up, not to be apprehended together. Or had the whole business of the policemen been a joke? They decided to go a certain distance hand in hand; then if all had gone well they would separate – Hafiz to go to Leila's nightclub to see if he could find Leila and discover what was happening: Maisie to the police station to ask about her passport. So they walked in the street like lovers; and like this would they stand out, or would people be too taken up with their obsessions to notice them? In the flat they had spent so many hours together in the half dark that it seemed to them that they had generated a glow like that of fishes that live in the deep sea; or something that would brush off from them like pollen. Maisie had begun to wonder if she were pregnant.

Hafiz said 'But you will be all right at the police station on your own?'

Maisie said 'The man with the scar on his chin must be very attractive?'

'Are you not anxious that I may fall in love again with Leila?'

'That will keep me thinking of you while you are away.'

'We do need your passport.'

'Oh yes, we're going to the Red Sea.'

They stopped on a corner, and put their arms round one another. A stream of people flowed past them as if they were a rock.

When Maisie left him Hafiz recalled a conversation he had had with her – The Red Sea was where Egyptians were drowned. – Is it called Red because there was so much blood? – I don't know: it's a place for honeymoons.

Hafiz reached the nightclub just as some of the evening staff were arriving – cleaners and cooks to start preparing food. He found Leila sitting at the bar staring at the ceiling as if entranced or drunk. He said 'Oh I'm so glad I've found you! Was it you who was so angelic as to have brought us that food?'

She said 'What's this strange way of speaking you've fallen into!'

'I was afraid you might have been wanting to stay at the flat.'

'But you two looked so angelic! And I've been all right staying here. I've been fine! Euphoric!'

'I'm so glad!' He thought – And I don't mean sorry –

– Though I suppose I would have liked just once to have made love to you.

She said 'Have you seen Richard?'

'No, is he back?'

'Yes. And he's had some mystic revelation.'

'Is that why he didn't come to the flat?'

'He thought he saw Maurice Rotblatt on the side of a hill.'

'That's another of his stories?'

'Well he's just saying he had the impression that that is what he saw.'

'And why have you been euphoric?'

'I'm going to marry Leon.'

'Oh I see.'

'I thought there was a time when you'd be put out by that.'

'Indeed there was.'

'So where did you find her?'

'In the café across the road from the apartment building.'

'Leon wants to have children.'

'Oh yes, we've discussed that too.'

'So aren't we lucky.'

'But what about Richard?'

'Well Richard's had his revelation. I can't really see Richard wanting to have children, can you?'

'No.'

'As a matter of fact I think I'm pregnant. I must have been pregnant for quite a while.'

'Have you told Richard?'

'He didn't seem surprised. He's gone to see Leon.'

'Ah.'

'No, he seems more interested in some Israeli girl who's disappeared.'

'What Israeli girl who's disappeared?'

'She's been missing for some time. Oh yes, you've been out of touch. Richard was asked to try to find out about her by someone in Jerusalem.'

'Where's Richard? I must see Richard!'

'I told you, he's gone to see Leon.'

'Oh yes, but I thought you meant about you.'

'She's not your girl, is she?'

'No. But there was another one.'

'What do you mean, another one?'

'I've been hoping to God she's all right.'

'You look as if you've had a mystic revelation.'

'Well so I have, in a way. And so do you.'

'I'm fed up with being a dancer. I want to have babies.'

Hafiz thought – A mystic revelation seems to be the experience that in spite of, or because of, wild uncertainty, everything is all right.

In the police station Maisie found a man who knew about her passport and said he would get it for her. When he returned he was with one of the policemen who had come to Richard Kahn's flat. He said 'Captain Leon would like to see you.'

Maisie said 'And I'd like to see Captain Leon. Thanks.'

The policeman led her up some stairs and along a corridor to another part of the building. Maisie was thinking – But can one live forever like this? As if the balloon has landed and one is within all the shapes and patterns on the ground.

In a small office on a top floor there was a desk and computer equipment and two comfortable chairs in one of which was seated a large grey-haired man with a scar on his chin, and in the other a slightly smaller man with curly brown hair and holding a stick between his knees. Maisie thought – That must be Richard Kahn. Both men stood up when she came in. The man she thought was Richard said 'You don't know me, but you've been staying in my flat.'

Maisie said 'Yes I'm sorry, but I was asked to give you a message as soon as you got in.'

'That's all right. But what was the message?'

'I was also told it was all right to say it in front of Captain Leon.' Maisie waited.

The others stared at her for a moment. Then Leon gestured to the man who had accompanied Maisie, and the man went out of the room.

Maisie said 'The message was – I think they are up to something, but no one seems to know exactly what, so we can probably say what we like.' Then – 'I'm not sure if I've got that last bit quite right, but that was the gist.'

'We can say what we like –'

'Yes. I suppose that means what we think best.'

'Yes. This message was from Hafiz?'

'Yes.'

'And what does Hafiz think is for the best?'

'I'm not sure. But as he's here now you can ask him.'

'Hafiz is back?'

Leon said 'I told you.'

'Did you? There's too much happening.'

Maisie said 'I suppose it means that whatever we do will be for the best.'

'I suppose it does. Where is Hafiz now?'

'He's gone to see Leila at the club.'

First Richard, and then Captain Leon, seemed about to say something; and then stopped. Maisie said 'I wondered if I could have my passport.'

Leon said 'Oh yes, you can have your passport.' And then to Richard – 'What was it that you could say what you liked about?'

'Oh, that weapon they were supposed to be testing.'

'You know there are stories that there is something happening.'

'Yes I know.' Richard stood up. He said 'And I suppose people are saying what they like about this girl.' He turned to Maisie. 'Not you. Another girl.'

Maisie said 'I see.'

'There's a girl disappeared some time ago in Jerusalem.'

Leon stood up. He opened a drawer in his desk and handed Maisie her passport.

Maisie said 'Thank you.' Then – 'Can we go and see Hafiz?'

Leon said 'Yes let's.'

Richard said 'Yes indeed.'

On their way out of the building Maisie was thinking –

There's a girl disappeared some time ago in Jerusalem? She is the one that it is important she is all right?

When they were in the street Richard suddenly stopped and turned to Maisie who had almost bumped into him and he seemed about to say something; but then he did not.

They moved on and almost bumped into Leon, who had stopped and was staring at something across the road.

Hafiz and Leila were at the far side of the road. When they all saw each other there was a moment as if they were all alarmed. Then Leila and Hafiz began crossing the road.

Maisie thought, as she had thought before – They are like a brother and sister.

Leila and Richard embraced. They remained quite still. The others stood around watching.

Eventually Leila left Richard and stood by Captain Leon. Maisie went to Hafiz and held his hand. Leila said, looking at Richard who was on his own 'I cannot bear it if you are not all right!' Richard said 'Of course I am, if everything is all right.'

Maisie wondered – This is a state of grace?

# XLV

Ben and Julie and Ben's father and mother were on a hillside overlooking the Red Sea. An overhanging rock formed a cave which sheltered them from the heat of the sun. They were seated on rugs on the ground and had been having a picnic. Gaby was holding the baby.

Ben said 'But when was this supposed to have happened? Two or three months ago?'

His mother said 'It seems so.'

'What exactly was it that Laura said?' And then to Julie 'Mum's got this friend in England called Laura who keeps in touch.'

Melissa said 'She said there's been this stuff in the papers about a girl in Jerusalem who disappeared. She's thought to have been kidnapped.'

'I didn't see it.'

'You weren't seeing any papers.'

'Yes we were at the site.'

Gaby said 'That was me.'

Ben's father said 'What?'

Julie said 'Well the baby's just two months old.'

Gaby was sitting cross-legged and looking down at the baby on her lap. Ben was thinking – She's become a sort of icon.

Ben's father was thinking – There should be a film of this: not just of the tunnel, the fall of rock, the birth of the baby: but of wars and the rumours of wars; of the chance of everyone being wiped out, and this getting closer.

He said 'Gaby, the sensible thing for you to do would be to go back to Jerusalem and tell them what happened, or all you can remember of what happened. Say you were knocked on the head and then drugged, and that's all you can remember. Then we may find out more of what actually happened.'

Ben said 'How would that be finding out what actually happened?'

Julie said 'And why should Gaby want to do what's sensible?'

Ben's father said 'Exactly.'

He was thinking – Well all right, the chance of seeds on the wind: the fish leaping up waterfalls.

Melissa looked from one to another. She was thinking – I suppose I thank God you are like children.

She said 'But we've all got to go home. To settle down. Gaby can't stay a refugee for ever. She hasn't got any papers.'

Julie said 'She is a refugee. I am a refugee.'

Ben said 'Mum, you and Laura can charm those old men. You can get her some papers.'

Melissa said 'And anyway, Gaby, you don't want to go back, do you?'

Gaby said 'I'd like to let my family know that I am alive.'

'Yes. But they may try to keep you.'

'They might try to disown me. I'd like to let the man who rescued me know that I am alive.'

'You don't even know his name.'

'I don't think that matters.'

Ben thought – An icon is something that makes sense without it needing to be known what the sense is?

Julie said 'And then you can come with us.'

Ben's father was looking down the slope towards the Red

293

Sea. He thought – All those Egyptians in pursuit and then – lo and behold! – the waters not coming down!

He said 'There should be a film. Or anyway a story. About the proximity of war. The prevalence of war. But then about it not being this that really matters.'

He seemed to be waiting for someone to ask a question, but when they did not he went on – 'I mean a state of mind. How to live with it. To deal with it.'

Melissa said 'To deal with what?'

'Uncertainty. Seeing the point of it. Of what turns up.'

'You can make a film about that?'

Julie said 'Is that what you meant, Gaby?'

Gaby frowned, and looked down towards the sea.

Melissa said 'There was another story from Laura. That some old document has been discovered in a tunnel under Temple Mount.'

Ben said 'What old document? Who discovered it?'

'They were excavating. There was some sort of explosion.'

Ben's father said 'What?'

Gaby said 'Well I don't think that was me!' She smiled.

Julie said 'Could it have been you, Gaby?'

Ben's father said 'But what did the document say?'

Melissa said 'They're saying it's a forgery.'

'Of course they're saying it's a forgery.'

'Why?'

Ben said 'Perhaps it's the lost chapter of the book of Jonah.'

They seemed to be slightly embarrassed by this. The sun was setting. It was making a blood-red path across the water.

Julie said 'Gaby, if you met your Arab friend now, what would you say to him?'

Gaby said 'Nothing.'

'Nothing?'

'He would know.'

Ben said 'Know that everything is all right?'

Gaby said nothing.

Julie said 'Would you want to stay with him?'

294

'No.'

They waited, gazing at Gaby. Then Gaby said 'I mean, I would be with him in a way.'

They had begun to pack up their picnic things. They stood like nomads carrying rugs, bags, baby.

Melissa said 'Oh yes, the latest message from Laura, on my answering service, was that if we're not in the hotel now, when we get back we should watch television, for something that's happening in America.'

Ben's father said 'In America?'

'Some event. Some terror. That might change the way people see things.'

'She didn't say any more?'

'No. We have to see it for ourselves.'

'Well that might make sense.'

They set off down the hill towards their hotel. There was the red carpet on the water as if one might walk across it. Ben's father was thinking – You mean this might be the beginning of what Nietzsche called 'the great hundred-act play reserved for the next two centuries in Europe; the most terrible, the most questionable, the most hopeful of all plays'? Have I got that quotation right? It was made over a hundred year ago! So it's been going on, but now we'll see it? Not just the war between Jews and Arabs, because that has never been hidden: nor the war between capitalists and anti-capitalists, because that will go on for ever. But the drama about evil not being localised but pervasive, and people being trapped in their minds, and whether or not there is anything that an individual can do about this. The hope being that there can be a learning, a healing, going to and fro between the inside and the outside worlds; the terror being that this is an illusion.

They were on their way back to the hotel, which they would be leaving the next day – to set off to try to arrange papers for Gaby, to find the best way of letting her family know she was alive and well, without too much pressure being put upon her to do what she did not think it right to do. But there was an extraordinary sense of rightness about Gaby now: that of someone who feels they have been and maybe still are in God's hands. Julie and Ben had said they would go with Gaby to see her family; but they had assured her that they would just stand (this was Julie's image) like figures on the walls of the churches that they all three remembered.

The others had gone on ahead. Ben's father was following. He was not thinking any longer of a story or a film, but of a war in heaven which either could or could not be influenced by an individual. Also of what could possibly be the vision of an event which might offer them a chance of seeing things differently?

The others had reached a turning point in their path and had stopped; they were looking in the direction of where a branch-path joined it. Here two figures who had been coming down this path had also stopped; they were a young man and a young woman holding hands. He was dark-haired and Arab-looking: she was young and seemed unmistakably English. Gaby was in the process of handing over the baby to Julie. Julie was taking it. Gaby was going to the dark-haired man and was kneeling down in front of him. The young man had let go of the young woman's hand and was trying to lift Gaby. Then he too knelt, facing Gaby, and leaned so that their foreheads were just touching. There was such energy between them!

The others, including Ben's father and the newly arrived young woman, stood around, watching. They were like people observing a huge and fragile and immensely valuable painting being lifted high into place. Ben's father was thinking – Yes that is exactly right! I mean people will see that it is right! Then the two kneeling figures stood and stepped back from one another. Maisie went to Hafiz and held his hand again: Gaby rejoined Ben and Julie and Melissa. They all remained looking at the ground where the figures had knelt, as if it was a nest from which fledglings had flown. Ben's father thought – And this is happening!

# LANNAN SELECTIONS

The Lannan Foundation, located in Santa Fe, New Mexico, is a family foundation whose funding focuses on special cultural projects and ideas which promote and protect cultural freedom, diversity, and creativity.

The literary aspect of Lannan's cultural program supports the creation and presentation of exceptional English-language literature and develops a wider audience for poetry, fiction, and nonfiction.

Since 1990, the Lannan Foundation has supported Dalkey Archive Press projects in a variety of ways, including monetary support for authors, audience development programs, and direct funding for the publication of the Press's books.

In the year 2000, the Lannan Selections Series was established to promote both organizations' commitment to the highest expressions of literary creativity. The Foundation supports the publication of this series of books each year, and works closely with the Press to ensure that these books will reach as many readers as possible and achieve a permanent place in literature. Authors whose works have been published as Lannan Selections include: Ishmael Reed, Stanley Elkin, Ann Quin, Nicholas Mosley, William Eastlake, and David Antin, among others.

# SELECTED DALKEY ARCHIVE PAPERBACKS

PIERRE ALBERT-BIROT, *Grabinoulor.*
YUZ ALESHKOVSKY, *Kangaroo.*
FELIPE ALFAU, *Chromos.*
  *Locos.*
  *Sentimental Songs.*
IVAN ÂNGELO, *The Celebration.*
ALAN ANSEN, *Contact Highs: Selected Poems 1957-1987.*
DAVID ANTIN, *Talking.*
DJUNA BARNES, *Ladies Almanack.*
  *Ryder.*
JOHN BARTH, *LETTERS.*
  *Sabbatical.*
ANDREI BITOV, *Pushkin House.*
LOUIS PAUL BOON, *Chapel Road.*
ROGER BOYLAN, *Killoyle.*
CHRISTINE BROOKE-ROSE, *Amalgamemnon.*
BRIGID BROPHY, *In Transit.*
GERALD L. BRUNS,
  *Modern Poetry and the Idea of Language.*
GABRIELLE BURTON, *Heartbreak Hotel.*
MICHEL BUTOR,
  *Portrait of the Artist as a Young Ape.*
JULIETA CAMPOS, *The Fear of Losing Eurydice.*
ANNE CARSON, *Eros the Bittersweet.*
CAMILO JOSÉ CELA, *The Hive.*
LOUIS-FERDINAND CÉLINE, *Castle to Castle.*
  *London Bridge.*
  *North.*
  *Rigadoon.*
HUGO CHARTERIS, *The Tide Is Right.*
JEROME CHARYN, *The Tar Baby.*
MARC CHOLODENKO, *Mordechai Schamz.*
EMILY HOLMES COLEMAN, *The Shutter of Snow.*
ROBERT COOVER, *A Night at the Movies.*
STANLEY CRAWFORD, *Some Instructions to My Wife.*
ROBERT CREELEY, *Collected Prose.*
RENÉ CREVEL, *Putting My Foot in It.*
RALPH CUSACK, *Cadenza.*
SUSAN DAITCH, *L.C.*
  *Storytown.*
NIGEL DENNIS, *Cards of Identity.*
PETER DIMOCK,
  *A Short Rhetoric for Leaving the Family.*
ARIEL DORFMAN, *Konfidenz.*
COLEMAN DOWELL, *The Houses of Children.*
  *Island People.*
  *Too Much Flesh and Jabez.*
RIKKI DUCORNET, *The Complete Butcher's Tales.*
  *The Fountains of Neptune.*
  *The Jade Cabinet.*
  *Phosphor in Dreamland.*
  *The Stain.*
WILLIAM EASTLAKE, *The Bamboo Bed.*
  *Castle Keep.*
  *Lyric of the Circle Heart.*
STANLEY ELKIN, *Boswell: A Modern Comedy.*
  *Criers and Kibitzers, Kibitzers and Criers.*
  *The Dick Gibson Show.*
  *The Franchiser.*

*George Mills.*
*The MacGuffin.*
*The Magic Kingdom.*
*Mrs. Ted Bliss.*
*The Rabbi of Lud.*
*Van Gogh's Room at Arles.*
ANNIE ERNAUX, *Cleaned Out.*
LAUREN FAIRBANKS, *Muzzle Thyself.*
  *Sister Carrie.*
LESLIE A. FIEDLER,
  *Love and Death in the American Novel.*
FORD MADOX FORD, *The March of Literature.*
CARLOS FUENTES, *Terra Nostra.*
JANICE GALLOWAY, *Foreign Parts.*
  *The Trick Is to Keep Breathing.*
WILLIAM H. GASS, *The Tunnel.*
  *Willie Masters' Lonesome Wife.*
ETIENNE GILSON, *The Arts of the Beautiful.*
  *Forms and Substances in the Arts.*
C. S. GISCOMBE, *Giscome Road.*
  *Here.*
DOUGLAS GLOVER, *Bad News of the Heart.*
KAREN ELIZABETH GORDON, *The Red Shoes.*
PATRICK GRAINVILLE, *The Cave of Heaven.*
HENRY GREEN, *Blindness.*
  *Concluding.*
  *Doting.*
  *Nothing.*
JIŘÍ GRUŠA, *The Questionnaire.*
JOHN HAWKES, *Whistlejacket.*
AIDAN HIGGINS, *Flotsam and Jetsam.*
ALDOUS HUXLEY, *Antic Hay.*
  *Crome Yellow.*
  *Point Counter Point.*
  *Those Barren Leaves.*
  *Time Must Have a Stop.*
GERT JONKE, *Geometric Regional Novel.*
DANILO KIŠ, *A Tomb for Boris Davidovich.*
TADEUSZ KONWICKI, *A Minor Apocalypse.*
  *The Polish Complex.*
ELAINE KRAF, *The Princess of 72nd Street.*
JIM KRUSOE, *Iceland.*
EWA KURYLUK, *Century 21.*
VIOLETTE LEDUC, *La Bâtarde.*
DEBORAH LEVY, *Billy and Girl.*
JOSÉ LEZAMA LIMA, *Paradiso.*
OSMAN LINS, *Avalovara.*
  *The Queen of the Prisons of Greece.*
ALF MAC LOCHLAINN, *The Corpus in the Library.*
  *Out of Focus.*
RON LOEWINSOHN, *Magnetic Field(s).*
D. KEITH MANO, *Take Five.*
BEN MARCUS, *The Age of Wire and String.*
WALLACE MARKFIELD, *Teitlebaum's Window.*
  *To an Early Grave.*
DAVID MARKSON, *Reader's Block.*
  *Springer's Progress.*
  *Wittgenstein's Mistress.*

# FOR A FULL LIST OF PUBLICATIONS, VISIT:
# www.dalkeyarchive.com

CAROLE MASO,

LADISLAV MATEJ KA AND KRYSTYN… …, EDS.,
  *Readings in Russian Poetics: Formalist and*
  *Structuralist Views.*

HARRY MATHEWS, *Cigarettes.*
  *The Conversions.*
  *The Case of the Persevering Maltese: Collected Essays.*
  *The Human Country: New and Collected Stories.*
  *The Journalist.*
  *Singular Pleasures.*
  *The Sinking of the Odradek Stadium.*
  *Tlooth.*
  *20 Lines a Day.*

ROBERT L. MCLAUGHLIN, ED.,
  *Innovations: An Anthology of Modern &*
  *Contemporary Fiction.*

STEVEN MILLHAUSER, *The Barnum Museum.*
  *In the Penny Arcade.*

RALPH J. MILLS, JR., *Essays on Poetry.*

OLIVE MOORE, *Spleen.*

NICHOLAS MOSLEY, *Accident.*
  *Assassins.*
  *Catastrophe Practice.*
  *Children of Darkness and Light.*
  *The Hesperides Tree.*
  *Hopeful Monsters.*
  *Imago Bird.*
  *Impossible Object.*
  *Inventing God.*
  *Judith.*
  *Natalie Natalia.*
  *Serpent.*

WARREN F. MOTTE, JR.,
  *Oulipo: A Primer of Potential Literature.*
  *Fables of the Novel: French Fiction since 1990.*

YVES NAVARRE, *Our Share of Time.*

WILFRIDO D. NOLLEDO, *But for the Lovers.*

FLANN O'BRIEN, *At Swim-Two-Birds.*
  *The Best of Myles.*
  *The Dalkey Archive.*
  *Further Cuttings.*
  *The Hard Life.*
  *The Poor Mouth.*
  *The Third Policeman.*

CLAUDE OLLIER, *The Mise-en-Scène.*

FERNANDO DEL PASO, *Palinuro of Mexico.*

RAYMOND QUENEAU, *The Last Days.*
  *Odile.*
  *Pierrot Mon Ami.*
  *Saint Glinglin.*

ANN QUIN, *Berg.*
  *Passages.*
  *Three.*
  *Tripticks.*

ISHMAEL REED, *The Free-Lance Pallbearers.*
  *The Last Days of Louisiana Red.*
  *Reckless Eyeballing.*
  *The Terrible Threes.*

*Yellow Ba… Radio Br…k…Dr…*

JULIÁN RÍOS, *Poundemon…m.*

AUGUSTO ROA BASTOS, *I the Supreme.*

JACQUES ROUBAUD, *The Great Fire of London.*
  *Hortense in Exile.*
  *Hortense Is Abducted.*
  *The Plurality of Worlds of Lewis.*
  *The Princess Hoppy.*
  *Some Thing Black.*

LEON S. ROUDIEZ, *French Fiction Revisited.*

LUIS RAFAEL SÁNCHEZ, *Macho Camacho's Beat.*

SEVERO SARDUY, *Cobra & Maitreya.*

ARNO SCHMIDT, *Collected Stories.*
  *Nobodaddy's Children.*

CHRISTINE SCHUTT, *Nightwork.*

JUNE AKERS SEESE,
  *Is This What Other Women Feel, Too?*
  *What Waiting Really Means.*

AURELIE SHEEHAN, *Jack Kerouac Is Pregnant.*

VIKTOR SHKLOVSKY, *Theory of Prose.*
  *Third Factory.*
  *Zoo, or Letters Not about Love.*

JOSEF ŠKVORECKÝ,
  *The Engineer of Human Souls.*

CLAUDE SIMON, *The Invitation.*

GILBERT SORRENTINO, *Aberration of Starlight.*
  *Blue Pastoral.*
  *Crystal Vision.*
  *Imaginative Qualities of Actual Things.*
  *Mulligan Stew.*
  *Pack of Lies.*
  *The Sky Changes.*
  *Something Said.*
  *Splendide-Hôtel.*
  *Steelwork.*
  *Under the Shadow.*

W. M. SPACKMAN, *The Complete Fiction.*

GERTRUDE STEIN, *Lucy Church Amiably.*
  *The Making of Americans.*
  *A Novel of Thank You.*

PIOTR SZEWC, *Annihilation.*

ESTHER TUSQUETS, *Stranded.*

LUISA VALENZUELA, *He Who Searches.*

PAUL WEST, *Words for a Deaf Daughter* and *Gala.*

CURTIS WHITE, *Memories of My Father Watching TV.*
  *Monstrous Possibility.*
  *Requiem.*

DIANE WILLIAMS, *Excitability: Selected Stories.*
  *Romancer Erector.*

DOUGLAS WOOLF, *Wall to Wall.*
  *Ya! & John-Juan.*

PHILIP WYLIE, *Generation of Vipers.*

MARGUERITE YOUNG, *Angel in the Forest.*
  *Miss MacIntosh, My Darling.*

REYOUNG, *Unbabbling.*

LOUIS ZUKOFSKY, *Collected Fiction.*

SCOTT ZWIREN, *God Head.*

# FOR A FULL LIST OF PUBLICATIONS, VISIT:
# www.dalkeyarchive.com